Trinity Island

Enis St. John

TANNENBAUM PUBLISHING COMPANY
DOWELL, MARYLAND

Published by
Tannenbaum Publishing Company
P.O. Box 117
Dowell, Maryland
20629

First Printing, 2011

Copyright © 2011 by Enis St. John
All rights reserved

ISBN 10: 0978736966
ISBN 13: 9780978736965
LCCN: 2011932329

Printed and bound in the United States of America

This book is a work of fiction. Except for references to the real world meant to situate the fictional story, all characters, places, incidents, and dialogue were invented by the author and any resemblance to actual persons, living or dead, is entirely coincidental.

No part of this publication may be used or reproduced in any manner without the prior written permission of the copyright owner or publisher of this book except for brief quotes in critical articles or reviews.

www.tannenbaumpublishing.com

Table of Contents

Dedication v
Prologue ix
1. The Wolf 1
2. Trinity Island 6
3. The Parsonage 10
4. The First Sunday 15
5. The Walk Home 31
6. The Critic 44
7. Mockingbird in the Mulberry Tree 54
8. The Crabbers 60
9. *"La Belle Dame sans Merci"* 63
10. Pila 69
11. Hanging at the Bridge 77
12. Ruby and Luke Read the Rifle Scene 89
13. Charles Revises 96
14. The MG ride 101
15. Rose's Death 117
16. The Legend of Santasay 122
17. Ephraim's Sermon 129
18. Pila's Story 136
19. Rose's Confession 144
20. Andromeda 151
21. The Crab Feast 157
22. Pila's Skull 166
23. Crab Dance 177
24. Ruby Breaks Bad 183
25. Shabbats 190
26. Mikva 198
27. On the Rocks 204

28. Thou Shall Not Commit Tomfoolery 213
29. The Barn Burner. 218
30. In the Stars. 229
31. Old Souls 234
32. The Night of the Crystal Skulls 241
33. Carnival 252
34. The Final Act. 265
35. The Cast Party 275
36. Maestro's Letter 284
37. Water Spout. 292
38. "Autumn in New York" .299
39. Catching Fish. 310
40. Maestro Morte 315
Epilogue 317
Acknowledgements 319

Dedication

To my friends Howard and Patricia Klein

Trinity Island

Enis St. John

Prologue

We were hidden behind the trunk of a huge sycamore tree that had fallen across the deepest part of the swimming hole, its branches resting on the other side. The voices came from around the bend where we couldn't see them—splashing water, giggling, swearing happily at each other—and then they appeared, and they were naked as jaybirds.

There were four of them kicking and walking through the knee-high water, arms linked, stretching themselves bank to bank, dark triangular patches beneath their tender bellies, bobbing breasts. Gloria, Audrey, Annabel, and Laura came toward us, striding water nymphs. Gloria was sixteen and Reuben's older sister; the others were her friends. They kept coming, and we ducked behind the tree trunk, afraid we'd be seen. The tree lay just at water level, and we hunkered down, our mouths underwater, our eyes peeking through the opening between water and tree. We could have easily paddled unseen behind the log to the other side, grabbed our clothes and made a run for it, but we were mesmerized. Lord, they were something beautiful! Then they broke formation and Gloria came, high-breasted, directly toward our hiding place. Reuben looked at me in panic, let out a squawk, and swam frantically to the bank where the clothes lay.

"Come back here, boy! You come back here!" Gloria yelled. But Reuben was gone, jumping fallen branches, heading up the side of the hill where his pale body was finally obscured behind the chinquapin bushes. I could hear him thrashing through the fallen leaves until he disappeared over the crest of the hill, heading for home.

I crouched behind the fallen sycamore as low as I could, shivering down, hoping I hadn't been seen, trying to crawl under it, when I felt a hand on my head.

"Come on. Get up from there, Charlie Abell. Come on. We ain't gonna hurt you."

I raised my head and looked right into the bright blue eyes of Gloria on the other side of the log, her black hair stringy, her lips pale blue from the cold Mattawoman Run water, a little glob of snot dribbling from her nose.

"Hoist yourself up on this log where we can see you," Gloria said.

I leveraged myself up in blind obedience and stood on the log, water streaming from my head and into my eyes, forgetting for the moment that I was naked, too.

"Look a there," Audrey said, pointing a finger. "His winkie's getting up!"

Suddenly, I realized the excitement in my nakedness and quickly cupped both hands over my crotch and fell back into the water. The girls teased and hooted as I walked and paddled through the water to the bank where I grabbed my clothes and ran as fast as I could after Reuben. I was frightened and ashamed and suddenly felt a hand on my back and knew that Gloria had caught up with me. I was done.

I opened my eyes and Leigh was there, shaking my shoulder gently. "Good morning, Mr. President," she said, and bent down and kissed me lightly on the mouth. The dream slipped into the present, and I drew her down to me and kissed her again and she licked the taste from her lips and smiled.

"Thank goodness, it's you." I said. "I was being chased by a naked woman and I didn't want to be caught."

"There will be no naked women in here this morning. Here's your coffee. You have your first appointment with the Board of Trustees in two hours and you can't be late." She put the cup on my bedside stand. "Was the naked lady someone you know?"

"Of course," I said, and lay back on the pillow trying to regain the image, but it had slipped away, leaving only the swirling waters of my dream.

Yesterday, on the day of my appointment to the presidency of Southern Maryland College, I had mourned and buried my childhood friend, Reuben Gandy. The loss of Reuben had given me a way to put my own family secrets to rest—allowed me to pray for my own troubled ancestors and put their spirits in their graves—away, forever, with the songs of the ages. I sipped the coffee, and its flavors came to my mouth fully as if it were my first cup, the same cup that I sipped one morning in my youth in Reuben's kitchen when we sat at his mother's table with plates of biscuits overrun with dark molasses. Then I heard his voice singing that old Charlie Bowman song,

> Roll on, buddy, roll on
> Roll on, buddy, roll on
> You wouldn't roll so slow
> If you knew what I know
> So roll on, buddy, roll on

His thrumming guitar took off in a long riff that I tried to hum. I lay back on the pillow and tried to follow it into memory, but couldn't quite hold on as it faded. For a moment, I thought I could taste the molasses on that buttermilk biscuit, and then it was gone, leaving a vague earthy bitter sweetness in my mouth from the coffee and the song being sung far away and low in the background, "Roll on, buddy, roll on."

I struggled against rising consciousness, trying to regain the essence of the dream, and then I breathed deeply, relaxed again and let myself fall into a light sleep from which I thought I could quickly awaken. Instead, I was swept away into a dream of the weeks and years to come.

1

The Wolf

A day before I was to conduct my first graduation as president, I had received a letter from the Eastern States Accrediting Commission congratulating the college on its recovery from the neglect of the past administration and affirming its full accreditation. In a private note, Dr. Burns extended his personal congratulations for the quick and successful turn-around of the college and awarded me the mythical Rights of Spring Pan Flute Trophy.

We had all expected that our accreditation would be confirmed, but the actual letter of acknowledgement was an affirmation of our work that pronounced our legitimacy. My spirits soared, and I could not help but envision the work ahead of us. The staff chastised jokingly about resting enough to celebrate the completion of one task before taking on another, but my mind was already engaged in the next project so as not to lose momentum or become distracted by success—it was not a process that I could temper or suppress with a planning calendar—it came to me with the rhythm of the day and issued from a clavier of mind whose scales were unending.

As we worked through the next two years, the college stepped from the shadow of its inglorious and tumultuous past into a clear understanding of its mission and relationship with the community. The more we succeeded, the more confident and competent we became in developing educational services for the county. Our successes were being confirmed by students, parents, and the business community to such an extent that the Board of Trustees asked me to write a white paper informing the county commissioners of our progress. I did so with confidence, outlining and describing our contributions to the welfare of the county and the state. Among the exciting developments in our growth, I mentioned that we had been asked to join a consortium of other nearby higher-education institutions in producing the annual summer arts program to be held on Trinity Island, within our own county, and that we would act as a supporting host to ensure its success.

I was prepared to receive the usual official thank-you letter from the commission, without comment, or perhaps an invitation to further explain some of our programs, but I received, instead, a handwritten note from Theodora Blundt, president of the commission, a week later.

> *The increase in your activities are a cause for concern if they will have the effect of increasing your budget request to us. You should not make plans or promises for future development that you will be unable to keep. If*

people want to get educated, they will come to you. You don't have to beg them. Under no circumstances should you participate in a summer arts program when there are hard working people in the county who can't put bread on their tables. Trinity Island isn't a fit place for anything except eating crabs anyhow.

I read the letter again and was overcome with the feeling that all of our work was being eviscerated—the academic blood, sinew, and fiber ripped from the corpus of the college in Blundt's abattoir of politics. I sat in my chair in shock.

I had always been taught that hatred and loathing were counter-productive and personally corrosive, but I must admit that I wanted to put all of my pain and despair into becoming a vengeful creature who could be summoned from within me, fearless of evil, to devour trolls like Theodora Blundt who controlled the bridges of life.

I envisioned a wolf growing inside me that hungered for a simple animal existence and the taste of blood. I envisioned a life without ideas, cocked only with emotions that were fired in self-preservation, to live only for the next day, the next kill, and the next bitch in heat. I felt a dark shadow of another person growing inside me, quite different from the one my grandmother raised, one with pain in his mind and a growing appetite to destroy loathsome politicians.

The next day, when the hair on my fingers hadn't grown longer, nor my teeth sharper, I became more convinced that the college should participate in the summer arts program. The answer, of course, was to support it through a source other than the college General Fund. I could buy into the partnership with ten thousand dollars from the Cynn Scholarship Endowment, for instance, and Blundt couldn't very well stop me. And I could also explore other charitable organizations for gifts that would allow us to participate. Regardless of where the funds came from, it would mean the détente with the commissioners would be over.

Quite coincidentally, that morning I received a call from one of the directors of the arts consortium asking me to personally participate in the summer arts program. The resident director had been called to the West Coast because of family problems, and since I was conveniently close at hand, I was the obvious choice as a replacement. While other colleges had contributed presidents and deans to the task from year to year, our administrative presence had been prevented because of Commissioner Blundt's insistence that we not participate in the program. I would be the figurehead in charge, but I would also be part of the creative writing faculty. The other requirement was that I live for the summer on Trinity Island. A house had already been rented, and I would have to move into it as soon as possible. I could still commute to my office in La Plata each day, but it was necessary for me to have a presence on the island as the legitimate official in charge. I was told that I would only be given a few students to help tutor and that there were others who were responsible for preparing lectures. My participation would not require classroom preparation; a bit of advice that was ultimately wrong.

Despite Blundt's heavy-handed warning against college participation in the event, I found a certain amount of whimsy in the idea of spending the summer on the island without the approval of my political dominatrix, and I tentatively accepted the position pending a few hours for further consideration and the final approval by my wife. When I described the opportunity to Leigh, she agreed we should take the position and make it a working vacation for six weeks. After all, we would be only forty-five minutes from home, in a pleasant location where we could enjoy the river breezes and dine on fresh seafood. We could shuck daily routines and slough the shell of old habits and make an adventure of it—an adventure to Trinity Island.

My decision might ultimately result in open warfare with the commissioners: slashed budgets, well-placed letters to the editor, telephone calls to trustees, and politically purchased editorials. If there were too much abrasion and criticism, I might lose my job. However, I finally admitted to myself that the job wouldn't be worth having under the blind and thoughtless stewardship of the Blundt administration. I didn't hesitate—the wolf went all in.

I tried to remember the poem written on the Trinity Island brochure that one of the consortium members had brought to a meeting. Finally, it came to me:

> A breeze enchants the Trinity Isle
> It cools our blood and soothes our day
> In summer sun and flowing tides
> All our worries wash away.

2

Trinity Island

Trinity Island lies at longitude 76.844 W and latitude 38.260 N in the Eastern Standard Time Zone. Southeasterly of the Cobb Neck Peninsula, it is surrounded by three bodies of water: the Wicomico River on the southeast; the Potomac River on the southwest; and Neale Sound, a small, shallow body of water that cuts its way for a mile from east to west, linking the Wicomico to the Potomac and separating a one-half square mile of land from the Cobb Neck Peninsula to form an island. Originally called Cobb Island, it was renamed Trinity Island out of respect for Captain James Neale's determination to establish a Catholic colony in Maryland.

On a nautical chart, Trinity Island resembles the shape of a rib chop. To the more romantic viewer, Trinity Island appears to be a tear squeezed into the Potomac from the ancient swamp bed of Cuckold Creek. As described in the citizens association brochure, it is

> a place of natural beauty, a place where swans stop by just to say hello, a quiet place where herons wade, ospreys hunt, and crabs and fish swim in sea-green water at your feet, a place where blazing sunsets signal the end to another tranquil day.

There is an inherent sadness about a small island or a waterfront community that crawls out of itself in the spring, basks quietly in the warmth of the summer sun, and shutters itself in the winter—places where houses and cottages are only inhabited during summer vacation, or temporarily on weekends, or have been exiled by the probate court to heirs who no longer care. However, many of the small cottages of Trinity Island, grown shabby since having been built in the early 1900s, are being replaced or refurbished by unoriginal inhabitants. A gradual gentrification of the community is being stimulated by an increase in the wealth of those who no longer make their living from the water.

The island is about a ninety-minute commute to better jobs, and much of that time is spent driving through pleasant farmland bordering Route 234 and the moderate traffic that courses up the Crane Highway through pine and oak forests to La Plata, the debarkation point of a more frustrating forty-minute drive to Washington, D.C.

Trinity Island has a sense of isolation and social reserve that most homogeneous living places value and protect. Senior residents, fiercely protective of the island, fuss about the occasional long-haired renter suspected of harboring illegal substances or the newish neighbors who arrive late on Friday evening and vanish on Sunday night.

Approximately 825 people live in over 400 households, or so the demographic snapshot tells us. George Vickers built the first permanent home on the island in 1889, long after nearby Rock Point was a thriving community. The lack of a vehicular bridge to the island restricted its development until the early 1930s.

The first bridge was built of wood at the west end of the island. Eventually, a few houses and cottages were built on the mainland at a right angle from the bridge. They are separated from Neale Sound in the front and by a marshy canal in the back. The little development was jokingly dubbed Chigger City by the men who built the houses who were plagued by an overabundance of the invisible larvae of trombiculid mites that hatched in the grasses, invaded their flesh, and created itching on the skin that demanded to be scratched raw. Although not designated on the maps of the area, the name Chigger City stuck to the little settlement sitting curiously above the marsh, and the mites are still remembered, if not celebrated, for their contributions to the discomfort of the citizens.

Today, a quarter-mile from Chigger City, a concrete bridge arches over from the mainland to Trinity Island terminating in a small commercial area containing the post office, a general store, and a coffee shop/gallery on one side with a restaurant-bar and marina on the other. Continuing down the main street, one finds a church/community center/meeting hall and, across the street from it, the volunteer fire department. Compact and easily navigated, the rest of the island is a grid of streets divided into lots approximately a tenth of an acre in size, especially on the waterside where the houses are built cheek by jowl.

Each house front offers a panoramic view of the Potomac River, the Wicomico River, or Neale Sound. Most houses are equipped with a dock jutting into the water for fifty or so feet for the management of small boats and crab pots. On the street side, small lawns and clumps of shrubbery planted strategically hide a shed or divide a lot or simply make an individual statement.

Four marinas and their accompanying restaurants and bars are destination points for boaters and seafood lovers. They, together with a few other retail establishments, make up the economic base of the island. Trinity Island earned its place in history in December 1900 when Reginald Fessenden, a Canadian, sent the first radio transmission over the distance of a mile. However, in December 1906, Fessenden transmitted the first radio broadcast overseas from Brant Rock, Massachusetts, and the technical accomplishment at Trinity Island was reduced to a small note on a historical road sign, framed by crepe myrtle, at the intersection of Trinity Island Road and Potomac River Road.

3

The Parsonage

When Charles and Leigh arrived at the parsonage on Friday to receive their housing assignment, they were met by Mrs. Rose Caine, wife of Reverend Jesse Caine, housing administrator for the summer. Jesse also served as chaplain and a general clerk of the works for the visiting student artists. With no hotels available within fifteen miles, the consortium provided space for a hundred people, including faculty and staff, in private residences on the island or in nearby Rock Point. The proffered homes rented one or two bedrooms at a modest price with breakfast included; a few very small apartments were available with cooking facilities. One three-bedroom house accommodated five women studying cello, while another provided a room, bath, and studio for a painter in an attached garage.

Mrs. Caine, a pleasant woman of early middle age, long dark hair streaked prematurely with grey drawn back in a schoolmarmish bun, apologized for her husband's absence as he had gone to La Plata to lay in supplies for the camp's first weekend. The workshops and seminars had been in session since the first of the week, and although Charles had missed the opening orientation as a substitute director, Rose was happy to explain the summer's organization.

The artistic disciplines represented in the program included music (strings, voice), dance (classical and modern), writing (play and short story), painting (oil and tempera), and acting. An archeology study group had been added to support a nearby dig undertaken by the university. The archeologists were surveying and screening a site thought to be the original Wollaston Manor built by Captain James Neale, circa 1637, on Weir Creek, at Swan Point, three miles away. Some of the students established a camp near the dig, and a few found places on Trinity Island, but all of them were expected to participate in the same educational regimen governing the activities of the artists.

Most of the formal classroom activities were held in the old Methodist church. When the church membership moved to a newer, more modern structure on the mainland, the congregation removed the pews and the wooden pulpit, lovingly crafted by local boatwrights, to the new location, leaving a building that not so much resembled a place of worship as a lodge, beamed to the peaked roof by pine trees harvested from the lot on which it was built. The island civic association purchased the abandoned, hollowed-out church and its large wood-shingled parsonage for community use. The leaded stained-glass windows were replaced and a stage large enough to mount a dramatic production was installed. The original hardwood floor made a fine surface on which to dance, and on Tuesday and Thursday nights during the winter months, roller skating was enjoyed on rented wooden wheels. For the size and nature of civic activities engaged in by the island population, the old church was more than an adequate venue. The auditorium could hold two hundred people without compromising the rules of the fire marshal. Although the church was not air-conditioned, the high peaked ceiling sucked hot air up to its rafters while undulating floor fans created a comfortable space at ground level for students wearing shorts and T-shirts.

Two wings of the church extended from either side of the stage, or old pulpit area. In the left wing, a large room stored costumes and props, and beyond that another room contained a piano for training both voice and string instruments. To the right of the stage was a room primarily used for dance class, temporarily fitted with mirrors and an exercise warm-up bar, its wooden floor sanded and sealed to make a resilient dancing surface. An office currently in use by Jesse and Rose was adjacent and easily accessible to an outside doorway that led through a short, sunken, covered walkway to the parsonage.

Resembling a large farmhouse of the thirties, the parsonage had an ample living room, kitchen, laundry room, and grand piano room downstairs, and two bedrooms and baths on the second floor, the larger occupied by Jesse and Rose while the smaller room was occupied by a piano student/assistant named Ward who accompanied singers and pursued independent study. A large third-floor attic space had been converted into a bedroom containing a small shower, toilet, and sink that required prior planning to avoid bumping and bruising the body going through daily ablutions. Much larger than most student dorm rooms, it also provided a small desk, bed, chest of drawers, and closet. This top floor aerie was occupied by Ward's friend, Luke, a general graduate assistant who helped in the theater, performed odd jobs, and attended the writing seminars. He was nicknamed "Luke" because he has been given the role of "Luke" in a play being written and produced by a university playwright whom the students have dubbed "Maestro."

The parsonage, as everyone called it, acted as a general meeting place or "orderly room," with messages tacked on a bulletin board hanging outside the front door, or where small problems could be discussed and resolved inside. The large wrap-around porch served as a hang-out for students, especially since they were expected to remain on the island at their tasks for six days a week, with Saturdays usually spent in the more physical aspects of rehearsal, practice, and the exercising of their discipline.

Each Sunday evening, the Reverend Jesse Caine held court in the piano room, the porch, or the lawn for informal discussions of religion, poetry, or philosophy. It was also an opportunity for newly learned music to be presented. During inclement weather or darkness, the group would move inside the parsonage or to the hall if more room was needed. Attendance was not required, although each artistic discipline was expected to be represented by a student. It gave time for students to socialize and exchange ideas, and to perform before an admiring, non-critical audience of friends. Hot dogs and hamburgers were available and, if privately provisioned, wine or beer could be responsibly consumed by those of age.

Rose gave Charles and Leigh a brief tour of the parsonage and the church hall, and then informed them that the house they were to occupy was not located on the island, but across Neale Sound, on the opposite shore, in Chigger City. She assured them that despite the amusing name, the house was less than a mile away by road, closer by boat, and provided a high level of comfort and privacy. After giving them a key, she drew a little map, and assured them the house would not be difficult to find. Before they left, Rose informed Charles that he was scheduled to conduct a seminar on Monday in the firehouse and that she had been assigned to him to receive personal tutoring. Although a little surprised at hearing of the assignment, he thanked her for the information and confirmed that he would be at the parsonage Sunday evening and would see her Monday morning at the seminar.

Charles and Leigh drove the short distance to the house in Chigger City and found it to be as she had described. They unloaded belongings and food supplies from the car and stomped around the little house as though kicking tires on a new car. On Saturday, they cleaned and primped the house a bit, sat on the porch, and watched the boats enter and leave Neale Sound. They opened a beer, raised one bottle neck against the other, and toasted their good fortune.

Following the celebration of Mass on Sunday, Leigh traveled up-county to check on their grown children and spend time with her sisters. As evening came on, Charles walked the mile past Capt. John's and Shymanski's marinas, over the bridge to the island, and up Trinity Island Road to the parsonage to attend the evening of fellowship. Smoke rising from the grill in the backyard carried the smell of cooking meat on the air. A few students lounged on the porch listening attentively to another playing guitar and singing folk songs. Charles stopped for a moment to listen, and then Rose opened the screen door and beckoned him in.

4

The First Sunday

Charles thought Rose looked different from when they had first met on Friday. Her hair seemed light and wavy and her face seemed to have a pleasant glow about it that Charles had not noticed previously. Perhaps it was make-up, he thought, but he was not expert enough in those applications to tell without staring uncomfortably. Somehow, she was not the same drab character that had greeted them a few days ago.

"Come in, Charles, and meet my husband, Jesse," she said. Jesse, leafing through sheet music arranged on a shelf in the music room, turned to Charles, smiling, and reached for his hand.

"How good it is for you to be with us this summer. I know you're giving up a lot of your normal work to be here, and we appreciate it and trust that it will be a good experience for you as well."

"Thank you. I've always wanted to do this, and I'm finally getting the chance." Jesse shook his hand warmly and motioned Charles into a large room containing a Steinway grand piano surrounded by futons, folding chairs, hassocks, and canvas chairs. Paintings, photographs, and posters hung on the walls with only a semblance of order and forethought. Obviously a room decorated by students for students, Charles thought, as he scanned the collection.

"Normally, no one is exempt from participation on these Sunday gatherings. Everyone who attends may be called on to perform in some way, but inasmuch as it is our first session this summer, you are probably excused from participation," Jesse said. "However, there is no privilege of rank here. When you enter this room, you are a performer of some kind, so be prepared. The other rule is that we offer no group criticism of the performance on this particular evening. You will have to beg that from someone at another time. We are all obligated to make objective assessments that may be helpful rather than harmful, but if you want flattery, you are in the wrong place. The sense of competition is pretty high. Alright with you?" Jesse asked.

"Does that preclude any group discussion of the performance, Reverend?" Charles asked.

"Pretty much, with the exception of exploratory questions asked in the spirit of discovery. And you needn't call me Reverend. Call me Jesse. We are all informal here. I can assure you that no one will call you Mister President."

"I understand," Charles said, thinking that the rule might make for some very intellectually bland evenings if no arguments could be heard or developed.

"I'll round up everyone and we'll get started in a few moments," Jesse said.

Students filed into the room and searched for places to sit. Charles went to a far corner, turned a straight-back chair around and sat down, his arms braced on the seatback in front of him. As a student he had liked sitting in the corner to watch the action of the class, and today he reverted to the old habit. He watched new arrivals jostle and squeeze into places that would make him uncomfortable. They were of the flexible age between twenty and twenty-five, still sacrificing comfort in the name of art. Jesse stepped into the room and welcomed everyone, going over the rules and apologizing that not everyone might be heard during this first evening since opening attendance was larger than expected.

"I think I will begin each of these evenings with a little prayer or a thought for you to carry with you throughout the week to help and encourage you in your studies. We have had a splendid opening week and tonight my heart is full of the wisdom and beauty of our Lord, Jesus Christ, and I am brought to wonder at the simplicity of the words of John. As I read this short passage from John 15, think of what he is saying that will bear fruit—the fruit of your art.

> This is my commandment, that you love one another as I have loved you.
> Greater love has no man than this, that a man lay down his life for his friends.
> You are my friends if you do what I command you. No longer do I call you
> servants, for the servant does not know what his master is doing; but I have called
> you friends, for all that I have heard from my Father I have made known to you.
> You did not choose me, but I chose you and

> appointed you that you should go
> and bear fruit and that your fruit should abide; so
> that whatever you ask the Father
> in my name, He may give it to you. This I command
> you, to love one another.

"Amen. Now, because I have listened to him practice all week and know that he is prepared, we'll start this evening with something from Ward Boswell," Jesse said as he moved away from the piano to the doorway.

Ward shuffled in from the kitchen, adjusted the seat on the piano, and began Chopin's "Prelude in E Minor," played with a sadness that touched Charles deeply. When the piece ended, the room burst into applause. Ward raised his hand to quiet them and moved quickly into the D-minor prelude, the music born out of the bass with incessant runs—cascading scales fell over one insistent stabbing note—notes reaching, denying, and finally falling to three strikes of the low D, reminiscent of a tolling bell. The dramatic effect of the music exploded in Charles as he leapt from the chair and applauded the last fading note. He had forgotten that such an experience was still available to him, and he was embarrassed at how vulnerable it made him feel, as though his presidential exterior had been stripped away and replaced with incautious and unlimited enjoyment.

Ward rose from the piano stool and bowed deeply from the waist, smiling, tossing bouquets with the tips of his fingers, and comically enjoying his moment. Shouts of "Encore! Encore!" sent him back to the piano stool where he sat, head lowered, contemplating the next piece until the room became still in anticipation of another performance. He raised his head slowly and, with exaggerated animation, plunged into the first chord of a Pogo song, "Baby Don't You Sugar Me," written by Walt Kelly to a rolling ragtime tune. He sang the tricky lyrics that ended with the saccharin advice, "Don't sugar me...cause us is throon." The audience laughed and howled in appreciation of the change from the deeply romantic mood Ward had created to the wacky vaudevillian rhythm with which he ended his presentation. Charles was taken by the humor of the artist who would play Chopin and Walt Kelly with equal sincerity and intensity. It is the glorious impudence of youth, he thought.

Ward remained at the piano and motioned with his head toward Jesse, who slipped through the door and took up a position standing beside him. Ward sounded a B, which Jesse immediately picked up as the first note of the song, and with Ward accompanying him on the piano, Jesse sang the first line of the Mendelssohn Oratorio, *Elijah*, "Draw near, all ye people, come to me!"

The room fell again into silence, listening to Jesse's baritone voice plead to the people of Israel to recognize the God of Abraham. His rich and supple voice singing the message turned into the voice of the prophet insisting that they "let their hearts again be turned." After finishing this prayerful and dramatic piece, Jesse simply dropped his head and walked back through the doorway having given a performance that exceeded the normal perception of his ministerial persona.

On their first meeting, Charles had thought Jesse was just another member of the Protestant clergy pleasantly engaged in an artistic community activity; when he looked again, he saw a man of talent and deep feeling whose voice had more than an emotional effect on the people around him. Charles looked at him carefully, wanting not to miss something this time. He found a man of ordinary stature, although a dynamic flow in his body movements made him appear larger. Jesse's broad chest carried a large head with a prominent brow beneath a full hairline. His straight nose, small for his face, tended to enlarge his dark brown eyes. A thin and tidy moustache grew above full lips that parted easily into a disarming smile. In repose he appeared quiet and reflective. His mellifluous and compelling speaking voice caused Charles to think that perhaps Jesse's sermons were well-attended by his parishioners back home.

Jesse stepped into the room again and received more compliments and applause from an appreciative audience; they soon subsided into general conversation. Several students rose from the floor, disappeared from the room, and reappeared moments later with a hot dog in one hand and a beer in the other. Charles leaned his chin on the chair back and thought that what he had just experienced was a family celebration of art. He didn't know if the performances had been spectacular or if his parched aesthetic sensibilities had been simply grateful for the downpour of creative talent. It didn't matter. For the moment, he was absorbing sensations that were not new to him but that had been revitalized, lifted, and separated from among the memos and the papers and the speeches and the reports that had become his métier over the years, and while he enjoyed the performances, they also rang a sharp note of warning of things that had been missing from his life.

As conversation bubbled around the room, Jesse walked to the corner where Charles sat and handed him a book.

"Why don't you read to us aloud the poem I've marked."

"But you said...."

"I know. I said 'probably,' but I decided we need you to do this." He clapped his hands to gain attention, and when the hubbub receded, introduced Charles as a mentor in the creative writing group.

"I've asked Charles to read this poem as a sort of benediction over this portion of the evening. Charles, please." After quietly clearing his throat, Charles read the poem:

> No man is an island, entire of itself.
> Each is a piece of the continent,
> A part of the main.
> If a clod be washed away by the sea,
> Europe is the less.
> As well as if a promontory were.
> As well as if a manor of thine own
> Or of thy friend's were.
> Each man's death diminishes me,
> For I am involved in mankind.
> Therefore, send not to know
> For whom the bell tolls,
> It tolls for thee.

"As written by John Donne," Charles explained, "from his Meditation XVII."

"Thanks, Charles," Jesse said, leading the polite applause. "I know you weren't prepared to perform tonight, but I wanted you to see and experience the spontaneous spirit that we're trying to generate here this summer. We have left our academic self-consciousness at the door, and put on the cloak of artistic license and creative spontaneity. The more we practice it, the more relaxed and better we will feel about our art and ourselves. Let's take a little break and come back and see what the string group has for us."

People stood and stretched and found new sitting places around the room. Luke watched the red-haired girl rise from a cross-legged sitting position and start for the kitchen with smooth athletic grace. With a lithe little hop to square her balance, she slipped through the doorway. He stood from his chair to follow her, but by the time he stepped over and around milling students, she had come back through the doorway and stood directly in front of him. For a moment they just looked at each other. He noticed she had one bright blue eye on her right and a darker eye on the left—over its blue iris was a speckle of color, not hazel, but simply a shade of darker blue. At first her face appeared unbalanced by it, and then he decided it added a touch of mystery. Earlier, when he had first entered the room, looking for a seat, he had noticed her sitting in the corner in what he perceived as an aura that set her off from the others. Her hair was red: dark, rich red falling around her shoulders, touched in places and made lighter by the sun. She wore no make-up.

"Tea or beer," she said, holding both hands out to him—one held a ten-ounce can of Budweiser and the other, steaming black tea in an off-white cup with a brown spider crack running down the side from a small chip on its lip.

"I'll have the tea," Luke said.

"Good, I'll drink the beer. Want to sit on the porch?" she asked, indicating the exit at the side of the room. "We can hear the music from there.

"Sure. I'd like that."

They sat down on the top of the steps that ran down one end of the porch.

"What brings you here?" Luke asked, immediately regretting he had asked the question for fear of appearing clumsy and ordinary. Every newcomer was asked the same question—the special circumstances that brought each to the summer arts workshop were worth telling and hearing.

"I'd rather you go first. I'm Andora, by the way. I've been wanting to meet you, but haven't had the chance. Everyone is so busy," and she reached out and shook his hand in greeting. "Who are you?"

"Everyone calls me Luke because that's the name of the character that I act in the play, but my other nickname is Shake." He let her hand fall gently from his.

"How did you get that name?"

"It's a long story about the influence of my grandfather. His library consisted of two classical writers, Milton and Shakespeare, so he pressured my parents to name me Shakespeare in honor of the bard. I haven't encouraged anyone to use it here. It's a little pretentious for an unaccomplished writer to call himself Shakespeare. As a summer name, Luke is as good as any."

"Okay, tell me about yourself, Luke."

"There's not much to tell. I just graduated from the university in December with a major in English and a minor in philosophy, and after the summer I'm going to NYU to study dramatic literature and philosophy for a master's. The good old G.I. Bill let me finish in three years so I have some financial eligibility left. Otherwise, I'd be back trimming cabbage in the produce department of a grocery store. In New York, I'll be rooming with Ward, the fellow who played piano, but he's going to Julliard and I'm going downtown to Washington Square. He and I are old high school friends. I'm with the creative writing group and we're doing a lot with stagecraft right now. I was helping Lonnie, the girl who plays

Ruby, with her lines. When Maestro saw me read with her, he cast me as Luke on the spot. He said it was a good pairing. And you. What about you?"

"Jesse and Rose Caine are the only ones that Will and I know here. We knew them in New York and when we found out they were here, we sailed in to see them. Will is my husband. We sail around a lot in his boat—that pretty little Bristol Channel Cutter at the marina is ours. The one without a name. Will took the name down to repaint it some time ago and he hasn't gotten around to it yet. We came down from City Island, off New York, to Annapolis for some motor repair, and then came here to lay over while Will does a total reconditioning. When he found out he could get some decent help working on the boat at the marina, we decided to stay for the summer. I'm a painter. Since my husband will be working every day on the boat—our home when it's not torn up—I decided to rent a cottage and join the painting group of the arts camp if they would admit me. I submitted some drawings and a few canvases to the faculty and they let me in despite the fact that I really have no formal training. I've taken a few night courses, but nothing more. I was painting at the marina and when Maestro saw me and found out that I was in the painting study group, he recruited me for his theater. That's how I became involved. Now I'm also painting sets."

"I'm not doing exactly what I should be doing, either. I'm supposed to be a writer, not an actor, but another professor of mine, Oliver, a good friend, pushed me to apply for a fellowship here, and then I think he convinced Maestro that I should have it. I know nothing about writing drama, but in the interview, he made the argument that the best way to learn to write was to act, so he cast me in his play and promised that I would have plenty of time to write, which so far isn't true. I'm working on a short story, but studying the play script and learning lines takes more time than I had imagined."

The sounds of violin and cello, slow and mellow, came to them from inside the house, so they said nothing more and listened.

Finally, Andora asked, "How long were you in the service?"

"Four years, with a nice three-year tour in Germany."

The music ended, followed by enthusiastic applause. They heard Jesse thank students for playing the adagio from Mozart's "String Trio E Flat Major," and announced that they would adjourn to the theater for the final production of the evening. People rose from their places and started making the transition from the parsonage to the auditorium.

"Well, it's my turn," Luke said. "I'm in this reading. Are you coming?"

The stage had been set without flats and with a minimum of props. The absence of walls normally used to define dramatic spaces would not be critical for this particular reading. From the audience viewpoint, a fireplace was positioned on the left around which sat two rocking chairs. A small wooden eating table accompanied by two basic wooden kitchen chairs sat in the center. A door frame stood by itself as portal to a room with a wooden bed and a bare dresser. To one side of the doorjamb, a standing clothes rack held hanging night clothes. There was no other furniture.

The house lights were raised and an elderly man, favoring his right leg, walked to the center front of the stage, his face framed in a neatly trimmed grey beard, wearing a long-sleeved white shirt—buttoned to the top on this warm evening—and a black string tie. He waited for the audience to be silent, and then he said, "Good evening. My students call me Maestro. Although I am not sure how I deserved that appellation, I wear it proudly since it was the invention of a demented undergraduate's mind." The crowd laughed politely.

"As you might know already, one of the assignments of the creative writing group is to study an old novel that I wrote by the title of *Ruby* and to adapt it to the stage. Some of you will act in it as we progress. While I can assure you that this is as precarious a task for me as it is for you, the final exercise of the assignment will be to rewrite the closing scene of the play entirely. To be honest, I have never been satisfied with it, and so I've thrown it open to the writers as a contest; the best scene will be chosen for production later this summer. But for now, we will play a short scene for you that has given us some technical problems. Our actors may not yet have all of their lines, so please ignore the prompting should it occur, and forgive them if they glance at a script hidden up a sleeve. If this scene doesn't work, it could be rewritten tomorrow—making art better is the only reason we are here. Now, in order to set the scene, let me give you a little background.

"Our hero is Luke—take a bow, Lukey." Luke walked on stage carrying a black coat over his arms, dressed in a white shirt and black pants. He nodded to the audience, placed the coat over the back of the chair, and sat at the kitchen table facing the audience.

"Luke has sort of won the right to court the female lead, Ruby, by winning a jousting tournament the week before and crowning her the 'Queen of Love and Beauty'—it was quite a thing in 1890 for a young belle to receive that honor. He wooed her and subsequently married her a few weeks later. He is in love with her, but she had been indentured by her father to a hotel owner to get her out of the house, and she married Luke as a practical way to leave the drudgery of washing dishes to live on a good farm, Elysium, where there was plenty to eat and a place of her own to sleep. However, life can also be hard at Elysium. It is months beyond their wedding night and they have not yet consummated the wedding vows. He sleeps beside her on some nights but is not allowed to touch her. On other nights, he sleeps in the hayloft of the barn. Abruptly, Luke's older brother, Raymond, the light of his life, dies suddenly of the grippe acquired while oystering the Potomac River on a cold and wet winter day. This scene opens after Raymond's funeral when Luke and Ruby have come back to their cabin in mourning. This is a scene from Act I."

{The stage is dim, lit primarily by a burning fireplace. Ruby is sitting in a chair rocking mindlessly. Luke comes in, takes off his coat, lifts a pint bottle of whiskey from the side pocket, and takes a swig. He stands by the corner of the fireplace, whiskey bottle in hand.}

LUKE. It don't seem right that the Lord would take him just like that. *{Snaps his fingers.}*

RUBY. Your Lord didn't have nothing to do with it. He stayed out oystering in bad weather 'til he near froze, and he got the grippe. That's what took him. The grippe.

LUKE. I know the Lord works in mysterious ways, but it didn't seem to be Raymond's time. *{Pulls cork from bottle and takes a swig.}*

RUBY. The Lord must choose to do a lot of His mysterious ways on the river in the wintertime then.

LUKE. *{Looks hard at Ruby and takes another swig. Sets bottle down. Puts his head in his hands, rests for a moment as if he has been thinking, and then appears agitated.}* Raymond was so good to me, Ruby. Why was it him that had to die? I remember the night he took me and Tom to hunt snipe and left us in the woods holding the bag while he said he was gonna drive the snipe into it. We half froze ourselves, and when we finally decided to go back to the house, there was Raymond, tucked in the bed while we had been left miserable holding the bag waiting for the snipe. He was fun like that. *{He laughs and coughs.}*

RUBY. Sounds like fun alright.

LUKE. *{Takes another swig. Turns his back to Ruby and sobs. He turns toward her again, eyes full of tears. He wipes his eyes, reaches in his pocket and draws out a whistle.}* He carved me a little whistle out of a green hickory branch and taught me how to toot on it so people could hear me and I would never get lost. *{Toots whistle.}* I kept this whistle in my pocket all through school. *{He sobs.}* We'd play chase, and, and, when we came in from swimming in the run, he'd hug me to get me warm again. *{Folds his arms around himself in pantomime.}*

RUBY. *{Rises abruptly.}* Stay here and get drunk if you want. I'm going to bed. *{She goes to a corner of the bedroom, puts out the lamp, undresses in the semi-dark light of a candle. The lights come up gradually showing her in a matronly nightgown. She slips into bed.}*

LUKE. *{Blubbers, moans, finally stands before the fireplace and undresses. In long underwear, he drains the whiskey and tosses the bottle in the fireplace. He goes into the bedroom, reaches for a nightgown on a hook, but puts it back. He strips off his underwear* *and gets in bed with Ruby and wraps his arms around her, cupping her to him.}*

RUBY. *{She rouses and attempts to push him away, but he holds her tight.}* Stop it! Stop it!

LUKE. I need you Ruby. I need you bad. *{Ruby resists.}* I need you to hold me. *{He cries.}* I just need you to hold me.

RUBY. *{Kicks at him trying to get him away.}* Go away! Git out of here!

LUKE. I'm not going to hurt you, Ruby. I'm just going to be your husband. I'm just going to be a man tonight in this bed. *{He rises up over her and pins her arms above her head. He rips the nightgown down her body and sinks his mouth deeply into her neck and presses down on her.}* I've waited long enough. I ain't gonna be your sister anymore. If I can't be your husband, then you won't have one. Do you understand? I'll set you loose! *{Spreads her legs and enters her roughly. She emits a little scream. He pins her under his thrusting pelvis. She groans in pain. He comes to climax, shivers, falls on her, then rolls over and gets out of bed.}* I'm sorry Ruby. I didn't want it to be this way, but I can't take it anymore. If I can't be your husband, then you won't have one. You'll have to go. *{He staggers, due to the whiskey.}* I'm going to the barn. *{He grabs his clothes, goes to a shelf, pulls down an old horse blanket, throws it around him, and leaves the house.}*

RUBY. *{Rises from the bed trying to stifle her tears. She lights a kerosene lamp, throws a blanket over her shoulders, and sits at the table, head in her hands. She sobs, finally rises and goes to the fireplace and takes a rifle that is lying on the mantelpiece. She turns toward the rack where Luke's clothes are hanging, cocks the rifle, aims at Luke's clothes and pulls the trigger, which falls with no explosion, but with an audible click. She cocks the rifle, aims, and dry-fires it again. Stage lights dim.}*

The audience sat quietly, silenced by the scene until the house lights came up and the actors walked out on stage, and then everyone broke into applause. The actors bowed deeply, still wrapped in blankets, and Maestro joined them and they bowed together. Jesse came in from the wings.

"Thank you, everyone, that concludes the program for this evening. There will probably be some songs over on the parsonage porch so we'll see you there, and Shirley Cannon, there's a message on the bulletin board for you. Good evening."

5

The Walk Home

The students left the auditorium and settled on the parsonage porch in small groups, chatting and joking among themselves. Although they had been on campus for a week, their time-consuming studies meant extra time for socializing had to be stolen from the day. They were still talking about the play and speculating about the significance of the rape within the historical context of a title like "Queen of Love and Beauty." Inside, someone was strumming the guitar. When Luke left the theater he looked around and found Andora sitting on the steps of the parsonage, drinking from a can of Bud.

"Want a swig?" she said, offering him the can as he approached her.

"That business made me thirsty," he said, and took a long draw from the can.

"That was a dandy scene you played—a bit rough—but it was effective. Nice performance. Very, very authentic. When was the last time a woman wouldn't let you in her bed?"

Luke was stunned for a moment by the question, and then she smiled at him playfully.

"Well, Ruby knew how to resist so that helped a lot, and Maestro worked hard on me to be excited and clumsy because I am usually more tactful in my seduction techniques." He backed up quickly as she took a swing at him with the back of her hand. The beer sloshed over his sleeve and fell from his hand to the ground.

"You egotistical jerk. You've spilled my beer." Andora growled, feigning anger at him. Silence fell, and they became aware that other students were watching to see what they would do next.

"Just mind yourself and sit quietly up here beside me," she said, patting the space on the step.

"Don't mind if I do," he said, and sat down.

"Where'd you pick up that country dialect?"

"In the country. I was raised on a farm on the western side of this county. My parents died when I was a wee child so I was raised by my grandparents. I didn't know that it showed."

"Oh, it's not offensive. I'm not being critical. I thought it was nice—not overdone—subtle and effective."

"Thanks. Whatever effect it produced was purely unintended. I was concentrating on remembering the lines. We haven't rehearsed much."

"I know. I've been painting flats in the back. I've seen you a few times. You're very convincing."

Lightning flashed several miles downriver, followed by rolling thunder that sounded ominous. Jesse stepped onto the porch from the house.

"It's gonna storm," he pronounced "Does anyone need a ride home before it gets here? Charles? Dr. Abell?" He called into the kitchen, "You live off-island, and I'd better give you a ride. Anyone else?"

The students lounging around the parsonage gathered their things, formed into walking groups, and headed toward their cottages. Andora rose from the steps and stretched.

"I'm going home before the deluge. Which way do you go?"

"I've got a room here at the parsonage, upstairs." Luke said. "How about you?"

"I'm up a couple of streets and then down toward the sound side."

"Well, I'll walk you home, if you like. Will your husband be looking for you?"

"No. He stays on the boat most nights, and with the storm coming, he won't leave it tonight. He loves foul weather. Let's just stumble along before the rain gets here," she said, rising from the steps with him. They walked down the sidewalk, out of the light thrown from the windows of the parsonage, into the narrow street and increasing darkness. The night was black, lit only by the occasional flashes of lightning and the rumble of thunder as they were swept slowly along by a cooling breeze that stirred the smell of honeysuckle and lilac blooming in the yards of cottages that bordered the street.

They said nothing in the darkness. Her fingers brushed his side and caught his fingers lightly at the tips and they walked, hand in hand, down the street, turning into another, even darker lane, until they stopped in front of a cottage. She pushed the front gate open and the barely audible squeak of a rusted hinge sounded to him like a symbol crashing in the night. She coiled his fingers in her hand and led him toward the house. With difficulty seeing objects, he stumbled slightly over the porch steps, but recovered quickly, and she turned to him. Her hand went up his arm and then down into the small of his back where it opened him as though it had touched a secret lock, and then she pulled him slightly to her and pressed herself against him. He put his arms around her and she was naked, her thin summer dress around her ankles, shed completely in a slow kick step, and she pressed even closer. He felt her lift his T-shirt over his head and her hands slipped slowly over his chest down to the stretch waistband of his cotton shorts, and she slipped them onto the floor. He felt, but could not see, her movement as she sat down on the worn carpet that led to the front door, and then she pulled him down to her, into the night that blinded him. He could not say what it was that happened next or how it happened—only that he was wrapped in darkness and the woman, deep into ecstasy, into a sublime feeling that ran through his body—a current cutting deeply into his source of pain and pleasure, and then the thrust and the light burst and the spasm. No grunting or rutting sounds interrupted the crickets or the chorus of frogs that sang in anticipation of the coming storm. He rolled over, and after taking deep, filling breaths, he lay still, on his back. In another flash of lightning he saw her face, momentarily, smiling down at him. Then she pulled him up with the touch of her fingertips and took his face in her hands and kissed him gently. Luke reached to wrap her in his arms, but she was gone, slipping through his ardor as though she had never been. He stood there and heard the door close quietly behind him, and he was alone. Reaching for his shorts and shirt, he strained for sight and another flash of lightning led him to the screen door and the yard gate. A few drops of rain hit him and then they pelted the macadam, raising smells of tar and earth and hot grass and the warm gravel from the road.

The rain quickened, chilling him slightly, but he stepped languorously toward the parsonage, unmindful of the storm and the rain. Luke reached his room on the third floor and kicked off his canvas loafers, tossed the rain-soaked T-shirt and shorts into the shower stall, and toweled himself dry. He fell damp and naked into the bed, and the sleep that covered him was born by the night and the sweet smell of the woman who had etherized him. He fell freely into the unconsciousness of his pleasure and did not awaken until after the sun had risen.

Jesse was singing a song at the piano and Lonnie and Charles were listening when the thunder rumbled again and the lightning momentarily lit up the room. Jesse went to the front door and looked into the sky.

"There will be some wind and rain in a few minutes. Why don't you let me take you home in the car?"

"The walk isn't far. Don't bother, I don't care if I get wet," Lonnie said.

The rain began to pelt the lawn, raising little dust storms in the light of the porch.

"Too late. Rose!" he yelled. "I'm taking Charles and Lonnie home. Be back in a minute."

Charles ran for the car and jumped into the rear seat and Lonnie took the front.

"Lonnie lives at the other end of the island, Charles, so I'll take you home first. Do you need something at the market? It's still open. We could stop on the way."

"Thanks, but I don't think so."

They drove for a few minutes in silence, the awkward moment when people, unfamiliar with each other, are thrown together in close quarters. They listened to the noise of rain on the roof and splashing tires. Finally, Charles said, "That was quite a little jam session you had tonight. Thanks for inviting me."

"Oh, I think they'll get better as everyone improves their study. What's your particular talent other than being a college president?"

"I'm a writer who hasn't written much worth reading and a teacher who hasn't faced a class in several years. My professional practice of late is planning and financing college buildings, which is not exactly what you might call a performing art."

"I think you're wrong there," Jesse said. "It's a combination of all of them. You dance and sing for your supper, write the dialogue, and paint the pictures for your audience of contributors, and you'd better be good at it or nothing happens."

"I suppose you could make those analogies, but in the end, they simply don't hold together. It's wishful thinking. I just think of it as making buildings. That's enough."

Lonnie turned and looked at Charles in the back seat. "Is that what a president does?"

"It's mostly what I have been doing since I've been president, yes."

"I thought the president sat in his office thinking lofty thoughts and writing profound things to other scholars and caring about the students," Lonnie said.

"I'm sure some do," Charles said, "but I haven't had the luxury. I generally get to care about the students after they have gotten into trouble; otherwise, I'm building their classrooms and labs, and I care about them when I try to hire the best instructors that I can, but when I write to my colleagues, it's generally about strategies for obtaining more state or federal funding—not very romantic." They pulled slowly into the graveled road to Chigger City, crossed the little bridge, and pulled into the first driveway that showed a single light through the downpour of rain.

"Thanks for the ride. See you tomorrow," Charles said, and quickly left the car, slamming the door and running toward the house. When he disappeared into the front door, Jesse drifted down the driveway and turned toward the road leading back to the island.

"Now let's get you home, Lonnie," he said.

"He seems like a pretty regular guy. Not the stuffy presidential type," Lonnie said. "I watched him during the recital, and he got pretty charged up."

"I don't think he gets a chance to be this involved with students. He was probably loosening up a bit."

"There's really a lot that I don't know," Lonnie said, "A lot I don't know about people. My folks didn't like me to be with groups of people, especially artists, because they thought that's where trouble started. But I've met some people here that just blow your mind. You know—take you right out of where you live."

"Well, when you are open to other people, you get to know a lot about yourself. That's where the lessons begin."

"Are you a chaplain and a counselor for the students this summer?"

"Yes, I am. I am a certified counselor and a minister of the Christian faith who is trying to become a better singer. That's also one of the reasons that I'm here this summer. I'm a student like you are a student and I double as director of housing. You can come to see me if you're having a personal problem or if there are bedbugs at your place; otherwise, I am singing for my supper. How about you?"

"Oh, I'm a half-senior. I only need eight more credits and I can graduate. I shouldn't be here because this is for graduates only, but I'm an honors student and decided to concentrate on acting, and so I'm a special student of the Maestro's. He believes I have a talent, so they let me in because he wanted me to take the lead in his play. Usually, I'm sympathetic with the character pretty early and develop the role without much trouble, but this Ruby part is tricky and I'm having trouble getting around it."

"Doesn't Maestro help?"

"He's terrific—really knows character—but I'm just not getting it right now—I will eventually, but right now it's like I'm too much in the role; he wants me more between the lines. Taking stuff away from the part is a lot harder for me than putting stuff into it. I think I'm just resisting getting rid of parts of me to get at the real Ruby in the play, that's all. Maestro said it would take time and work, but we don't have a lot of time, so I've got to get into it where I'm comfortable."

"If you need voice coaching, maybe I could help."

"I do. I've got to do a better job whispering so that it's heard in the back row."

"I can help you with that. I can project a whisper. It's in the diaphragm, down here," he said, patting her gently beneath the chest. "There are some exercises for it. When did you say you were coming to see me?"

"I didn't say, but I suppose I should. Talking to you might help me. Our minister at home didn't like to hear about people's troubles and feelings, and you could help me learn to whisper. When do you have time?"

"I always have to do paperwork on Monday evening, so I'll be in the office anytime after supper. Say, seven o'clock?"

"Good. I'll see you then. You can let me out in front of that yellow house where the flagpole is."

"See you tomorrow," Jesse said, watching her run toward the house in the rain. He sat for a moment, saying the name Lonnie over and over to himself. What if that's it, he thought. What if that's what it means. He would have to check the charts. He began to sing the chorus from "Bringing in the Sheaves" with gusto and drove back to the parsonage, windshield wipers banging furtively in rhythm against the end-stop of their arc.

As soon as the players and audience had emptied the auditorium, Maestro threw the main switch controlling the stage lights and the lighting control board. He gathered up the soft leather case containing the script and note pads and walked through the auditorium and into the street. Many of the students were hanging around the parsonage porch. He could hear someone on the piano playing a ragtime tune, and he paused, thinking that he might go in for a beer, but remembered a bottle of Chateau De Lavernette Cremant cooling in his little refrigerator and passed up the opportunity for more socializing. He liked late-night talks with students, but tonight he preferred being alone.

Maestro had rented a little cottage on the waters of the Potomac, next to people he had gotten to know through the years. He felt the stiffness in his knees and hips and settled into a comfortable pace for the ten-minute walk. In the mailbox at the sidewalk entrance, he found a letter, but couldn't read the return address in the darkness. There was a flash of lightning and then a roll of thunder down the river that reminded him to close the windows before he went to bed. Distracted by the letter in his hand, he absentmindedly sat in an overstuffed chair that he would have ordinarily avoided because of his difficulty in rising from it. But done is done, and he sat back and peered at the return address on the letter and opened it. It was on stiff stationery with an embossed seal at the top. He read it and sighed heavily. "Shit," he said, and returned the letter carefully to the envelope. Then sliding to the edge of the chair, he thrust himself from it with no difficulty.

From the refrigerator in the corner, he took the bottle of wine, read the label—smiling at a fond memory—and twisted the cork from the neck with a slight hiss. From an overhead cupboard, he fetched a small jelly glass and took it and the bottle to the table against the wall that served as his writing venue. He didn't pour the wine, but put the bottle to his lips and drank from it in several throat-tingling gulps. There was a yellow business tablet on the table, and a ballpoint pen with which he began to write a letter:

> *Dearest and Best,*
> *It is the end of our first week, and tonight we staged a brief scene from the play. I am blessed with inexperienced players who are quick-witted and eager to learn and improve with every rehearsal and reading. We have to work on the opening pace—needs to quicken, but the short rape scene we did tonight was successful despite it being very difficult to make convincing. Our leading lady a young woman named Leighanne, but pronounced "Lonnie," of all things,*

has more raw talent than I have ever seen. Whether or not it will take form is another matter because she is just coming into the world, so to speak, and her energy and enthusiasm seems boundless and undirected. How frequently we have seen talent rise on a creative thermal and fail to realize that it must find another one to take them higher, and another one more difficult than the last, that will take them higher into the thinner air above us all.

She is a pleasure to watch, carving shape and form with her movements and gestures that add meaning to my dialogue. She articulates it more clearly than I can write it. It is not that she walks nicely from this blocking cue to that one—the space that she is about to occupy seems to reach out and wrap itself around her as if she had magically just appeared there. I can only watch in astonishment as my words are expressed in her movement—she breathes life into the character. And she doesn't have the character yet. Not yet. It's something we are working to understand. If anything, she is overplaying it, but she will have it. I can tell.

Much is the same on the island since our last visit so many years ago. The river flows through Neale Sound with barely a ripple until it hits the bridge and merges with the Wicomico. Across the Potomac, the Virginia shore we called "Marseille" still twinkles at sunset and forms the stuff of dreams. I am an old man, and yet on this island, the blood runs through me as ripe and warm as it did in our youth. I remember our cottage at Chigger City with such fondness that I wonder sometimes if I am here on the island by myself or there, a mile away with you.

> *I dreamed last night of standing beside a railroad track that ran off into the horizon and I saw clearly every station of my life along the way. And places where I thought it stopped, it didn't. The curves I thought were dangerous were never there, but the track continued straight until the train reached me and I thought it would stop and I would get on and be carried away to my next station, but it didn't. It slowed respectfully and moved on without me, leaving me to write another letter to you of my love and to celebrate it as the stuff that heaven is made of.*
>
> *I was going to pour myself a glass of Cremant to celebrate all of our summers when I received a letter of sad news. You remember my other true love, the young girl that I traumatized in grade school only to have her become my soul mate and then a celebrity among the American ex-pats in Israel. I received a letter from her friend telling me that she was blown up in a bus that was on its way to a political rally in the Golan Heights. Why anyone would visit or live there is beyond me, but she was ever the optimist. My loves are disappearing, one by one, into the damp cave of my memory and I can only salute them. And so I shall. L'chaim!*

He stopped writing and poured wine into his jelly glass and drained it, then poured another and another, drinking all three in a ceremonial gesture to the memories of women he loved. He didn't take up the pen again, but left it lying across the yellow-lined pad and turned off the lamp. Walking carefully through the dark to the rear door of the little cottage, he opened it. The rain was slowing. Going back to the little dresser in which his clothes were laid, he brought out a small paper box containing two others. From the last box, he drew out a ring, held it in his hand, and walked from the rear door of the cottage, down the steps, to the end of the dock. The low clouds were leading the rain toward the west, and he could see the brightest lights of Colonial Beach appearing through the overcast. Holding the ring to his lips, he kissed it, and then dropped it in the water. "Goodbye, my love," he said, with a tear in his eye. Maestro turned back to the house, wiped the moisture from his head and face, and sat down at the desk in front of the unfinished letter. He decided not to write anymore. There was Cremant in the bottle, so he poured another glass.

"Here's to the loves I have lost; let us hope it was not the last," he said, raising the glass and drinking it down.

6

The Critic

"Hi, Lonnie, I'm Jesse," he said, reintroducing himself, reaching for her hand and taking it lightly. "Just call me Jesse. Quite a rain we had the other night, wasn't it? It's nice to be working with you. Here, take a seat, why don't you, and tell me a little about yourself, so we can get to know each other better." He sat down facing her.

"I'm just an ordinary student trying to find out what I want to do in life," Lonnie began. "I started majoring in journalism and then my advisor told me to change to English because I was smart enough to do the work, and I enjoyed reading the plays in class, and ended up in Maestro's interpretation class. He told me that I had the voice and movement of a potential actress and asked me to become a drama major, and that's like letting an English major out of jail. I fell in love with it. My mother always called me an overachiever, by which she meant that I was active in a lot of things rather than being a brain, you know."

"Your mother and father are still together? I mean, so many that I meet are without that kind of support. I just wondered."

"Yes, I'm an only child, so both of them work at good jobs. Mom and Dad are active in church life at home, so I come from what you might call a very ordinary background, which means that they are not too thrilled about my becoming an actress instead of a teacher or a banker or something practical like that. They think it's a phase I'm going through and that I'll give it up eventually."

"Do you think you will?"

"Not now. It's too exciting. Performing in front of people is a thrill of its own, but that's not all of it, just one of the things that makes it super. I mean acting is a difficult and exacting craft to master—revealing a character to an audience—like, *you* know about the character, and you want *them* to know, and I'm beginning to understand it, and I like learning how to do it, although I'm a novice at it. No, I think that acting is an artistic expression that I can be good at and that's important to me. Like the part of Ruby I'm playing for Maestro. I think she is the exact opposite of my natural personality; I'm not close to being her physical or mental type. She's a virgin because I don't think she loves anyone. I don't mind telling you that I'm a virgin so it should be easy for me to be able to play the part of a virgin, but this is a different kind of virgin than I am."

"Look, you don't have to...."

"That's alright. I'm just making a point. We had what they called a 'Cherry club' among the kids at church for some of us to choose celibacy instead of invasive sex—kind of a

Virgins Anonymous, where we could talk out our problems and get some counseling. I had steady boyfriends and all, and sometimes the petting got pretty heavy—most of us knew what an orgasm felt like—but we'd say a prayer or think of other things, or just walk away from the situation, you know. We were full of desire, but just didn't execute, if you know what I mean—not like the character I'm playing. Ruby has no feeling inside. I have to play a kind of bloodless virgin—without the blood that I feel running through my veins every day, and that is a different thing. I have to shred every speck of life right out of me to the level where Ruby lives. It's something I've never done."

"I'm sure you'll get it," Jesse said. "It'll take a quiet mind, like the mind of Mary. You'll have to be absolutely still as though the miraculous slept inside you," Jesse said, lowering his voice to a spoken whisper.

"The what? Oh, yes, that would really be hard to do."

"Did you want to practice some whispering exercises?"

"If you have the time."

There was a knock on the door. When Jesse opened it, Charles Abell was standing there.

"I was looking for your wife, actually. We have a session this evening."

"I think she's over in the kitchen, Charles, baking cookies for you," Jesse smiled.

When Charles reached the kitchen, he knocked on the doorjamb to announce his entrance.

"Is this where we're meeting?" he asked Rose, who was taking a hot cookie sheet from the oven.

"This is the place, if you want to have a hot cookie and a cup of coffee?"

"It's not something I can turn down," he said. She waved an arm for him to take a seat at the table and then slipped out of her apron and hung it on a wall hook.

"What will you take in your coffee?"

"Nothing, thank you." She poured and placed the coffee in front of him and brought the cookies to the table, hot and fragrant, resting in the cookie pan.

"I don't have a cooling rack to put them in, so for the time being, let's munch out of the pan." She slid a metal spatula under the cookies and bulldozed them to one side.

"They're like me, just plain oatmeal from the recipe on the box. Please, take what you want."

He let her remark slide and took a cookie, chewed, and made appreciative savoring noises.

"I like to keep them around for the kids who drop in. Gives the place a touch of home."

He thought for a moment that he could easily spend an hour over cookies and coffee talking pleasantly about the events of the day, but he became anxious to begin the evening's work or lose the opportunity in the aroma and pleasant surroundings of the kitchen.

"Which writers do you like most to read?" he said.

"Milton, Shakespeare, Racine...."

"Racine?"

"Yes, and Thomas Mann, Dostoyevsky, Tolstoy, Hawthorne and Melville, and James, and...."

"Okay. I get it. You like everything you've read."

"Not everything. I still don't like James Joyce and that mindless trip through Dublin."

They laughed at her reference to *Ulysses*.

"Is there a particular style that you admire enough to copy, if you could?"

"F. Scott Fitzgerald writes beautifully and so musically. I love to read him just for the language. And Milton, when I need to be reminded of who I am."

"Was there anything in this morning's seminar that you want to ask me about?"

"Not yet. I've been writing all afternoon, and I have a few pages for you. Do you want to see them now?"

"Sure. If you'll pour me another cup of coffee, I'll read over it and my comments might help you to finish it." Rose handed him three typewritten pages, and then refilled his coffee cup. Charles scanned the pages silently. He put a half-eaten cookie in his mouth and swished coffee around it. He reached in his shirt pocket for a pen clipped there, then put it back without writing anything. He finished the third page and set them in front of him. He "harrumphed" like a whale forcing stale air from his lungs during a breach.

"Do you have the *The Elements of Style* by Strunk and White, or a stylebook that you use for reference?"

"I don't have that, but I have a few things like *Fowler's Modern English Usage*, yes."

"Get Strunk and White. Read it. Read them all again. Read Fitzgerald again and pay close attention to syntax and the way he uses language to support his ideas. You may have a story here, but it isn't at all interesting, at least in what I've read so far. Do you remember what I said this afternoon? Pick a subject with which you are absolutely familiar and present it clearly without clutter, without grammatical excuses, without false notions of propriety. Don't write like a writer imitating a writer writing. Does that make sense?" Rose hunched her shoulders, not answering the question.

"Why don't you just start again? Don't try to repair this one, just make a new start for a new story in which you do not obscure the inner voice. Okay?" Rose shrugged and raised her brow as if such a thing he was demanding was far from her reach. The blood drained from her face and she stared at his left ear without making eye contact.

"Look Rose, I'm trying to help you write better. What I have to say about your writing is not personal, and you have to remove the feelings about yourself from your writing as well. You have to reach a place in writing where you can see what you are crafting—putting together and creating—not something you're giving birth to. You have to grab the language and work it as much as Rembrandt or Renoir manipulated their brushes. Get rid of the parsonage prattle and use the language that will clearly tell the story and reveal your idea, whatever that was." His voice rose more than he intended and he paused a moment. He was angry at her without knowing why. He regretted that he had created a useless moment of anxiety contrary to his purpose and he wanted to resolve it. Was it the cookies? The domestic woman/writer in the kitchen? The unprofessional too-casual atmosphere? He continued his commentary in a less strident tone.

"Do you like what you've written? I mean, does it give you satisfaction? Or is it just a story you've begun because it was an assignment? I'm sorry. I'm supposed to be teaching, not interrogating you, but I'm anxious for you to get the point, you see." Rose swallowed, her eyes wandered from side to side as though she were going to say something, but couldn't.

Oh no, she isn't going to cry, he thought, not over this, and then he said the unforgivable, the thing he wanted not to say.

"Rose, what you've written isn't worth crying over. Don't do it."

Her head tilted downward. She didn't look up as he rose from the table. At the kitchen door, he paused and said, "I'll see you tomorrow afternoon in seminar. Good night." He walked noisily down the driveway so he might not hear her crying. When he passed the hall and Jesse's office, deep in thought over his session with Rose, Charles heard a voice that he thought at first was a recording, but then he recognized it as Jesse singing a verse from *South Pacific*: "Younger than springtime, are you, softer than starlight, are you...."

The voice, rich and smooth, made Charles wonder if Jesse was practicing by himself or whether he was still helping Lonnie. Thinking no more of it, Charles walked over the Trinity Island Bridge, preoccupied by his unproductive session with Rose.

After Jesse had instructed Ruby in the practice of whispering and warned her repeatedly that when done incorrectly it could ruin the voice, he asked her to sing something to clear the tubes and exercise her vocal chords. She sang, "Some Enchanted Evening," from *South Pacific* since she had done it for a university production last year, and he listened with interest and appreciation.

After Ruby finished her rendition, Jesse could not help but sing "Younger than Springtime" to her as if they were in a B-movie from the forties. They were trying hard not to act like lovers, but a stranger looking into the room would have been convinced otherwise.

When he finished, Lonnie blushed slightly, and blurted, "I loved that show! I could sing those songs all night, they are so romantic, especially since we are on an island—'Here

I am, your special island, come to me, come to me," she sang, holding her arms out to him. His eyebrows raised in expectation.

"Oh, sorry," she said, "I was just singing that phrase about the special island, I didn't mean...."

"It's okay," he said, "We're just enjoying each other and the music. No harm done. It's good that you're learning how to express your inner feelings without feeling guilty about them. That's great! Look, I'm doing some research studies in the use of astrological phenomena to better interpret heavenly intentions. If we know the cards we've been dealt, so to speak, we can understand ourselves better and direct our personal freedom. It would be great if you could tell me about the important dates in your life, like the date and time of your birth, and that of your father and mother, and the essence of the important milestones of your life. You can write them down, chronologically, if you like, in short sentences so I can work with them in building your chart for the future."

"You can tell from that what my future will be like?"

"Not exactly. But I believe I can tell you some things about yourself that will give you direction that will open up possibilities for the maximum use of your talents. I'm using new methods that are proving to be very exciting, and you seem to be a perfect candidate. I want to do some others, too—the fellow who plays opposite you, for instance. I've already done Andora and Rose, and it's already proven to be effective."

"Okay. When do you want it?"

"How about at rehearsal? I also have a part in the play. I believe we have some lines together. Maestro typecast me as the minister, Ephraim, and I get to preach a sermon and sing some hymns. My lines with you are in the third and fourth acts, I think, unless they're eliminated by the writers' group. I'm looking forward to it. With rehearsals every day, we'll probably see a lot of each other. We'll have plenty of time to work on the voice stuff as well as your chart. If you're ready, I'll walk you home and we can talk."

When Charles walked over the bridge, he saw Shymanski's Seafood Restaurant and Bar directly in front of him, and he made for it as though it were a beacon of safety in an otherwise sad and reckless night. The bartender was watching the wrestling channel with another patron at the other end of the horseshoe-shaped bar. Charles took a stool where he couldn't see the TV and ordered a shot of Jameson's and a National beer on draft. He had not had a shot and a beer since he was a freshman in college and worked construction one summer in Erie, Pennsylvania, but the frustration prompted him to it again.

He reviewed what he had said to Rose. Charles knew he was right, of course—correct in his criticism of Rose's story—but wrong in the way he had delivered it. What had he been thinking? He wondered if Rose would survive the summer as a writer. More importantly, he wondered if he could emerge again as an instructor who could help students, or had those skills been ground away in the machinery of college administration? Perhaps he would see it differently tomorrow, but tonight he was kicking himself for his display of rudeness.

Waving to the bartender for another shot of Jameson, Charles thought of old Gus, his Norwegian boss in Erie, who had worked him and criticized him and taught him, and how they had visited the noisy bars and clubs after work for a shot and a beer, arriving home, arm in arm, without the lingering worry over a hard day's work. Holding the whiskey up level with his eyes, he thought, "To you Gus," and tilted the glass to let the whiskey slide down his throat, then he sipped the beer. He wished Rose were here so he could explain it to her again, differently. Although he was about to order another whiskey, he decided against it. There had not been enough time for the booze to reach his brain, so he would leave it alone for now.

After paying, Charles left Shymanski's feeling no effect of the drink and a little less reproachful of himself. As he shuffled along the shoulder of the road, he recalled Jesse's melodic voice singing from *South Pacific*, "Younger than springtime, are you, softer than starlight, are you, warmer than winds of June, are the gentle lips you gave me...," and he couldn't remember the rest. As he reached Chigger City, the effect of the alcohol became more pronounced. He climbed, whiskey-tired, up the stairs to the front porch, opened the door, and entered the house. "Hey, Momma!" he yelled, drunkenly, "Your bad boy's home!"

7

Mockingbird in the Mulberry Tree

Tuesday morning, the mockingbird singing loudly in the mulberry tree awakened Luke. The piano-playing of a Chopin scherzo from below brought him from half-sleep to full consciousness, looking at the ceiling. Rolling over toward the window, he saw Andora in the butterfly chair, gazing idly out of the window, watching a squirrel jump from limb to limb in the mulberry tree. The sun splashed over her face and shoulders, firing her red hair and casting her neck in shadows. When the bed creaked, she looked over at him and smiled. He extended his arm in a gesture that drew her out of the chair toward the bed. She took his fingers, holding them to her lips, kissing each one slowly and deliberately. He sat up, reaching for her, but she stepped away and went to the chair, turning her back to him and unbuttoning her blouse. It slipped to the floor and, with a flick of her hand behind her back, her brassiere followed. She plucked one hairpin from the back of her head, and the hair tumbled scarlet onto her shoulders. She thumbed down the elastic on her skirt and removed the pink half-slip beneath. Standing there, one leg slightly raised on its toes, she looked like Aphrodite—perfect Greek statuary of body lines flowing continuously and smoothly into a dream-like image of attraction and beauty. Then she turned a little more so that he might see her breasts—comely, firmly shaped and perfectly ripened. After an eternity of expectation, Andora turned and came back toward him. Luke could not wait and swept out of bed to embrace her.

The intoxication of that morning, in the sunlight with the summer breeze tracing over their skin, was new to both of them. The energy in those romancing bodies was knitted with the sound of Ward's piano-playing in the room below—after the climax of the scherzo, he finished softly with the prelude in E-flat minor. When the music was finished, Andora dressed and went to the door. "I came to get you to help work on the set," she said. "We have to paint the scrims today and fix that doorway so it will close." Then she left him.

Luke lay back, languorous, unwound, full of the sense of the miraculous. Downstairs, Ward's playing turned from lilting Chopin to the crashing, discordant sounds of Schoenberg. Eventually, Luke put on the shorts draped over the chair, drew a fresh T-shirt from the duffel bag on the floor and, stretching it over his thin frame, went downstairs to find Andora.

"You'd better take a cup of coffee with you," a voice said as he passed the kitchen doorway. Luke stopped and peered in and saw Rose sitting at the kitchen table. She pointed to her left, "Cup's in the cabinet, second shelf. Milk's in the refrigerator."

He went in. "Thanks anyhow, I take it black." He took down the cup and poured the coffee.

"Have a sit-down for a minute," Rose said, motioning him to a chair. He paused and sat down and sipped at the steaming cup. She was quiet and distracted, and he felt as though something unpleasant had happened and he didn't know what it was. He wanted to escape an awkward moment.

"I have to get over to the stage. Andora's waiting for me to help her."

"She'll wait," Rose said. "The next time you come down, bring your sheets. I'll wash them for you. No trouble. Nothing like clean sheets to make a fella feel comfortable. Are you feeling comfortable up there?"

"I'm very happy," he said, smiling at her.

"I can see that," she said. "It gets a little hot on the third floor in the daytime. How's the writing coming?"

"Not well. It's not that I'm stuck, I just can't find the time for it between working on the set and learning lines and all the other stuff."

"Be careful Luke, It's the other stuff that'll get you," Rose said, without expression.

"May I ask you something personal, or at least something that may not be my business?" Luke asked.

"This morning, there is not much of me left that's personal. What do you want to know?"

"Do you know Andora very well?"

"Fairly well, I think, although I'm not what you would call an intimate friend. She was in a youth church group when we were on City Island and Jesse counseled her once when she had a spot of trouble. She was in the church choir, but she couldn't sing a lick—voice sounds like she's just getting over bronchitis. You could tell she was there because of Jesse, all moon-faced and goggle-eyed, hanging around in the atmosphere of the Christian spirit." She winked at Luke. "The young girls think the world of Jesse. Andora worked with her father in a ship's store after her mother died. That was tragic. She tells people that her mother died of cancer, but honestly, the woman just walked off the pier one day and drowned. Hit her head or something. Kinda mysterious. Not long after she began working with her dad, she met Will in the store and married him. He is a very good marine architect, got a little money, and frankly, I think he's a little eccentric...." She was interrupted in mid-sentence by Ward coming into the kitchen.

"Luke! Andora needs you at the stage," Ward said.

"Maybe we can finish our conversation later; I'd like to hear more," Luke said, pushing away from the table.

"Why don't you ask her," Rose said, "She isn't a very forthcoming person, but she might tell you what you want to know."

He blushed again. "I will, I will," he said, and left the kitchen for the theater annex.

Rose motioned for Ward to come in.

"Sit down, Ward. Take a break. You're driving me nuts playing that dreadful atonal stuff."

"I know, I know, but I have to show them I can do it— that my playing and interpretation is flexible."

"It's okay. I'm just a little out of sorts this morning. My tutorial last evening didn't go well, and I feel terrible about it. I failed completely. Charles advised me to start over. I don't know if I can do that. I feel as though nothing I write will be of any value now, so what's the point? For whom shall I start over? Nobody will read what I write anyhow."

"Don't be down on yourself. If you need a guinea pig, do it for me. I'll read it gladly. I'm a good proof reader. If I'm not motivation enough, I'll throw in some bonus points. Start it over for me, and I'll cut down on the Schoenberg practice time. How's that?" She looked at him as if he were joking. "That shifts the focus," he continued. "Now I'm the reason for you to start over, and if I ain't reason enough, lady," he said twisting his non-existent moustache in imitation of Groucho Marx, "I'll throw in the Bach and Chopin that you like so much. If you haven't written a goodly amount by the end of the day, I'll go back to Schoenberg and you can scrub floors. Is it a deal?" Without waiting for her response, Ward got up from the table, took her hand and shook it gently as a sign of agreement. "Deal! Let's do it."

At the end of each day, the students who were not eating home-cooked meals with their landlords gathered on the parsonage steps around 6 p.m. Ward, practicing later than usual, rolled through the Bach toccata imperfectly, but without interruption. He'd been at it since morning and was tired. Without reaching the end, he crashed the piece in a jumble of discordant notes and began to riff and sing the song advertising Pabst Blue Ribbon Beer. "Pabst...Pabst Blue Ribbon...Pabst Blue Ribbon Beer...." With a sustained and sanctimonious "Ahaaaaaaa Mennnnnn," Ward finished with a final tremulous chord from the right hand.

"Woo damn!" he exclaimed, and made his way to the gathering crowd on the front porch. "Where are we dining tonight?"

"Half-priced burgers at Scuttlebutt's," someone said, and the group began walking down the road toward the little stucco bar located to the right of the bridge.

Rose, who had been sitting at her Olivetti portable all day, stopped writing when the music stopped. She had written and rewritten ten pages, double-spaced, and had corrected and edited until the copy was a blur, but she had made a start. Despite wanting Ward to read the pages, she stacked them neatly beside the typewriter and left the room. She was tired, but pleased she had worked her way into the new story and she experienced growing satisfaction that she hadn't put herself in the dumper. Instead, she had struck a vein of her imagination, and it was working—at least so far. She didn't know if she liked the new story, but compared with how she had felt that morning, she knew it would be better than anything she had previously written. She had gone from nothing to something, and although it was unfinished, it felt good.

Deciding that the kitchen was not a good place for her to write, Rose moved the table and typewriter into the bedroom, working late each night for the remainder of the week and awakening early, determined to have a story to give Charles Abell by the weekend. Each morning as the dawn lightened her room, she heard footsteps quietly ascend the staircase and the unmistakable squeak of the hinge on the door to Luke's room. The sheets, she thought, would need more than one washing.

8

The Crabbers

Each morning, Charles drank his coffee at the table overlooking the rock jetty marking the entrance to Neale Sound. He watched the crab boats haul the wire pots from the water and empty them on a culler, slide the keepers into a barrel, pitch the undersized crabs and the females back to the river, empty the old bait and replace it with new, gun the boat motor, then slide to the next float and repeat the process. Gulls dove and dipped around the boats as the old bait was thrown overboard. Although there were numerous crab pots around the mouth of the jetty, two or three crabbers could work their pots in rhythm, passing each other, bow to stern, with easy grace.

Charles thought crabbing must be hard and boring work—up early each day, tending pots on the changing tides, providing constant attention to pots and floats. What pleasure was in it other than the inherited desire to be on the water, taking food from it? Most crabbers barely made a living from a season that lasted only eight months, and much of that in bad weather. Perhaps making a "life" on the water kept the crabbers satisfied, if they ever were. Charles knew they were always at the mercy of rising fuel prices, a public's fickle eating habits, and the inconstancy of the numbers and quality of the crab population. State regulations constantly contained and trimmed crabbers' behavior, and a special commission of Maryland and Virginia officials placed further restrictions on licenses and catch. The notion of having a romantic occupation on the water as viewed by an outsider did not take into account the responsibility and tangled net of paperwork that the waterman endured. Pretty to watch from a distance, Charles thought, sipping coffee, but out there it was a constant push against a tide of difficult circumstances.

Only on the island for a week, he was already breathing a heady air of freedom from social constraints that normally bound his life to a singular purpose. Each morning of his presidency, Charles swam into the tide of public affairs and fished the pots that held resources for building the college—the screw-spinning, gear-screeching work of finding another pot down the line, culling and dumping, and missing the float with the boat hook and circling back for another stab at it, the gulls swirling and screeching to be fed. Here, on the porch of a house in Chigger City, looking down the jetty at the crab boats and the birds wheeling around them, he was beginning to free himself from the responsibility of working with the tide. He did not miss the irony of his finding beauty and enjoyment in the crab boat, driven by necessity, like the college president, to repeat the process of catching and keeping.

Charles tried to spend his mornings editing the stories and scenes produced by the students. For the remainder of each day, he studied and prepared notes for the next seminar, the kind of work he enjoyed, but had not been able to do for many years. Since the incident with Rose on Monday evening, he was more circumspect in his commentary to the writers assigned to him. He had conducted only one other seminar since that time, but Rose had not been an active participant. She had listened intently and taken notes; Charles had not called on her and she volunteered no comments. Thinking of Rose again, he wondered if she would shuck enough self-pity to become a writer or would she again lapse into the dull and maudlin prose characterizing her first story. Would she work at the craft of writing, or was "writing" simply a romantic notion in the head of a minister's wife? The student strings across Neale Sound began tuning for practice, and he quickly forgot Rose and listened in anticipation of their music.

9

"La Belle Dame sans Merci"

Each morning of the week, the parsonage steps creaked as Andora padded softly to the third floor just as the sun was rising. Under normal circumstances, lovers would be sneaking out of rooms at dawn, but her times with Luke were guided not by the rules of deception and subterfuge, but with freedom and openness. She would lie with Luke quietly until he awakened. Eyes closed, he would reach to free the hair from her face and kiss her lips tenderly. In the folding and unfolding of their bodies in the morning sun, there was no rush of purpose, no struggle to overcome, just the easy motion of love as if on quiet water. When they had rested, Andora would leave to attend her painting class and Luke would make his way to the theater.

On this morning, he found Maestro sitting onstage, not in the canvas chair with "Maestro-Director" written on the back, but in a more comfortable upholstered chair. After greeting each other, Maestro poured coffee from a thermos into a plastic mug.

"Would you care for coffee? I have no cream and sugar. They seem to be an unnecessary complication. There's another cup on the windowsill over there," Maestro said. Luke took the cup, wiped it clean on the bottom of his T-shirt and held it out until Maestro had filled it up.

"Have a seat, why don't you?" Maestro suggested, and Luke pulled up the director's chair. "This feels good," Luke said. "Now, if I only had a megaphone!" They laughed and sipped their steaming coffees.

"You know, I believe I taught you when you were a freshman not terribly long ago."

"Yes sir. You did, in English 102."

"And you wrote an excellent paper on '*La Belle Dame Sans Merci*,' did you not?" Luke clasped his hand across his breast and recited with emotion:

> O what can ail thee, knight-at-arms,
> Alone and palely loitering?
> The sedge has wither'd from the lake,
> And no birds sing.

"That's it, that's it. You remember."

"I do because it was one of my first college papers, and the first one that got an A."

"I remember that as well. You were an A student in that class. Were you as good in all the other classes as you were in mine?"

"Not nearly. But I have a confession. I plagiarized a reference in the paper. I didn't know what plagiarism was at the time. I should have known, but I did it out of ignorance, which is no excuse, of course, in a college English class."

"No it isn't, but you see, I knew it too, and I didn't have the heart to break you for plagiarism. I can't remember the passage, but it had been written by a colleague of mine in a paper with which I was familiar, and had nothing to do with your analysis of the poem. I thought you might have copied the passage from one of the departmental books on reserve and forgot to make attribution. Students frequently do. I started to reject your paper, but I gave you a reprieve because it was otherwise the best paper in the class. I meant to discuss the mistake with you, but never did for some reason. It's a nice poem. You should read it again. It reads like a fortune cookie for you. Do you remember the fourth stanza in which the knight tells the traveler why he is palely loitering? He says,

> I met a lady in the meads,
> Full beautiful—a faery's child,
> Her hair was long, her foot was light,
> And her eyes were wild.

"Is that not a familiar description?" Maestro asked.

"Yes, I remember it now."

"I'm not talking about the poem, Luke. Is there not a resemblance in those lines to you? My God, you are even our official resident knight-at-arms. Don't you remember? In the play, Luke wins the jousting contest as Knight of Elysium and earns the right to name Ruby the 'Queen of Love and Beauty?'"

Luke looked at the bottom of his coffee cup as if something was going to appear there.

"So you've noticed."

"One would have to be blind not to. It's a very small place, Luke, and with Jesse Caine encouraging a new style of Christian creative intimacy, our attention is drawn to those who love each other with fervor more generous than perhaps the message Jesse intends. It's none of my business, of course, but my colleague, Oliver, told me in his recommendation that you were a good writer with a fresh slant on the creative process. I enjoy your role as Luke in the play and appreciate your helping Andora with the sets and your obvious attention to her, but shouldn't you also be writing? If you have been, I haven't seen anything."

"I've been making notes for the church scene that I think will show Jesse's voice better and explore the collective guilt of the congregation a little more. It's the type of scene I'm familiar with and I think I can make it more authentic."

"Fine, fine, then do it. If there's too much traffic in the parsonage for you, go to my cottage. I've got an extra bedroom and a shower with plenty of hot water. Take a change of clothes and make yourself at home. There's a typewriter there and no one to bother you. There might even be some wine and cheese in the refrigerator—help yourself. I'll need the scene in two or three days, so you needn't come to work here until it's finished. I'll tell Jesse where you are, so don't worry about meeting your fellowship duties. The only stipulation is that you can have no visitors. Is that a deal?"

Luke was taken aback by Maestro's aggressiveness, and it made him speechless for a moment. He was flattered by the older man's attention and his insistence that he isolate himself until the scene had been rewritten.

"I guess. If that's what you want."

"That's what I am recommending you should do in order to fulfill your writing commitments to the workshop. While this place exudes the languor of a vacation in paradise, it really isn't, you know. There is work to be done."

"Yes, sir. I'll slip up to the room and get my script and then I'll be off. You did mean right away, didn't you? No waiting around for the muse to bemuse me?"

"An interesting idea, but you should do it now. The muses are less fickle and hardier than we're led to believe."

Luke drank his remaining coffee and looked at him. There was a hint of a smile tucked in the corner of Maestro's mouth, an expression of firmness overlaid with kindness and an intimation of understanding—a sense of confidence in having moved Luke in the desired direction with little effort. Luke went to his room, gathered up the script and a note pad, a change of shorts and T-shirt, and wrote a note for Andora.

I have been captured by the muses and taken to the writing dungeon. Do not try to find me. Luke.

He pinned the note to his pillow and began to feel the loneliness of being without Andora for several days. Not several, perhaps one, he thought, and maybe not even that if she found him sooner. The scene he was to write was in his head. He had only to script it out. That wouldn't take long. He would miss her, surely, but then there would be the reunion.

When Andora showed up that afternoon with members of the stage crew, she inquired of Luke's whereabouts. Maestro informed her that he had been given a personal task to do and would not return for some hours or perhaps a day or two.

He pulled her aside. "Listen," he said, "I talked to Will last evening, and he could use some help on the boat for a couple of days. Why don't you give him a hand, and when he doesn't need you anymore, come on back. You've caught up with the painting here anyhow."

"I should. I haven't been there in days. Although I don't think he misses me, he might need a hand if he's down there working in the bilge. There's always something that you can't reach and need help doing. Where did you see him?"

"At Scuttlebutt's. We had a beer and then went over to Captain John's for a soft-shell crab sandwich. It was delicious."

"Did you find anything to talk about?"

"Diddling conversation of men who don't want to talk about anything important: about boats, the America's Cup, and how good help is hard to find these days. He said you were a good hand to have aboard, and that if I saw you to ask you to drop down if you weren't busy and give him a hand."

"Alright, I don't mind. I've just finished a canvas, so I'll take a little break. Thanks." Maestro watched her go down the stairs, her body like silk flowing in the sunlight, and he thought that perhaps Luke's passion for her was well-placed. How could one not want to hold her and caress her? Then he turned to take a sip from his cold cup of coffee.

10

Pila

The living room of the parsonage was jammed and there were people on the porch chatting. A string quartet had set up on the lawn in front and had been playing Mozart for half an hour, attracting not only students but many of the islanders out for a Sunday stroll. A full-throated motorcycle roared up the street, heedless of the occasion and eager to drown the sound of the strings in the lusty roar of Harley-Davidson pipes to the annoyance of spectators on the lawn and porch. Across the street, volunteers were propped on chairs outside the firehouse, smoking and listening, not unhopeful that a call would come through in time to destroy the sound of the fairy music being played. Inside the parsonage, Jesse circulated among the students moving toward the piano, preparing to start the evening with his usual welcome and mini-sermon. Students on the lawn were soon drawn to the porch in anticipation of the Sunday evening program while the island folk drifted along on their original paths.

Luke was in the music room, leaning against the wall closest to the piano stool in anticipation of turning music pages for Ward, who would be accompanying Jesse in another song from *Elijah*. Having finished the scene for Maestro, Luke left it spread prominently on the writing table for the master's inspection. He then showered and left the cottage, eager to find Andora, whom he had not seen for two days. He scanned the room, the porch, and the lawn outside, but didn't see her. When he asked around, Ward hadn't seen her nor had anyone else. Maestro would know where she was likely to be, but he was next door in the theater, and Luke was becoming anxious over her absence.

Suddenly, a young woman stood in the doorway of the parsonage searching through the maze of faces for one that was familiar. She wore soiled jean shorts, sandals, and a clean white T-shirt. Her black hair, cut short and tight, swept back and revealed pouting pink ears. Through her naturally dark skin color, a reddish glow marked her cheeks and forehead as having worked in the sun. She stood there, looking. Then she saw Luke talking to Ward at the piano.

"Shake!" she screamed, and barged through the people milling in her path like a fullback intent on a first down. When she got to Luke, she threw her arms around him, knocking him into Ward, who was sitting on the piano stool.

"Shake, you fool, it's you!" she screamed. Luke hugged her and tried to disengage but she continued to squeeze and hug him. "It's me, Pila. It's me, it's me!" she cried, and then she tried dancing in a circle with him but was prevented by the close proximity of a chair and several bystanders. She hugged him and kissed him practically everywhere there was skin to kiss. Finally, laughing, Luke grabbed her hand and led her back through the front door and onto the porch.

"Oh, I've found you, I've found you," Pila shouted.

"But Pila, I wasn't lost, and I'm so glad that you're here," and he kissed her lovingly on the lips. They moved to the corner of the porch, away from the coming and going of the doorway traffic.

"Let's sit here on the steps. I'm in a performance later, so I have to stick around. Why don't you tell me why you're really here."

Pila pulled a folded piece of paper from her back pocket and waved it at him. "This is why I'm here—this suicidal letter."

"You mean you worried about me and came looking for me?"

"That and some other things."

"I told you in the letter I wouldn't commit suicide. It may be one thing to feel empty and worthless and another thing to want to end the pain of existence. I felt dumb, without value, a homeless soul."

"What else could I think but that you were really contemplating suicide? Listen to how you ended it: 'Give love and life is found; in man's own blood, man must drown.' If that isn't suicidal, what is it?"

"I don't know. I suppose you might think that, but I was just down in the major dumps. It was a rotten patch that I had to get over. Not many nights after you left, I was alone in the basement on Knox Road. In a moment of clarity, I felt my life was not there—there was nothing left inside. I felt like a hollow drum—empty. And then I heard a sound like a small ball bearing rolling from side to side. I just sat and listened. Finally I realized that I was hearing my courage, and

I cried. The more I heard the sound, the more I knew it was something in me that I had not put there—something not of me, not of my creation, but of my essence, of my being, tolling inside me. It was my eternal being, my God, the stuff of which I was made. The feeling it gave me was euphoric—I had been given back my life. I scribbled on a piece of paper, 'A falling star spent life and fell into my lap among the many seasons.' I knew I had received a part of the universe that would be eternally with me. That's what I've got now, and that's what I'm trying to keep. If that sounds a little screwy, that's okay, because I think that I have discovered the freedom to love life for its own sake and to have it love me in return."

"Wow, that's very poetic, not screwy at all, but how did it help you?" Pila asked.

"It gave me courage, but let's not talk about that anymore. Why are you here?"

"I came here hoping to find you, but also because I got a good summer archeology internship and a chance to learn some skills I'll need later. If I found you, I thought we'd have a beer and talk old times like we did before you sent me that stinking letter and left me without a proper goodbye. What a schmuck you are to send me something like that, and then end it with those lines: 'Give love and life is found. In man's own blood, man must drown.' What the hell kind of romance is that?"

"But, Pila!"

"Shut up! You, with the loose ball bearing, do you know how it made me feel? I was desperate for you, and yet I couldn't rush to you because if it was just a writing funk you were going through, you didn't need saving from it. But then I began to worry that it wasn't just the doldrums, but something more permanent, and the thought of losing you got to be too much, so I decided to find you. I was afraid for you and I needed you, and here you are going around inventing a religion out of a ball bearing for crap's sake. Find an altar—Jewish, Catholic, Protestant, it doesn't matter—and pray to a God already invented, one you don't have to dress in your own inadequacies. You need to pack up your doubts and come with me."

"Is this still your thing about the kibbutz you used to talk about? Your desire to make a new Israel in the land of milk and honey?"

"That's it."

"Oy vey," Luke said, and held his head in his hands.

"Come on, new man who has found his courage, I have plans for us."

"Pila, couldn't we talk about this later?" Luke asked. Inside the house Jesse began talking, so Luke shushed Pila and the conversation between them in order to hear Jesse.

"Many of you will be leaving us at the end of summer to go to other schools and places to practice and hone your art. I am also planning to go back to New York to start a new ministry and hopefully find work singing in an operatic company, perhaps the Metropolitan. Although I am working to build my vocal skills, those of you who know me understand that my ministry is equally important. The work of Jesus Christ is not finished and it takes many people with messages of faith to advance the Word brought to us over two thousand years ago.

"My particular interest in the revelation of Christian history and thought has become one that is dependent on an understanding of the universe and all of its meaning. If God made the world and the universe then it is obvious that there is a plan for man's destiny written within it. One of our fears lies in the presumption that if we can predict what will happen in the future, it will negate our understanding of free will; yet no one here would likely contest the notion that the more we know about ourselves, the better we may exercise our free will. The more we know about the astrological phenomena surrounding our conception and birth, the more efficacious our free will becomes. It is that simple.

"Much that we read and are taught about Christianity speaks to the end of things rather than to the future. We wait for the Second Coming and have created a ministry of soothsayers who have fed themselves predicting that there will be an apocalypse that will end the world. But I believe there is a larger vision, a vision beyond the shortsightedness of our generation, a vision that has been given us in the stars, and it is to the understanding of that vision that I am rededicating myself.

"You can help me in my studies, if you will, by stopping by my office when you have some free time and talking with me about your vital dates and critical occurrences in your life thus far. This will help me chart the characteristics that make up your character and point out the incongruities that may lie on the path to your success. It will only cost you a little time, and, of course, all of the information is confidential and only shared between us. Now, if you will lend an ear, Ward and I will do a piece from the Mendelssohn oratorio, *Elijah*, the story of that fabulous prophet who dared to change the course of religion."

As Ward played the piano, Jesse sang the piece with a controlled emotion that was spellbinding. He finished, took a bow, and for an encore launched into the Arlen and Mercer song written in the forties, "That Old Black Magic." The audience's mood in the room changed quickly and became charged with a youthful excitement. When he reached the last stanza, instead of ending with an up-tempo finish, Jesse squeezed his voice down and whispered the lines seductively.

> Down and down I go
> Round and round I go
> In a spin, lovin' the spin I'm in
> Under that old black magic called love.

As if in a night club, the crowd cheered and whistled as Jesse and Ward took another deep bow. Then Jesse announced that a scene from Act Two of the play would be performed in the theater in fifteen or twenty minutes once the cast was assembled.

Sitting next to Luke on the porch, Pila looked at him in astonishment. It was her first exposure to a Sunday evening at the parsonage and her introduction to the skills of Reverend Jesse Caine. "What the hell was that?" she asked.

"I really don't have a good answer for you. It's just part of the flavor of the summer arts program as it's being played out on Trinity Island. Every Sunday evening is a kind of 'Showtime.' There are always surprises. Everyone has to participate in some way or the other. Some of it is good, some is off the wall. I don't know what you're going to come up with from your archeology dig gig. Maybe you could just sing an ancient song while you sift dirt into a bucket, kind of like a 'Joan Baez digs dirty artifacts' thingy." He laughed at himself.

"You are such a putz."

"I'm sure you'll think of something," Luke said with a smirk.

"Listen, I've got to get back to camp because we're opening a new section tomorrow, early, and it's going to be a hard day."

"When will I see you next?"

"Next Sunday night maybe, if I can get a ride. If not, I'll ride a bike. It's only five miles down here, I think. I haven't finished explaining my plan to you, so don't run away."

"Okay. Come back. We can have a long talk."

"You could come to the dig to see me. I have a private tent and a 'Johnny on the Spot' and pure spring water in toxic plastic bottles and everything. All of the comforts. We would be serenaded by the cicadas with the stars above. You will be enraptured."

"I know. That's why I'm going to stay away."

"In the meantime, don't make any commitments, because you're mine."

They hugged vigorously, and Pila walked to an old pickup truck parked in the lot behind the firehouse and drove away toward Swan Point. Luke watched her drive over the bridge, wondering how he could tell her, and then he walked toward the theater.

11

Hanging at the Bridge

When Luke reached the front door, stagehands were setting up more chairs for the people standing around the perimeter. The crowd was larger tonight, probably as a result of word being passed around about last week's performance. There were also more islanders in attendance. The crowd grew noisier and, finally, the house lights flashed on and off, and then began to dim slowly. The crowd hushed.

{A spot gradually illuminates stage right; a gaunt man walks in carrying a cobbled-together leather case from which he extricates an old fiddle. He tunes it quickly.}

EZRA. My name is Ezra Gandy. I'm a fiddler and good friend and neighbor of the Adams family. I live over in that house yonder. Broadus Adams and me fought in the war together—that was the war between brothers. That's how I come to be where I am—because of Broadus.

I know pretty much the goings on around here on account of I walk the roads and play music for everybody and do special jobs when they need 'em done. I'm here to tell you about the hanging at Tobacco Styx Bridge, on account of I wrote a song about it that you still hear every now and then. This is a kinda long story I reckon, so if you just pretend that I'm singing it, it will help me get through it. I normally sing my stories because talking them makes me nervous. *{He plays the line of a tune ending with a suggestion of "take me out to the ball game."}*

It started at a baseball game. The Pisgah Blue Jays whipped up on the McConchie Marvels something awful, nineteen runs to nothin', and as hot as it was, Tom Adams pitched a one-hitter and Luke Adams hit two home runs. After the game we were celebrating and dancing. *{Baseball players in rag-tag uniforms shuffle out of the wings and gather around the bench drinking water from a big pot with a dipper. Ezra plays "Dixie" and some of the players and spectators dance around. After a few minutes, a ball player carrying a catcher's mask and wearing a vest walks into the scene.}*

DORSEY. Hold it down for a minute, y'all. Let's have a meeting here for a few minutes. I've got a few things to say and then we can all go home. This meetin' is for the ball players, so the rest of you all just go on over there in the shade or go home, we won't be but a minute. *{The spectators shuffle offstage, leaving uniformed ball players gathered around the bench. Ruby and Ezra stand away, but are still within hearing distance. Dorsey stands on the bench and addresses the men.}* I don't know if you heard yet, but they got Ted Cockrel down at the Chandler Town jail. They brought him from Baltimore, and since the new jail in La Plata ain't gonna be ready for a couple a weeks, they're gonna send him to the one in St. Mary's County. That means he won't be tried for a couple a months, maybe not for a year, or maybe not ever. Next thing you know, he'll be walkin' out of there a free man and nobody down there'll give a damn. He killed both my sisters in cold blood, and my daddy still can't talk from the stroke he had at their funeral. Y'all saw him go down—I tell you he's pitiful, slobbering and crying all the time. If we don't do something, they'll let that damned Englishman get away, I'll bet on it. Then nobody's family'll be safe. You're gonna have to lock your doors away from your neighbors and watch careful over your wife and children. *(The ballplayers grow agitated.)* I ain't gonna let that happen. It's gonna stop right here. I'm gonna stop it tonight. I ain't askin' anybody to do what I ain't gonna do myself, but I'm gettin' that murderin' sonofabitch out of jail and do what no judge in Charles County will do. I'm gonna hang that sonofabitch! *(The ballplayers applaud and finally someone speaks.)*

VOICE. When you gonna do it?

DORSEY. Midnight at the bridge. I'll be there if anybody wants to help, and we'll just go do it. *(He looks around and sees Ruby at the edge of the crowd.)* Let's be a little careful. Wear a mask, or better yet, wear some ladies' clothes so the sonofabitch will know that it's my sisters coming for him. Let's do that.

VOICE. Good idea. That'll teach 'em they can't mess with our womenfolk. That'll give 'em a message.

DORSEY. Let's get home and do what we have to do. *(The crowd begins to disperse. Luke walks up to Ruby and pulls her aside.)*

LUKE. You weren't suppose to hear any of that. You can't know any of it.

RUBY. Well, I heard it, and I agree with Joe. I'm in on it now, so's there's not a lot you can do about it.

LUKE. Shut up and get into the wagon. Where's Tom? *{Ruby walks offstage. Tom comes from the other direction with Ezra following behind him.}*

TOM. Ezra needs a ride home, too. We got plenty of room. *{They walk offstage to the sound of a horse and wagon driving away. Stage blackens for a minute. Finally, a match is struck and a lantern is lit stage left.}*

LUKE. Everybody asleep in the big house?

TOM. I hope so. Waughnetta's tossing and turning and talking in her sleep. I hope she doesn't have a nightmare that wakes her up and she finds me gone, that's all.

LUKE. She feeling any better?

TOM. I don't see how. If the baby's getting bigger every day, I think she's gettin' sicker. She can't keep anything in her stomach and she looks pale like there's no blood in her. How's Ruby comin'?

LUKE. She's feeling fine. You hardly know she's going to have a baby. She spends half the day with that squirrel rifle her daddy gave her, shooting rats and birds. Have you seen many cats lately? I think she's taken to shooting them too. Maybe Waughnetta will feel better when this heat calms down. It's so damned hot, I don't feel like putting on this dress. I'm taking off my overalls first. *{They both disrobe and put on dresses and bonnets that almost cover their faces.}*

Feels funny doesn't it, not wearing pants? *{The lantern light fades and the light is gradually shown downstage right where there is a railing made of tobacco sticks and timber raked across the corner. Men in dresses, some holding lanterns, are facing toward the corner of the stage with their backs to the audience. Tom and Luke enter stage left to the rear of the crowd and stand with their backs to the audience.}*

TOM. They've already broke him out of the jail. *{A man without a dress or hat and a handkerchief over his mouth for a mask, obviously Joe Dorsey, holds up his hand for quiet. He is facing the crowd and the audience.}*

DORSEY. Thank you for coming. My sisters and my daddy are proud of all of y'all. But before we go on, let me say that if you don't want to be here, you should go home now. Every man standing here now is a hero to us and to those murdered girls and every woman who's been taken advantage of in this county. Nobody can take away the guts it took for you to show up here. If you stay, you are helping fix the law they took away from us. Okay. Stand up, Ted Cockrel. *{He motions for the kneeling man to stand. Cockrel is bound hand and foot with a handkerchief tucked in his mouth, which Dorsey removes. The crowd slowly parts to the left and right allowing the audience to see Cockrel's back and Dorsey's front. Dorsey pulls a piece of paper from his pocket and reads by lantern light.}*

DORSEY. On the night of April 23, in the year of our Lord 1896, you did murder and butcher both my sisters with a hatchet and then pretended that it was someone else that done it. What can you say for yourself?

COCKREL. This isn't a trial. This is murder, that's what this is. I will say nothing to you. You are not the law!

DORSEY. The prisoner can't even say he didn't do it. He can't deny it. It was his hatchet, and the blood of my kin was all over him. He said he was beat up and knocked unconscious but there was barely a scratch on him. He tied himself up and pretended he was hurt, but a baby could have untied those ropes. And the bump on your head didn't even bleed because you put it there yourself, you liar. That blood on your pants didn't come from you, it came from my sisters, alright. No doubt about that. You got anything to say for yourself?

COCKREL. I told you I wasn't going to say anything to you. This isn't a trial. You have no right to judge me. I will tell the judge what happened at the proper time.

DORSEY. Do you want to say your prayers before you go?

COCKREL. I told you I wasn't saying anything.

DORSEY. *{Raises arms to crowd. He dips his finger into a small jar and paints a cross in red on Cockrel's forehead.}* Everybody on your knees and let's pray for his damned soul. *{The crowd kneels around Cockrel and they repeat "The Lord's Prayer." When they are finished, a man walks out of the crowd and throws one end of a rope over a tree's overhanging limb and ties it tightly to the railing of the bridge. He positions the end with the noose over Cockrel's neck.}* Put him up on that rail. *{Cockrel is forced to stand on the rail and balances precariously.}*

COCKREL. I didn't do it. I'll tell the judge. Get me down from here. It wasn't me who done it. It was one of you. I know who it was. I can show you who it was.

DORSEY. Say the name and save your neck. Say it now and we'll take you down. *{Several men move close, prepared to help him down.}*

COCKREL. It was.... *(The crowd moves in as if to hear better and a figure in a dress lunges at Cockrel and pushes him from the bridge. He falls. The rope tightens. We hear the snap of his neck. The crowd rushes to peer over the bridge and the person who pushed Cockrel disappears. The rest look at each other in surprise.)*

VOICE. What happened?

SECOND VOICE. We were going to take him down. He was going to show us who did it....

DORSEY. He had enough time to tell us. He was stalling. Don't worry, he got what was comin' to him.

LUKE. Oh, God help us. Look what she's done now.

TOM. What? I couldn't see what happened. Is he dead?

LUKE. He's dead. It's over. Let's go home. *(The crowd quietly leaves the bridge. The lights diminish to a single spot on the bridge into which Ezra walks with his fiddle and plays "Nearer My God to Thee.")*

As the house lights came up gradually, the capacity audience applauded. The actors came out for their bow. Backstage, Maestro was furiously writing in his note pad the corrections he wanted to make in the scene. Luke waited for him to finish. Finally, Maestro looked up from his writing.

"The action right before and after he gets pushed has to be slowed down a bit," he said to Luke. "It's too fast—boom—he's over the rail and it's hard to see—it's hard to realize what has happened and then the scene is over before you can gather your thoughts. We can make a little more business right before—maybe they should make a move to take him down and then she rushes in to push him over—that will probably help. What do you think?"

"You're right. We can put in some shuffling business; a couple more lines from Dorsey would help," Luke said. "By the way, did you get my manuscript?"

"I saw it there, but I haven't read it yet. I'll do that tonight. Are you coming back?"

"I might. It depends. If I see a light in the living room, I might drop by. Otherwise, I'll see you in the morning."

"Come by if you have a chance," Maestro said. "We'll open another bottle of Chateau de Lavernette and work a little."

"Maybe I'll see you," Luke said and walked from the stage and out of the building into the warm night air. He had been tempted to ask Maestro if he had seen Andora, but he didn't want to appear overly concerned about her. His steps took him automatically toward her cottage and when he reached it, no lights shone from the inside. There was no sound or light. She's not home, he thought. Luke retraced his path from the cottage, passed the parsonage and theater, and walked into Scuttlebutt's. Ward was there drinking beer with students from the string ensemble. When he saw Luke, he raised his hands and shrugged his shoulders as if to say, "I haven't seen her." Luke stood at the bar until he had looked around the room, then he waved goodbye to Ward and headed for the marina.

From the road above the marina he could see the boats docked in rows, their masts swaying in the gentle summer breeze. He walked down the path toward the berth of the Bristol Channel Cutter. The dock light illuminated a boarding ramp, but only ambient light from the portholes illuminated the deck. Through the portholes he could see figures moving inside and he caught a glimpse—a flash of red hair—and then nothing more. He waited and watched. A hum of an air-conditioner and the sounds of patrons on the deck of Scuttlebutt's filled the night, but nothing else.

Finally, he walked away from the marina. It was late, and he knew that Andora was going to stay on the boat overnight and that she had probably been staying with her husband. His heart sank as he headed back toward the parsonage.

Instead of going to his room, Luke walked up the road toward Maestro's cottage, passed the Fessenden marker, and saw a light still burning in Maestro's living room. He knocked and Maestro rose from the chair where he was reading the script and let Luke into the house.

"Couldn't find her?" Maestro asked nonchalantly, reaching in the refrigerator and extracting a bottle of wine.

"I think she's on the boat with her husband," Luke said

"Probably. She's been helping him down there for a couple of days."

"Oh," Luke said.

"I've read your scene, and I like it. It's well done. I'll tweak it a little tomorrow and make copies for the others and get started on it. We can have it ready for next Sunday night. The sermon's a bit long, but Jesse can read much of it from the pulpit without trouble."

"Thanks. It came to me without much difficulty. I think the shooting scene is going to be technically hard to pull off, though."

"Maybe not. If we change it a bit. Suppose she doesn't shoot a hawk on stage but Luke finds out that she probably shot the family dog?"

"That's good. That would really piss him off, and he could still take the scene to its climax. Do you want me to make the changes?" Luke asked.

"Okay, then I'll stay out of it. You'll have to do it here again, I insist."

"Alright. I don't know when I'll see her again. Hell! Maybe never."

"Here, have some more champagne," Maestro said, filling his glass. "Think about the work. I can't stand despondent lovers. They're so damned useless."

"Easy for you to say."

"No it isn't—not easy at all. I have a junkyard full of painful love affairs among my reminiscences whenever I care to visit them, each one more foolish than the first. I'm not going to tell you that I know your pain or that I've been where you are because it doesn't matter. What matters is what you're going to do about it."

"I do love her. I've never known another woman I wanted to spend the rest of my life with until now."

"You've known her what? Two, three weeks? Hardly enough days from which a lifetime can be writ."

"I just don't know how it could get better."

Maestro paused for a moment and then drank all of his wine and held the jelly glass out for Luke to pour more. He looked at Luke and squinted his right eye as if it contained the wisdom of the universe.

"I can understand that. She is one of the most delectable married woman I have ever known: young, vivacious, talented, slightly soiled, and undoubtedly a terrific lover, no? But those things are the price of admission; they aren't the show. Do you think that because you love her more than anything that it is enough to carry the baggage she has collected in her short life?"

"What baggage?"

"You see. You don't even know! You are ready to open yourself wide, to give her all of yourself in return for her love and you don't have any idea how large the payments are. When you vomit love it's almost always from a badly cooked meal. Take some time to see what comes from this relationship. You have no idea what she wants from life, what she dreams about. You want to be with her; she smells good and she walks with a grace and beauty in your eyes that are unparalleled, but why has she been wasting away in a boat sailing around the world with a husband who can't carry a conversation without talking about the geometry of a sail?" Then softly, Maestro repeated a verse from the poem:

> I set her on my pacing steed
> And nothing else saw all day long
> For sidelong would she bend, and sing
> A faery's song.

"You are listening to the faery's song, Luke."
"I can't give her up."
"First of all, you don't have her. You only want her. Secondly, that's okay. You don't have to stop wanting her, you only have to hold back something of yourself, something that you can give her six months or a year from now. Hold something in reserve. Like a fine wine, it will improve. It will deepen and develop character and continue to improve with age. But when you lay yourself open, when your raw affections fall out in a jumble, it will take a lifetime to put them together again. You will forever be looking for the thing which you have dissipated and you will not have reserved enough to make more. You will have nothing and the nothing will destroy you. If you give her all of yourself now, you will not get it back, and her thirst for you will be insatiable. It is what a truly dangerous woman does to a man. She leaves nothing for him to love in himself. Develop

something strong and durable in yourself; something that you may also love. Give Andora only the measure of yourself that she needs, and not more, and she will love you forever. When you are blinded as you are, you think the apex of your life is within reach; you embrace the lyrics of that stupid song: 'All of me, why not take all of me.'"

Luke drained the remaining wine from his glass and rose wearily from the chair.

"Bullshit," he said, "I'm going to bed."

12

Ruby and Luke Read the Rifle Scene

"Who was that woman you were lip-locked with for hours last Sunday night?"

"Come on, don't exaggerate, Lonnie. That's Pila. She's just an old friend who showed up unexpectedly."

"It looked like she was gonna jump your bones right there in the living room."

"No, we're not into that; there is no physical relationship between us."

"Not with you maybe, but she sure acts like she wants to bust your buttons."

"She's an excitable woman, that's all. We are simply close friends. She wants me to go to Israel with her and work in a kibbutz. I would rather not, but if she insists, I will have to do it. It's a long story."

"Tell it to me. Please. We have time."

"I know her briefly from grade school, then I met her again when we were both sophomores on the literary magazine at the university and we became friends. I bunked in a basement apartment behind the sorority houses with a desk, a portable typewriter, and three other roommates. I was not looking for a physical relationship, not even an easy one. I was already committed to my studies and to writing and sex seemed to me to complicate everything. That made Pila my perfect companion. We shared study time and careless beer-soaked hours filling ourselves with poetry and good feeling. We wrote and criticized and applauded and encouraged each other to do finer things, but we found each other around campus in yo-yo fashion, tethered to the same emotions and the same length of intellectual string. We hugged and occasionally we kissed, but most of all, we liked each other's company. Maybe that was because she was Jewish and I was from good Protestant stock of the hymn-singing, Bible-pounding variety. But what's not to like about her? She's almost as tall as I am, wide shoulders, ample bust, narrow waist, nice hips and legs. Her ankles are thick enough to hold that athletic body firmly in stride. She is *zaftig*, a heroic figure of a woman unlike the campus chicks with cute little figures and pouting lips."

"Stop fantasizing. I saw her, remember."

"I was just making a point. I was the scruffy guy in the beard and peacoat stalking the campus with the happy Jewish Amazon with the dark upper lip and ears that poked through her curly black hair. We hung out, talking stuff that ordinary students aren't interested in or can't understand. In the beginning of my senior year, I found that I could graduate at mid-year because I had been taking over twenty credit hours a semester and had accumulated enough to graduate in December. I was reluctant to leave, but I needed to work and earn enough money for graduate school the following year. I said goodbye to my mates, bought a six-pack of Iron City beer and sat on the back stoop with Pila and we talked. We talked mostly about nothing. We talked around our leaving each other because we had never ever talked about being together. Since we never admitted to being a couple, it was absurd to suffer the feelings that close couples suffer when they part. So we sat there, drinking beer and not saying what was smoldering inside us. Finally we finished the beer and I crushed the last cans, trying to make a statement, and Pila leaned over and kissed me lovingly and passionately until we ran out of breath. Then she gave me a great line. She said, 'Write me a suicide note, because you're gonna kill yourself when you finally realize what you've missed.' She smiled and walked down Knox Road in the shadows of the trees. 'Goodbye Pila,' I said, and suddenly felt like shit, and then I felt like shit for a very long time."

"Is that it?"

"It's enough."

"I don't have any deep relationships like that," Lonnie confessed. "I don't know how to get one."

"I don't think you can just go out and get one. That's part of the whimsy in life, isn't it? Things happen when you least expect them, and then they are not always what they seem to be. Like this play, whose lines we have only two more days to memorize."

"Okay, but I have one more question about the relationship between these characters, Ruby and Luke. Do you really get angry when Ruby won't go to bed with you?"

"Sure, I'm supposed to. You're my wife."

"Ruby is your wife."

"Which did you mean, Luke, the character, or me, the actor?"

"Both, I guess."

"Well then, hell, I don't know what the question is now, but yes. The character Ruby makes me angry when she won't commit to her conjugal vows. It's part of this farmer's life. It's part of the earth he tills and the food he grows that he must bed his wife and hopefully produce a son that will follow him. It is part of the cycle of the father and the son, and the ghosts of the men who came before them that drive his seed. It's not only Luke that needs to bed his wife, Ruby, it's the spirit of those others in him, driving him and the people at Elysium to renewal and completion. The Father and the Son and the Holy Ghost lay in the womb of the Virgin. That's what this play's about," he paused. "I think." He chuckled with uncertainty.

"And I thought she was just being a bitch. I can play the bitch, but wow, all that other stuff about the Virgin...."

"You do it very well."

"When we first did the rape scene, I was frightened. You scared me, but I don't feel that anymore."

"You are becoming an actor when you can express fear without feeling it personally."

"Maybe. I didn't say I didn't feel something; I just said it wasn't fear. Oh, well."

"Let's read through the rifle scene. We've got to make sure that the audience understands the differences between us although our characters don't understand it themselves. The tension keeps pushing them apart. Ruby's aloofness is palpable—it's almost a loathing.

"Okay, it's after church and I come back to the cabin to confront you. You're sitting at the table cleaning that little rifle. Here, use this yard stick until we get the rifle."

LUKE. I thought you were coming to church in the carriage with Mama?

RUBY. I didn't feel good. I felt sickish.

LUKE. You should've been there. It was important. Ephraim knew all about the bridge and the hanging. He said that God would forgive us killing a man like Cockrel if we went to the altar and prayed with him. You should have been there especially.

RUBY. Why me? We went to the bridge together.

LUKE. But only one of us pushed him over. And that 'one' was you. They were going to let him tell who killed his wife and sister. They were going to let him down from that railing, but you pushed him over.

RUBY. Everybody had a dress on. It could've been anybody.

LUKE. Not everybody had on the same dress that you had on at the ball game. Not everybody was in a blue dress and not everybody looked like they were carrying a baby, either.

RUBY. Well, nobody can say that they saw me, and you're not gonna tell anybody that you were there, so it don't matter none. He deserved to die.

LUKE. Nobody deserves to die like that, Ruby. He might have been an innocent man.

RUBY. He wasn't innocent of beating her, was he? Wasn't that why she sent for her sister to stay with her? Because he beat her?

LUKE. She never told the sheriff that, Ruby. You don't know that for sure.

{Ruby takes a cartridge from the table and slowly puts it in the rifle.}

RUBY. Everybody knows he deserved to die. That's why we was all down there. What do you care for anyhow?

LUKE. I care for the same reason I care about you shooting up the farm animals. Mama told me that she's seen fewer and fewer cats at milking time. Shooting crows is one thing, Ruby, but you can't go round shooting the cats. You're pregnant, for God's sake. The cats are like family, Ruby. And what about old Ranger? Did you shoot the dog too? Nobody's seen him for a month. Did you shoot him, too? *{Luke steps toward her menacingly.}*

RUBY. Whoa, son. *{Ruby places the barrel of the .22 rifle on his chest.}* I'd hate to mess up that shirt after I just ironed it. Just take yourself back a little. You try to lay a hand on me and you'll end up like Cockrel. *{She cocks the rifle. Luke's shoulders slump in resignation. He turns away from her but quickly turns back, snatching the rifle from her hands. He unloads the shell and, taking the rifle by the barrel, he smashes it on the fireplace.}*

RUBY. *{Jumping on his back and screaming.}* No! No! No! You can't do that. That's the only thing my daddy ever gave me. It's the only thing I've got. *{She tries to fight him and regain the rifle, but he pushes her away.}*

LUKE. Listen to me! Listen to me! You're carrying my baby. You can't go around killing everything on this farm you don't like. I'm not going to let you do it.

RUBY. But it was mine, mine! My daddy gave it to me and you had no right to break it. It's the only thing he ever gave me. I'll get it fixed.

LUKE. *{He grabs her arms and shakes her.}* It can't be fixed—you can't be fixed—and I'm tired of trying. You'll never see this piece of metal again, so get it out of your head.

RUBY. Then I'll see you in hell for it!

"Then I exit stage right with your broken gun, and lights go down with you sobbing into your hands. Okay?" Luke said.
"Alright, what do you think about the scene?"
"I think you've got to be a little more insane, somehow."
"I can redo the hair and make it more wild."
"No, I mean in the voice. Maybe after the first scream, you start screaming inside—but containing it and squashing it into a whisper that is evil—especially that last line."
"I'll work on it with Jesse."

13

Charles Revises

Tacked on the bulletin board on the parsonage porch was a flyer advertising a summer "float-in" sponsored by the Trinity Island Yacht Club for the enjoyment of all the yacht clubs on the Potomac River. Visiting boats were expected to arrive on a Friday evening at the end of August and leave on Sunday afternoon after attending events being held for their benefit. There was also an announcement under Jesse's signature that the students of the summer camp would participate by staging concerts, art shows, poetry readings, and a portion of Maestro's play on that Saturday, during the fifth week of the arts workshop.

The theme of the weekend was the "Crystal Skull," announced tongue-in-cheek, a mysterious artifact said to have been buried with pirate's treasure somewhere on the island. Members of the yacht clubs could search for the treasure at designated spots where the twenty-five events were being held. For the islanders, it was a summer celebration, and for the students, a dress rehearsal for their final programs in the following weeks. Not only would the weekend provide eager audiences for student performances, it would create a positive distraction from the student grind of study, practice, and rehearsal, or from writing, editing, rewriting, etc. The announcement about the float-in created an air of excitement and a tone of seriousness that always accompanies preparations for a performance.

Charles changed the venue of his Monday morning seminar to Linda's Gallery and Coffee Shop where he treated his six students to lattes and fresh pastries of their choice. As they sipped and blew on their coffees and settled into the leather couch and the overstuffed chairs in the corner, he sensed a considerable easing of the tension that had characterized last week's session. Rose was still quiet, but she looked relaxed and attentive, and he saw her smile during remarks by another student. Glad for the change in tone as the discussion progressed, he wondered if a simple cup of coffee in a different venue was the cause. When the seminar ended and students were chatting with each other on unrelated subjects, Rose handed him a manila envelope containing her manuscript.

"Ahh. You've finished," he said to her, smiling.

"Not finished, of course, but a first draft."

"It feels more substantial," he said, hefting it in his hand. "Look, I'm sorry the way our session went the last time...."

"Don't mention it," she said, breaking in. "You were right, of course; I think I over-reacted to your criticism. Finally, I decided that you were frank because you wanted me to succeed. It took me a few days to figure it out, but I'm alright. I've been through worse."

"Of course," Charles said. "Please accept my apology. I suppose we won't meet again tonight. I'll just get back in touch when I'm ready to go over the story with you."

"Shall I bake cookies again?" she asked, teasing him.

"Sure. It was nice there in the kitchen. Less academic than usual, I will admit, but very comfortable. I would enjoy that."

"Okay. Give me a ring when you're ready."

"I understand you have another project in the works," Charles said, preparing to leave.

"Yes, I'm trying to rewrite the last scene of the play for Maestro's little contest. Writing for the stage is a new experience, and I think I'm going to enjoy it."

"Well, if you need help with it, give me a call; otherwise, I'll be in touch when I finish the critique of your story."

Charles left the coffee shop and walked down the macadam road in the sun, hoping there would be a breeze that might alleviate the oppressive heat. The first boat of the morning was unloading crabs at Captain John's restaurant and men were wheeling the bushel baskets down the dock and into the outside walk-in refrigerator. Giving a wave of recognition to the workers as he passed, Charles walked on, trying to decide whether or not he should make a trip to the office today to check on college affairs. The work for the new semester and upcoming year had been substantially completed in the spring and most employees were away on vacation. A new building was about to go up, but it wasn't out of the ground, and his inspection of the site would be of no consequence. Perhaps he would make a few telephone calls to staff to give the impression that he was on top of campus affairs although he wasn't physically present. He felt uneasy when he couldn't feel the press of college business at his back. Then he realized it was his own need to feel important that was fueling the question of what to do, and he felt slightly embarrassed at catching his ego naked. He smiled and chuckled at himself, walking up the road to Chigger City trying to feel important.

"Fuck it," he said aloud to himself. He was shocked at having said it and looked around the road to see if anyone had heard him. No, it's okay, he thought. "Fuck it," he said again, this time deliberately, although under his breath, within the confines of his relaxed stride. If they needed him, they would call. Besides, he was curious as to how Rose had rewritten her story.

When he reached the house in Chigger City, he found that Leigh had set the table with a clean white tablecloth and was putting the finishing touches on lunch. He put his blue canvas briefcase by the table he used for writing and, on the way to the bathroom to wash his hands, pecked his wife on the cheek. She served a crab salad made from the backfin lump picked the night before, and they sat down to eat facing Trinity Island and the breakwater at the entrance to Neale Sound.

"What do you have to do this afternoon?" she inquired.

"Edit a story, correct a few papers. Remember the session with Rose, the minister's wife, I had a week or so ago when I staggered in from Shymanski's?"

"Did you really stagger?"

"Maybe just a wobble or two, but I felt like staggering. Anyhow, she has submitted a story and now I have to spend time with it—very carefully spend time with it. I dismissed her work the first time because it was trivial. I hope she didn't just rehash the old stuff and hand it back. If she did, I will have wasted a couple of shots of Irish whisky at Shymanski's and she will anger me again."

"Why does her failure to perform upset you?" Leigh asked.

He considered the question for a moment. "For some reason, I feel as though she needs to succeed at this herself—apart from the dubious aspirations of her husband. Not to mention this is supposed to be a graduate-level program, requiring a high standard of performance. I'm a little upset with sloppy work, that's all."

"I was thinking of picking up a few groceries uptown. Want to come?"

"No, I have Rose's paper to read, and then Maestro gave me Luke's finished script to look over. Have fun. I'll be here."

It was nearing sunset before Charles stopped reading. He had made copious notes in his copybook, and now he paused to let it all sink in. He had read Rose's story a half-dozen times, and still he could not wrap himself around it completely. There were things she needed to do to improve it, but he was loathe to suggest them to her now. He could tell her how good it was and praise what she had done without damping her enthusiasm. The changes he thought necessary would come during her rewrite.

He enjoyed reading Luke's rewrite of the third act, but that was a work of a different kind. Some stilted conversation remained in the script, probably a characteristic of writing short stories, but that would be simple to fix. Charles suspected that Luke had not spoken it through enough times and was in a hurry to complete it. Of course, he was correct, although unsuspecting that the cause of Luke's sloppiness was the missing Andora.

14

The MG Ride

Luke harbored no special appreciation for automobiles in general, but he loved his red MG TD convertible. He had sold all his earthly possessions to purchase it when serving for the U.S. Air Force in Germany and had toured in it through the Rhine River Valley as well as through Austria, Italy, and Spain. The little roadster had been taken to Majorca on the deck of a ship carrying goats and chickens, and he had driven it through the vineyards of southern France. It had been geared up and down the Swiss Alps, and he made the fabled run to Monte Carlo in it. The car shared a history with him; it wasn't just an English sports car.

On this hot and sunny evening, Luke washed and cleaned it, a thing he rarely did. After wiping the car dry, he started the engine and tinkered lightly with the carburetors until it sounded more like a racing machine than a hay bailer, and took it for a test drive around the island. At least that was his conscious intention, but underneath his thin mask of nonchalance he was searching for a glimpse of Andora. Motoring slowly by her cottage, he didn't stop because it projected emptiness.

At the tip of the island he saw her, with easel and portable canvas seat, painting the marsh grass and breakwater at the entrance to Neale Sound. He pulled around the cul-de-sac and shut off the puttering engine. He went up to her, looked at the nearly finished painting, and playfully shook his head.

"Well, what do you think?" she asked.

"That's a terrific oak tree," he said, jokingly, because there was no oak tree in the painting. Taking the brush in her hand, she wiped it across several blobs of paint on the pallet, turned and swiped at him with a sword stroke that made a brilliant red and yellow streak across the middle of his white T-shirt. He stared at his stomach, fell to his knees, and rolled on his back, pretending death.

"My liege, my liege! I am finally brought down by vermillion and cadmium yellow," he said, breathing his last dramatic breath, the streak of paint glistening across his stomach. Andora stood over him, pointing the brush. "Get up, you ungrateful varlet or I'll paint you all over." She laughed, leaning over him and brandishing the brush. He groaned and leaned on one elbow, reaching for her hand to give him a boost up, but she ignored him and went back to her painting.

"Are you finished?" he asked.

"With the painting, yes. I'm losing the sun. But with you, I am obviously not finished! What do you have in mind?"

"I've missed you. Throw that stuff in the boot and let's take a spin."

She ignored his reference to their time apart. "Will you buy me something to eat?"

"I would if I could, but my eagle has not yet landed and I don't have a dime. If I did have money, I would have to buy gas with it."

"What a lover you are," she said. "I get to feed and water you for a ride in an ugly little English car."

"Right now, I think it's the best offer you've got."

"You're not nearly right," she said, smiling. "It's the only offer that I want—even if I have to buy it."

She stowed her gear behind the seat of the little car.

"Stop at the house for a moment so I can wash up and get some money."

When they reached her cottage, she motioned him in. He had never been inside the place she maintained apart from her husband, but he wasn't surprised when he found it to be as sparsely furnished as most beach cottages. He followed her toward the bedroom where she stopped in the doorway, put his face in her paint-stained hands, and kissed him tenderly. She looked at him.

"What?"

"I've left my mark on you," she said.

"Then I guess it'll have to stay there," he said. "If I wipe at it, I'll smell like turpentine." Taking a rag from her back pocket she cleaned the smudge of paint from his face.

"There," she said, closing the door in his face and disappearing into the bedroom. He wandered to the far wall, where a large hanging painting looked as though it had been done at night. It was dark with large indistinguishable shapes appearing in the background as if they were trying to find release from the canvas. The signature in the corner was hers, "Andora." He didn't like the painting and walked away from it. On a side table he spotted a small box in the shape of a sea chest, expertly crafted and inlaid with colorful bits of shells.

Expecting to find a few trinkets of memorabilia, he opened it. A few photographs lay loosely atop a folded piece of soft blanket: Andora and Will posing on the boat; Andora and Will swinging a child between them; and then a close-up of the child's face, who bore a close resemblance to her mother. Then Luke saw something else, a familiar expression... Andora stood in the doorway.

"Put it back!" her voice came at him sharp and hard. "It's nothing to do with you. It's private! Put it back!"

Luke placed the photos in the box and closed it quickly. Andora came over to the table, picked up the box, and took it hurriedly from the room. When she returned, she left the house without a word and got into the passenger side of the car. Following her, Luke closed the car door and got behind the wheel, feeling as though he had just done her some injury by opening a box that lay invitingly in the living room. He wanted to apologize, but didn't. Instead, he headed quickly over the bridge and off the island. She said nothing until they had driven twelve miles to the intersection of Route 301 and he took a left turn that would lead them south to Virginia.

"Where are you taking me?"

"You'll see soon enough."

They crossed the Harry Nice bridge over the Potomac and, after filling the tank with gas, turned left at the sign directing them to Colonial Beach. They drove to the eastern tip of the peninsula and pulled into a parking place at Point Payne where they had access to the beach as well as a view of the twilight afterglow.

"Why did we come here?" Andora asked. Luke pulled a small blanket from behind the seat and motioned her to follow him. They headed for the beach, found a smooth spot of sand, spread the blanket and sat down. He pointed to lights on the distant shore.

"See over there? That's our island. Over there where the red light is blinking? That's Fessenden Point. When we stand over there and look over here, it looks far away, as if it were another country. It's only Colonial Beach, but it could be France or anywhere in our imagination. And what does our island look like to you?"

"It looks like Trinity Island," she said. "Were you hoping it would be Capri?"

"I don't think so. I was just looking for another point of view of our island, another angle that would give me more clarity. I've missed you terribly these last couple of days. I thought maybe that seeing the island from here would change the reality of the life I've been living lately. I don't know if I am real over there, or if the real me is sitting here, or are they both fictions of imagination?"

"What do you find unreal about living over there?"

"Your disappearance for one thing; us for another. It's as though I've walked into a fantasy world that keeps opening doors with experiences and feelings that are unreal to me. I need to know if you are real before we go on."

"Go on?" Andora asked. "Go on where? Go on to what?"

"That's what I want to know. I feel as though I'm in a dream. I don't want to guess, and I don't want to dream. I want to know that you won't disappear if I should suddenly wake up."

"Crikey," she said. "I stayed on the boat with my husband for a few days to help him do some work. I didn't disappear. Will and I talked a little. Well, we almost talked a little, but there was nothing else. Don't make a big deal out of it. I have to spend time with my husband—he is my husband—and don't pry into my personal affairs."

"I had no intention of prying. It was idle curiosity that made me open the box, but now I realize that I want to know more about you. I could just let it all slide—lay back and enjoy the pleasure of being your lover—but now my feelings are growing for you in ways that go beyond that...into deeper water."

Andora clasped her hands around her knees and rested her head on them and lapsed into a moment of contemplation. She didn't normally speak at length. Her voice was not the instrument that revealed her character as it was with so many other students in the camp. When she labored to say something important there was a twisted croak in it, as though there were a hurt animal in her chest laboring to get out. When she held her silence, her eyes gave him thoughts the voice could not sound, and it enriched what they did not say to each other. Tonight, however, there were many things that needed telling.

"I'm sorry to have upset you," he said.

"Talking like this doesn't upset me. I want you to know me as much as you like, if it helps us go on, but if I tell you about myself, I'm afraid you'll make an end of it and leave me. I am in such a dark place sometimes that I'm not sure that anything can be done. There are things that will always be there—between us—and they won't go away. Sometimes I think that I can resolve them, but I know that they will never be forgotten—cannot be forgotten—and I am locked in the nightmare that lies inside that box."

"The box I opened at your house? There were only photographs in it. Why did that upset you?"

"It upset me because I wanted those photographs—those memories—to stay there, especially away from you. I haven't opened the box for a while because I didn't want it opened—didn't want to be haunted by those memories—and then you were there, uncovering, letting them out, and it was as though I felt the pain again, and it was you hurting me, and I couldn't help myself. I wanted you to stop."

"I didn't see anything unusual. I thought I might find some shells."

"You found the shell of my life and didn't recognize it."

"Can you talk about it?"

"I don't want to for fear of losing you. I have made a lot of mistakes that don't seem to be redeemable, and I don't want you burdened with them. I want to come to you with a feeling of freedom that will give us a life together. Does that make sense?"

"Only if you realize that if you tell me about them, you may free yourself from them."

"You must be patient then, because some of it is hard for me, and regardless of how you think of me after, you still have to feed me and give me a lift home."

"Alright."

✦

"I was living on City Island in Pelham, off Manhattan, with my father who ran a ship's store down by the docks. My mother died with cancer, and I took her place working the store with my dad who had retired from the Merchant Marine as a supply officer. You know how islands are in the summer—like nobody cares—so I was caught smoking pot out on the pier with some other kids by this self-righteous cop and rather than being arrested, we were sent to the Reverend Jesse Caine, the Methodist minister, for counseling. After a couple of sessions everyone dropped going to him but me. I liked listening to him, and I would hang around the church while he practiced singing. His voice was exciting to me and it made me want to listen and understand. It was better than the pot, and I gave up hanging out and smoking with my friends. When he sang, he made me want him—not just to listen to him—I was drawn to him—I wanted to be with him. He didn't condemn me for being a delinquent. He sang to me and saved me and made me feel good about myself inside. One night, after church, he walked me home. We sang some hymns together and then in a dark corner of the boatyard, I stopped and kissed him and we lay down and made love. I was sixteen.

"After that, I hung around the church and the parsonage as much as I could and helped clean the church and made cookies with Mrs. Caine in the kitchen and made love to him every chance I got. We were very careful not to get caught, but within a few weeks I knew I was pregnant. I had only missed one period, but I knew he had impregnated me because he was a man who could not fail to change me in every way possible.

"Then Will Van der Falken came into the store to buy some boat stuff. He was a young god: tanned, rugged, confident, all the romantic looks of a man who's been sailing at sea. I was drawn to Jesse, but I knew when I saw Will that loving him, too, would be easy, and that it would be far better to let him have my baby. I married Will Van der Falken two weeks later. We lived on his boat—it was the *Galaxy* then—for a few months, and when I became larger with the pregnancy, we moved to Manhattan and occupied the second floor of a brownstone a block away from Broadway. Before the summer was out, we had a little girl that we named Tilley. If she had been a boy, her name would have been Tiller, of course."

"Then she is the little girl in the photographs? Where is she now?"

"Let me finish," Andora said, choking back an immediate response to the question.

"Will worked as one of a group of marine architects shaping boats, designing sails, redesigning and testing new ideas, and he loved it, and eventually I came to love him. I didn't know when we were married that Will's father had been a successful Dutch importer and had left Will a rather substantial legacy. The money, not to mention his talent, made it easy for Will to purchase a partnership in the design firm. Since Will was happily occupied in the ship-designing business, I was given the selfish luxury of raising baby Tilley. As other mothers rushed downtown to work in the morning, I pushed Tilley around the parks and looked for the sights and sounds of New York that I thought would please a happy child. Of course, I was expanding my horizons as well. I took her to museums and we listened to music and tasted the gelato from the corner vendor and I don't think there could have been a happier nineteen-year-old mother and baby in the city than us.

"On nice evenings, with Tilley tugging at my fingers, I walked through the crowds toward the subway to meet Will as he came up from the underground station. When he saw us, Will would play hide and seek with her, squeezing himself behind a lamppost, crouching behind a parked car, hiding behind the person in front of him, and, finally, Tilley would see him coming and scream and hold out her arms for him. She was just a toddler, a little more than two. We were walking down the street toward the station one day when she saw him coming toward us. I let her down so that she could run to him as he ducked briefly behind a parked car. She started bobbling toward him and then suddenly she veered to her right and ran between two parked cars and directly into an oncoming taxi cab. I think she was trying to play with him—to play the same game with him—but she was killed outright.

"I shouldn't have put her down, but I had done it before without harm, and it was just something natural for me to do. It was an innocent child's impulse to play that pulled her into the street and underneath the car. I was only a few feet away, but she was gone in a second—too far to reach. Will was devastated. He took her death on himself: we shouldn't have been living in the city; he shouldn't have been slow to catch her up; we shouldn't have had a child in the first place because I was too young to be a responsible mother—all of it. I didn't fully realize it then, but he put me aside. The moment she died, Will's love for me was gone, as though Tilley took it with her. That's when we moved onto the boat, out of the evil city and away from all those things that reminded us of her.

"We sailed back across the river to City Island. Will wanted to start going to church so we walked down from the docks to the Methodist church where Jesse was still the minister. He took us in with open arms and talked with Will and me about death and the life hereafter. Jesse gave both of us his love—a wholehearted love and understanding of our suffering. He prayed with us and sang to us and helped me understand and accept Tilley's fate, but he could not release Will from his grief. Jesse helped him a bit, but Will couldn't give up his pain to Jesse as I did. One evening, Will had stayed on the boat and I went to see Jesse by myself. Rose had gone to Manhattan, and Jesse was in the living room at the piano singing a song from *Elijah:* 'Night falleth round me, O Lord! Be Thou not far from me! hide not Thy face, O Lord, from me...,' and as Jesse sang, I could feel his love healing me. When he finished, I went over to the piano and leaned over and kissed him, and I could feel the pain leaving me, and then I gave myself to him without saying a word, and afterward, when I was walking away from the parsonage, I could hear him singing, and I knew that the pain in my heart over Tilley had been taken away.

"After that, we didn't stay very long at City Island. Will couldn't stand being moored at that dock. Every child he saw brought tears to his eyes until he couldn't talk it out with Jesse anymore. One day, I provisioned the boat at the old ship's store and had a hugging farewell with my father. He was old and sentimental and given to a quick tear, which was probably why Will wouldn't say goodbye to him despite the fact that we both knew it might be a while before we saw him again. That was five years ago and I have been sailing with my Flying Dutchman ever since—stopping here and there until the memory of Tilley would catch us up and then we'd float another tide and be gone again."

"But how did you get here? What brought you to Trinity Island?" Luke said.

"I had a revelation," Andora replied. "We were sailing off Bermuda one day. Will was still deep in remorse and I was becoming frightened because he would barely speak to me. Then I saw the box down in the cabin, the box that held the ashes of our Tilley, and I went topside and confronted Will in a fury, accusing him of sailing around the world with the ashes of Tilley and never wanting to put her to rest. 'The child needs peace!' I screamed at him. 'Put her in the ground. You can't keep her wandering around the ocean while you wait for her to come to life again. This is perverse!' I screamed, 'I won't let you do it, anymore,' and I attacked him. My hysteria woke him from his trance for a while, and finally we charted a course back to City Island.

"When we arrived, I went to the ship's store and found that my father had died shortly after we sailed and I had never received the message. He had retired because of a heart ailment to which I had paid scant attention in my youth, so the news put me into a little spin. I went to the Methodist church to see Jesse, feeling sure that he would have more details, but he had been transferred to a church on Long Island shortly after my father died. The world as I knew it had disappeared. I didn't know what to do. We found that my father had been buried in the Methodist church's cemetery although he had never been a member of the church. Jesse must have done that for us. But the new minister was also kind and offered to place Tilley's ashes next to my father's body and I was grateful and relieved. So, her ashes are there, on City Island, beside Dad. The minister gave us Jesse's phone number on Long Island, but I was told when I called that he had left that place as well. Then I was given the number of a bishop or a supervisor who told me that he was here, on Trinity Island for the summer.

"Will had to go to Annapolis for an engine repair, so when we completed that, we sailed down to Trinity Island. I think Will wanted to see Jesse to show him that his sorrow was being repaired as well the boat. It was something between them."

"My God," Luke said, "the cuckold searching out the adulterer to show him what a man he has become, and the ravisher, eager to assuage his guilt, commiserates with the victim to ease his own pain. What a shabby drama."

"Don't be snotty."

"I'm sorry," Luke said, rushing to recover his remark. "I didn't mean to be disrespectful. It's the irony of Will and Jesse uniting again like lost brothers that created a bittersweet scene. I wasn't mocking you. It's tragic. When I saw her picture in your house, I was struck at how much she resembled you, and then for a moment I thought I caught another expression in her that I couldn't place."

"Now you know," Andora said

"It was Jesse. Do they know? Do Jesse and Will know who fathered Tilley?"

"No. Will sees only the likeness of his dead Tilley and nothing beyond it. He cannot see beyond his grief. We never show the photograph. We rarely look at it now. We placed it in the box where her ashes had been as a kind of memorial just for us. We don't open the box for fear that all of that will suck the life from us again—that the tragedy and pain, the death and the loss will come back to us. We usually keep it on the boat, but Will needed it to be moved while he worked, so I brought it to the house. I should have put it in the bottom of the closet, but you are one of the few people who have been inside the house."

"And I opened it."

"I don't think it carries a curse, only sadness."

"What is Will going to do when he finishes repairing the boat?"

"I'm trying to convince him to stay, or at least find work in Annapolis, although we certainly don't need the money. He's talented enough to do that, but I don't think that I've convinced him that we can't sail out of her memory."

"Are you ready to spend the rest of your life on a boat? Sailing from place to place? Doing what? Carrying around your secret to comfort the man who wasn't the father of your child and has difficulty acting as your husband?"

"The moving around isn't the worst of it. There were weeks at sea when he didn't talk with me. I could see him crying inside, and he wouldn't let it out. It drove me to painting more—scenes around docks, boats, water, ocean, all of the old clichés—and I sold them in the little towns we visited. I have some over at Linda's Gallery now. People like them and buy them cheaply, and it makes me feel independent. When I'm not helping at the theater or with you, I spend most of my days painting, as you saw today. I would be lost without it. I'm beginning to think I would be lost without you, as well. As for telling him who fathered Tilley, I never will. It would kill him, and since you are the only other person who knows, I will kill you if you tell him. Does that answer all of your questions? Do you have a clear sense of reality now? Knowing what you know, is it possible for us to 'go on' as you called it?"

"Do you still have a physical relationship with Jesse?"

"You are getting tiresome. Suppose I asked you what difference it would make between us if I were screwing Jesse? Would you answer me? If the answer were, 'yes, I am still screwing him,' it would make you cry, wouldn't it? You would feel hurt and abandoned and lost, and in the end you would be outraged—so much for the depth of your selfless love, Lukey. Take me or leave me for what I am, not what I have been."

"There's the grand irony. I know less about who I am than you do. It's not finding out about you that will make us 'go on,' it's finding out something about me." Luke said, smiling weakly. "I don't blame you. I don't feel that I offer you as much as your husband or your Bible-pounding lover."

"Oh crap! It's true. You sing me no songs or hymns in order to make me your conquest. You don't blabber at me about sails and their relationship to hull shape and you don't need me to bear your personal pain and suffering when we're together. You believe in kindness and the goodness of the soul. But you want me to see the same beauty in life that you see and you want me to celebrate it with you—just as I am. That's what I thought you were, Luke, but since my secrets have spilled out of the box, you might have changed your mind. Am I still enough, Luke—enough to 'go on?'"

"Yes," Luke said. "But you also have to see what you're getting. I am an unaccomplished writer with no place to go, helping you paint stage sets in a dinky summer theater on an island that feels like it doesn't exist in time. My future is uncertain because I have mortgaged myself to a graduate school to study a subject that will not help me earn a living. I'm a mediocre writer who can't get published and whose prospects for the future are not encouraging. That's the sum of the person who wants you."

"You see," Andora pleaded, "that's what I love in you: the things you say you don't have are what attract me. You give me love and it fills me up; you touch my hand and my heart races; I look at you and I can't wait for our future to happen. I don't feel the same things about you that I did about Will or Jesse. There's a quality about you that I can't describe. After I've been with you, I want to paint, paint beautifully in bright colors and pleasing forms. I don't want to dig into the dark recesses of my soul, to hurt myself and bring my tears to canvas. I want to come out with you to dance and paint in the sunshine. I do want us to 'go on.'"

She looked at him expectantly, waiting for him to affirm her declaration. She waited, and he said nothing, so she continued.

"That's how I see us 'going on.' I don't know what decision it would take to make our future come true. Can we continue to work it out, to see where the 'go' will take us? If I get to the place where my freedom lies, I'll know it and reach out and take it. I need to come to you freely. It's that freedom that will give us our future, nothing less."

"Meanwhile, does Will care about my being with you as much as I am?"

"There's another irony. He cares because I am the mother of his dead child, and he will keep me from harm because of it. He won't interfere with my happiness. Will doesn't love me the way that you love me, but he wants to hold onto me until he has completely resolved her death and then he wants to make another Tilley. I am his mother-in-waiting, but his sorrow has made him emasculate. I am Jesse's discarded concubine but he has also become impotent. You are the lover that I want and cannot keep—you are the heart inside my own. That, my precious Luke, is how the secret will spill out of the box if it is overturned on Trinity Island. That secret will bring a raging storm."

"Look at the lights twinkling on the island. It's a pity we can't see ourselves as clearly."

"You're only looking at the dying light. It seems poetic, but it's an illusion," she said.

"I suppose so. Over there our lights burn from the inside; over here we only see the color without the heat and the passion."

She kissed him and then, holding his face in her hands, she said softly, "Right now I would trade you and all this poetry for a soft-shell crab sandwich. Don't say another pretty thing. Let's go!"

15

Rose's Death

It was after dark when Leigh came back from her visit to La Plata, and she could tell by the general disarray of the kitchen that Charles had made a sandwich for his supper, a crust of which remained in a plate sitting by his worktable. There was also a bottle of Jameson Irish Whiskey on the counter. In the small living room, she found him slouched in an aging overstuffed leather chair, a sheaf of papers in one hand, and an empty whiskey glass in the other.

"Have you been at it since I left?" she asked.

"More or less."

"Are you having any success?"

"Oh, a great deal, or at least I am convinced that Rose will have a successful story. It's very good."

"Wonderful. What changed it for you? Didn't you tell me it was so bad you became angry with her?"

"Yes, but this isn't the same piece. She must have started over, and this time, it is really well done—a little rough, but a very interesting draft. I hesitate to mark it up."

"That hasn't stopped you before."

"I know, but I think it's a little personal, so I want to be careful about suggesting editorial changes so as to avoid bruising her feelings anymore. I want to talk with her about it."

"Is the story that raw?"

"I think so. It's about a woman riding in a car with her husband when he clumsily involves them in a horrific accident. He survives with scratches; she's taken to the emergency room in a coma, barely alive. At one point she's declared dead, but she's resuscitated, and for the next two weeks she undergoes several operations just to keep her alive. Her coma persists, but when she finally comes out of it, rather than having lost her memory, as many accident victims do, it has been intensified."

"What does that mean, exactly?"

"She remembers what she has been thinking during the coma, a kind of a reverse amnesia. She remembers things as though having had a vivid dream. Before the accident she was the wife of a minister living the conservative lifestyle admired by the biddies of the church, but lying in her dream state, she built a new and different relationship with him. She writes him love notes—some of which are erotic—and gets him to go dining and dancing on their anniversary. Instead of wearing her grandmother's full-length nightgown to bed, she dresses in an eye-popping negligee in an attempt to invigorate the husbandry of their marriage. In her subconscious life she creates the independent behavior she has always wanted, including a loving and exciting sexual relationship with her husband."

"She had to be unconscious to do that?"

"Yes, because of the expectations of her social position. It's all told very cleverly and in the best of taste, although what she enjoys with him in her dream is less 'missionary' and more 'harem' than he expects. The subconscious life she's passionately living lasts but a short time in her coma. Her husband, meanwhile, prays day and night by her bedside that the coma will end. She eventually awakes, and he believes that his prayers have been answered—he has been the instrument of her recovery. Of course, he doesn't know what she's been dreaming."

"Haven't we heard this story before? Isn't this where Prince Charming lifts her from her death shrouds and sweeps her into never-never-land on his white horse?'

"Not quite like this. You see, she remembers the beauty of her life in the dream world, and she's anxious to continue it with the same passion when she's awake. Although her health progresses, she looks at herself in the mirror and sees the devastating toll the accident has taken. She is shocked and frightened by her ugliness. How can she continue to create a new sexual and spiritual life with a gruesome and repulsive image? How will she create her life, reborn in oblivion, and continue with confidence to make a new life with the man she loves?

"As time passes in slow agony, surgeons perform miraculous operations; she undergoes tedious therapies and an exhausting regimen of recovery. Because she has paid dearly for this new life, she is intent on having it. Her suffering is a long, arduous, and painful journey buoyed by a courage that is otherworldly. When her face and body have been completely restored and enhanced, and her enthusiasm for life regained, she begins to realize that her renaissance has had the opposite effect on her husband. She tries, with diminishing success, to recreate the relationship of her dream, but she cannot help but see that she's failing. He believes he's responsible for raising her from the dead, and his relationship with her has been consumed by his tormented spiritual desire to recover her life from the wreckage he has made of it. She tries but cannot persuade him that she was not only saved from death, she was also reborn in a new life. However, it becomes clear to her that he doesn't love her. She has become an icon, removed from the warmth and care of her husband's daily life.

"There's a terrific scene where she faces herself in the mirror, and as she watches, the positive effects of her operations are undone: the skin tears apart at the scar, the eye disappears into the skull cavity, a bleeding cut strikes across her cheek, her shoulder sags, her arm breaks and her hand is turned backward in a simulation of Dorian Grey in slow motion. She has difficulty breathing as a rib punctures her chest. Finally she can stand no more. She lies down on her bed, crosses her hands over her breast and dies."

"Wow," Leigh said. "Is that a true story? Was that Rose in the coma?"

"I don't know, and I'm almost afraid to ask. That's why I have to be cautious with my editorial remarks."

"This is some minister's wife you've got there, Charles. It really doesn't matter if it's her life story. Her imagination and creation of the story is the thing, isn't it?"

"It is. But if the story is autobiographical, I don't want her to complete the cycle of the drama by dying on me. She may need more help and advice than I can give her editorially. I really must talk with her soon."

"You'll figure it out."

"I feel ill-equipped for this one. If this is really her story, she might be a very sensitive and needy woman."

"Aren't we all," Leigh said, smiling at him. She walked over and kissed him on the cheek. "Just remember that when you get through giving her all of that heartfelt literary criticism you've drummed up, the sun goes down right here in Chigger City, podner."

16

The Legend of Santasay

As usual on Sunday evening, the living room of the parsonage was full of students waiting to see who would perform. Jesse appeared next to the piano where a pianist other than Ward had been playing Chopin waltzes. When she finished, Jesse waited briefly for the attention of the group before announcing that next Friday would be the annual crab feast produced by the civic association and the volunteer fire department for the enjoyment of all the students and islanders alike, an occasion in local gastronomy not to be missed. Admission was free to all students in possession of an ID card, and a friend or relative was welcome to participate for a five-buck donation to the fire department.

"Since we have another act of the play, *Ruby,* tonight, in which I have a role, I'm going to forgo my usual mini-sermon and song and hustle over to the theater. However, we have with us this evening a member of the archeological group that is excavating the site of Wollaston Manor up at Swan Point to make a presentation related to the history of the area. When she finishes, we will be reseated over at the theater for another scene of the play, which I am sure you will enjoy. Now let me welcome Pila Kravitz. Pila? There she is. Come up, Pila. Step through the bodies and come up here into the belly of this whale of a piano." Jesse gestured to her and relinquished his place at the corner of the piano.

Pila looked over the upturned faces and, with professorial seriousness, began her talk.

"Much of what we archeologists do before we ever break ground is study the region and the locale in which the dig might take place. We need to know as much as we can about the society living in that period in order to make valid assumptions about the use and value of any artifacts that are found. Many times there is no remaining written history of the period or place of the excavation, and so we rely on local folklore and try to patch together a picture of life during the period in order to better describe it. In such cases we are likely not to find the 'truth' of the period as we would like, but have to settle for events that are carried down to us in the telling of stories and tales.

"This is such a tale, and it begins at the time of Elizabeth, the Queen of England, when a heroic figure named Shane O'Neill, a Tanist, or successor to the king of all the Irish tribes, secretly pledged his loyalty to the queen. He lied, of course, as his real object was to clear the English Protestants out of Ireland.

He was defeated at the battle of Ballycastle and taken prisoner. He kept losing fights and drinking, and drinking and losing, until one day in an argument he insulted some Scots to the point where they couldn't stand him any longer, so they killed and dismembered him. His head was hung on a pole over Dublin Castle and he became an instant martyr for Irish Catholics. 'Pila, you may ask, what has that to do with anything?'

"As always in these Anglo/tribal matters, the story continues with the progeny. Shane supposedly had ten sons, two of whom were spirited away in the dead of night by a priest who escaped with them to the pope, who at that time, I think, was Pius the IV or V, I can't quite remember, anyhow the pope called on the Catholic kings of Spain and France to each take a child and bring him up in the royal court, and that's how one of Shane's sons was taken to Spain and reared by Spaniards. The boy grew up to marry a lady of the court, and his son, in turn, James Neale, became an admiral in the Spanish Navy. James Neale sailed the Caribbean obtaining gold and jewels for the Spanish king and found, in Grenada, a woman of rare beauty, named Santasay, whom he took to be his concubine. Santasay became devoted to the captain and was instrumental in helping him establish the newly forming Catholic colony of Maryland, and she is said to have named this spit of land in the Potomac River "Trinity Island" to further advance its religious personality under the auspices of Captain James Neale and the Catholic church.

"James Neale was a man of many talents and quickly became recognized as a leader of substance. He fell in love with and finally married a beautiful and upstanding woman of the colony named Ann Gill and sailed back to Spain to give himself to the service of the king of Spain as well as the Duke of York in England. To celebrate his marriage, while in England, he had a ring made for his wife encrusted with pearls with a secret compartment in which lay a tiny skull on bones shaped like a cross. Think of it—if we could find that in our excavation!

"When he returned a few years later, he bought two thousand acres of land with money called cobbs. Cobbs were pieces cut from larger silver coins and used as legal tender. That's why this whole peninsula is called Cobb Neck. But I have lost my bearing. Back to the historical tale.

"When Neale married Ann Gill, he placed Santasay on what is now Trinity Island, several miles removed from his home, Wollaston, on what is now Swan Point. There are no records or love letters that tell us whether or not the Captain continued to dally with Santasay, but our guess is that he kept her on the island rather than send her back to Grenada because he wanted to keep her close at hand as well as heart. Because Trinity Island and Swan Point were probably a single island at one time, and because of her stature in the colony, we believe that she simply lived apart from the Neale family at this time rather than having been placed in 'exile.'

"It is here that the story becomes a little less tidy. When Neale left again with his wife to return to Spain and eventually to England, he placed an overseer, one Tom Sloughter, in charge of his estate as well as making him the protector of the beautiful Santasay. One of Neale's commands to Tom was to see that Santasay was cared for on Trinity Island—fed well and kept immaculately chaste until his return.

"Tom Sloughter was not a thoughtful or compassionate overseer, and when Santasay produced twins, a boy and a girl, some eight months after Captain Neale left Maryland, Tom whipped her until her back ran with blood and then chained her in a shed where she was fed scraps shared by the dogs.

He took Santasay's babies, rowed them in a boat to the deepwater channel, stuffed them in a gunny sack, bound them with a chain, and dropped them into the Potomac River. Needless to say, the loss of her children, the deprivation of food and water, and the filthy conditions under which she was held prisoner drove Santasay mad.

"One night, with the help of Tom Sloughter's disgruntled slaves, she escaped her chains. She stumbled to the house and the bed where Tom Sloughter was sleeping and severed his snoring head from his body with an instrument not unlike a machete and hacked the body into small pieces. She stuffed the bloody remains into a hemp sack and dragged it down to the pier that extended into the river for about two hundred feet. She tied each of Tom's body parts onto a piece of stout twine—a forearm, a calf, the neck, the heart and liver, etc.—each about six feet apart—then made the end of it fast to the dock and threw the long length of twine studded with body parts into the Potomac to be eaten by the fishes and crabs. When she finished, she held her lantern high in order to watch the pieces of Tom Sloughter swing out with the tide, then she took a few steps and disappeared, lantern in her hand, into the deep water at the end of the pier.

"Her friends, watching this hideous scene from the shadows, remarked the next day that the light did not go out when Santasay walked off the pier. The light continued to burn under the water and moved down the shoreline as if Santasay were hunting for her children. The next night they swore they saw the same light in the waters on the other side of the island. To this day, the local fisherman will tell you that on a dark night they have glimpsed Santasay's light as she fulfills her destiny trying to find her drowned children, who were fathered by Captain Neale. And if you get into a deep conversation with some of the old fisherman here in Cobb Neck, you might hear them refer to the bait that they use on a trot line or in a crab trap—the eels, chicken necks, bull-lips, or alewives—as 'Tom's Body.' They call the bait 'Tom's Body' in memory of the beautiful and mad Santasay's dismemberment of her keeper, Tom Sloughter."

Pila paused and looked at the expressionless, silent faces around the room. She leaned into them and said, "On my sacred and professional Latin oath, *in vino veritas,* I swear to you, the assembled, as a certified student of archeological folklore for the Cobb Neck Historical, Croquet, and Chesapeake Bay Retriever Society, and as the editor of historical archives for the Trinity Island University Press, that Santasay walks under the waters of the Potomac River as they lap the shores of Trinity Island and Wollaston Manor. Just don't go swimming after dark."

The crowd was still for a second and then people began to howl with laughter and applaud Pila. They pummeled her with pillows and any soft item at hand. She covered her head with her arms, laughing, screaming for help, and then Ward struck a chord on the piano. He began to sing to an altered tune of "Yankee Doodle":

> Ohhhh, Santasay is fantasy
> Her light doth shine in water
> Looking for the kids of Neale
> Drowned by old Tom Sloughter

Santasay don't give up hope
Santasay my darling
Keep shining up and down the coast
And Tom will keep on trolling

Ohhh she trussed him up in old trot line
And strung him out in pieces
Now he's serving just desserts
For all the crabs and fishes.

Santasay don't give up hope
Santasay my darling
Keep shining up and down the coast
And Tom will keep on trolling.

Following a tremulous chord finale, Ward stood at the piano and announced, "That, ladies and gentlemen, is the ballad of the 'Ghost of Wollaston,' or 'Santasay Does Cobb Neck Underwater,' as presented to us by Pila the bone-digger." After a last rousing cheer for Pila, everyone clapped and laughed and then made their way to the theater to view another scene of the play, *Ruby*.

17

Ephraim's Sermon

Jesse had gone to the theater in preparation for his role in the play—a sermon given by the minister, Ephraim, to his congregation. As students found seats in the audience, actors milled around onstage, chatted, and then sat on benches arranged to simulate the interior of a small church. A three-foot-high railing separated the pulpit from the congregation. A large black space-heater occupied one corner, exhausted by a black stove pipe to an outer wall, and in the other corner stood an upright piano. For several minutes, a pianist played softly from a hymnal as patrons and actors took their seats. When everyone was settled, Jesse walked slowly up the aisle, onto the stage, and into the raised pulpit. He nodded to the pianist and the congregation on stage began to sing "Let the Sun Shine In." The minister turned to the theater audience and urged them to join in singing another verse. After the song ended, the house lights dimmed.

EPHRAIM. *{Sunlight streams from a high window illuminating his face; he raises his arms from the pulpit.}* It is a glorious morning in the house of the Lord, so we must open our hearts and let in the sunlight that Jesus brings—let it open your hearts to your neighbor or to the stranger passing by so that they may see and feel the goodness of Jesus Christ and the blessings that we have been given. Rejoice not in sorrow for the blood of the lamb, rejoice not in the death of the lamb, but in the everlasting life in the world to come.

Today I am reminded once more that evil can be found in the simplest of things: in our footsteps, in the beauty of the sunset, in the rough-tongued lick of the newborn calf, the cool drink that slakes our thirst, and the undying love for our family. Those of you who remember the war know that ordinary things can be the stuff from which evil is made. This land is our Garden of Eden, in which we build a life—in every little thing there is a choice we make between good and evil with a will that is freely given by God. Our God-given will separates us from the animals and creates the human mystery of life, the mystery that surrounds our freedom of choice.

My brothers and sisters, in this life it is hard to make a choice that is not tainted by evil. Without the spirit of Jesus dwelling in our hearts and minds to guide us, we are men blundering without sight in a world where things are never what they seem. In our world of free will, our best intentions sometimes have evil consequences. And so it was with the most honorable of intentions, Ted Cockrel's neck was broken on Tobacco Styx Bridge the other night and he was left hanging from that big sycamore tree until the sun came up. I have no doubt that many of you slept well that night because you figured that justice had been done. But things are never what they seem. *{Ephraim raises the Bible and presents it to the congregation.}*

There is nothing more important in this entire book than the covenant we made with God not to murder our brother. Nothing! But what of a man like Cockrel, whom we accuse of murder? Has he not disobeyed the law of God, and are we not correct in punishing him with death in God's name? Doesn't God reap revenge upon the murderer through the instrument of man's justice? Is this not our choice in the name of God? No, it is not! It is the choice of the Devil.

In the new covenant with God, through Christ, the old law of an eye for an eye and a tooth for a tooth has new meaning: your hate of your brother must be turned to love. Brothers and sisters, this is the burden of free will that God has given us, because when we fell from grace, our eyes were opened, letting us see the sins of our brothers as well as our own. Our worldly knowledge makes us say he is guilty of sin and must be punished, and our judgment turns to hate, and our hate turns to revenge, and we circle like vultures and land on the carcass of death and eternal damnation. We feed on it, but it does not nourish our soul. Revenge is the banquet of the Devil; in our hunger for it, we are cast out of the garden of eternal life.

But man is given hope, because of this covenant with God through Christ. Christ takes our sin unto Himself and transforms it into the redeeming source of God's love. *{He pauses, wipes his brow, looks into the congregation, and a smile spreads across his face.}*

I started by saying that evil can appear in the simplest of things if we make the wrong choice, but in the arms of God there is also salvation from those mistakes if we want to redeem that choice. There it is, my brothers and sisters. The Tobacco Styx Bridge, where some of you forfeited your soul a few days ago, is your bridge to eternal life. If your soul was given up in the murder of Ted Cockrel on that bridge, so shall you redeem it through Jesus Christ so that you may cross into eternal life. Let us pray.

Dear God, there is a burden here today that weighs heavily in our hearts where only You can reach and bestow Your healing touch. We who have sinned yearn for Your grace and Your forgiveness; we yearn to be lifted up again unto the Lord our God in the sweet name of Jesus. Help us to have the courage to come forward and unburden ourselves. Help us lift the anger and hatred from our hearts and place it in Your hands. Amen. *{Ephraim bows his head and shuts his eyes as the pianist plays the introduction to a song, softly. He raises his head and the piano stops.}*

When you step up to the altar, bring the burden of sin in your heart as a gift. Take it from the secret room in your heart and place it in the hands of Christ the Savior who will accept your sacrifice in the name of the living God. *{The pianist plays the hymn and Ephraim sings it lovingly}*

> Softly and tenderly Jesus is calling
> Calling for you and for me;
> Patient and loving,
> He's waiting and watching,
> Watching for you and for me.
> Come home....

{Ephraim raises his arms to the congregation. The pianist continues to play softly, but the singing stops. He looks out at the congregation. There is a shuffling among the benches as several men make their way up and kneel at the altar. The sound of weeping comes from several women.}

As you join me in our song for the ages, come up to the altar and kneel with me so that we may sacrifice your gift to God and receive the everlasting peace of forgiveness.

{The pianist changes keys and leads the congregation into singing "Rock of Ages." As the song is being sung, Luke and Tom make their way to the railing. Ephraim continues to sing the second verse. The railing is soon filled with men and Ephraim kneels in front of each one and prays, then takes each man's face in his hands and kisses the forehead lightly. Ephraim rises and the men return to their seats among the congregation.}

Dear God in heaven, we pray for the forgiveness of our sins which we have made through our own pride and ignorance. Restore our humility. Give us the courage to seek the righteousness of Your Word as we travel through this world of sorrow and pain. Lift up our hearts and give us the strength to work for everlasting peace in Thy name. Restore to us the promise of eternal life as we walk in the footsteps of Thy son, Jesus. Amen.

{The pianist plays "A Mighty Fortress Is Our God" with gusto. Ephraim walks from the stage down the center of the theater and out the door as the congregation follows, singing lustily. The house lights are gradually brought up. The actors reassemble outside of the theater.}

Pila, who had stayed for the performance, applauded vigorously and made her way outside. The actors were receiving compliments from members of the audience. She ran into Jesse, still in make-up, eager to shake hands and receive compliments from his admirers.

"Ah, our resident archeologist. How did your presentation go?" Jesse asked, greeting Pila.

"I was hooted at and run out of the room. But all in good fun," Pila said. "I hope they enjoyed it."

"They would have been very quiet and serious if they hadn't enjoyed it—they would have been embarrassed into silence at your attempt to play artist."

"Does having pillows thrown at me equal a good thing?"

"The very best thing. It signifies wholehearted acceptance."

"Then I'm in," Pila said, and clapped her hands.

"Excuse me," Jesse said, moving from her to greet others who wanted to congratulate him. Luke pushed through the crowd and gave her a hug.

"It's good to see you. May I carry your books?" he joked.

"Nothing I would like better, but I have to get back to camp. Another big day tomorrow. They think they found an old well, or at least a depression where an old well might have been. We're going to start work on it at dawn."

"Too bad."

"It is, because I really have to talk with you. We have to sit down and get a few things ironed out."

"Aww, Pila, we've never done that before. That's what's good about us. We never need ironing."

"I'm serious this time, Shake. When can we meet?"

"Can you do it next Sunday night?"

"I'll be here."

"Okay, see you then." He gave her a hug and watched her walk over to the pickup truck parked behind the firehouse and then leave.

18

Pila's Story

Charles walked to his rented house in Chigger City in an expansive mood. He mounted the steps, two at a time, and let the screen door of the porch bang behind him. Leigh, sitting in the living room, stopped reading the paper and greeted her husband.

"Well, you're happy this evening! Have a good time?"

"You remember those free-wheeling days as an undergraduate? Tonight reminded me of that—new experiences that lift you up and set you down in a different place—an altogether memorable evening. You'll have to come the next time. The music is sublime. We also had some storytelling. One was a ghost story told by an archeologist, a strapping young Jewish woman, and she was very funny. She reminded me of someone I had known in grade school, of all places."

"Where, back in Bryan Elementary, in the city?"

"Yeah, a long time ago. Did I ever tell you the story about catching the Nazi spy?"

"I don't remember it. Is it a true story, or one that you're going to make up to entertain me?"

"No, it's true. It happened back in the middle of World War II."

"Not a war story!"

"Yes and no, but more of a story about my callow youth."

"Well, that's better. Am I allowed to laugh?" Charles ignored her and began his story.

"Well, we lived on Bay Street, two blocks from the main D.C. jail, where they were keeping accused German spies and war criminals, and each morning we could hear sirens screaming, making way for a convoy of black vans escorted by Army jeeps with machine guns mounted in the back, driven from the jail at high speed up Independence Avenue to the courthouse downtown, and then, as we were getting off from school, they would come rushing and clamoring back down Independence Avenue toward the jail. The transfer of those war criminals every day made us kids feel like we were in the center of the war with all of its mystery and urgency. Then the convoys got bigger and were escorted by a machine like a tank with a rubber half-track, on top of which soldiers swung around in mounted turrets gripping .50-caliber machine guns.

"Our heads were full of stories of the heroism of our soldiers against the fanatical Japanese and iron-willed German armies. We were alerted to the possibility that miniature submarines could slink up the Potomac River at night and attack the Washington Navy Yard a few blocks away. My grandfather, who was about to retire, had been taken from the metropolitan police force and inducted into the Army as a sergeant and was thought to be fighting somewhere in Europe, although we really didn't know because we hadn't heard from him in two months. Although I thought he was out there distinguishing himself as a hero, the look of apprehension in my grandmother's eyes always told me it might be otherwise and that unnerved me.

"Our little gang of four—Mac, Diff, Hagie, and myself—couldn't do enough to help the war effort. We collected everything: cans, rubber, string, tinfoil, fat, leather, and cloth, especially clean white cloth that could be rolled into bandages and wrapped around the bleeding heads of our soldiers. Our expectation of engaging the enemy soared each morning and remained there until we bivouacked each night in our own beds. On Saturdays we left the block at 10 a.m. and went to the Beverly Theater on 15th Street or the Home Theater on C Street, whichever was showing a war movie, and didn't return until late afternoon after seeing the feature and the newsreels at least four times. Fueled by the news of our heroes, we thought we could fight for our country. We wouldn't hesitate to engage the enemy and kill him, and we talked amongst ourselves about how we would do that. While rummaging through my grandfather's underwear drawer one day, I found my weapon, a .38-caliber Smith and Wesson he had worn as a cop. In a little box next to tie pins I found the bullets. The other kids fashioned weapons from sharp sticks and old kitchen knives, while Diff preferred a bow and arrow, but I could boast of a real weapon,

"Our classroom at Bryan Elementary was frequently interrupted by new students or the disappearance of old familiar faces. They came and went as their parents moved or were stationed elsewhere for the war effort. One day there was a new girl from Poland. She was introduced to the class by the principal, and we soon found that she spoke little English. I tried to ignore her despite the fact that she sat directly across the aisle from me. She was a strange-looking girl with dark hair in tight curls, and I noticed she was hairier than most of the other girls in the class. Her eyebrows were heavy, and an abundant wisp of hair swirled around her ears. A darkness above her upper lip that I assumed was part of skin color or a permanent shadow finally revealed itself as a faint moustache. Not a man's moustache, but something feminine above the lip that seemed natural on this girl with an abundance of hair.

"As class ended one day, she dropped something in the aisle and tilted over to reach for it, and I glimpsed down the front of her dress and I saw what I thought was a suggestion of hair on her chest. I was stunned but I recovered, looked again and saw it again, and couldn't believe it. Then she reached behind her neck and fastened the tiny gold chain with a small gold cylinder she had retrieved from the floor. With her elbows turned up and flared behind her, I couldn't keep my eyes from where her breasts swelled, showing a substantial cleavage, unlike most of the girls in our class. I stared at the little cylinder tucked between the swells.

"A few days later, when it was my turn to clean the erasers after school, I saw the chain and gold cylinder lying on the floor, tucked tightly behind a rear leg of her chair. I picked it up, but since she had already headed home, I put it in my pocket. Later that evening, sitting on the front stoop with my friends, I remembered the necklace and pulled it from my pocket. I twisted the top of the cylinder and it came off revealing a very small piece of paper inside. When I unrolled the paper there were marks on it resembling foreign writing of some sort. Immediately, I thought it was German, and it didn't take us long to figure out that it must be a code of some sort being smuggled to the enemy by this strange girl with a strong accent and hair on her chest.

"The twisted fuse of our imaginations burned brightly, and we agreed on an immediate plan of action. We would confront her and make her confess her crimes against humanity and make sure she got a ride in the convoy to the courthouse downtown.

"She lived with her uncle only a block and a half away from where I lived. We put the plan into action that very evening. Three houses down from the corner deli owned by her uncle was the apartment where she lived, and just at dark, when she came out of the deli and headed for her house, we grabbed her. We put a white handkerchief over her mouth when she screamed, then stuffed it in her mouth to gag her, and hustled her across the street and into an alley. She kicked and freed one arm from Diff and hit him in the nose and he dropped his bow and arrow and let her go and suddenly she was out of our grip. She pulled the handkerchief out of her mouth and, without saying anything, backed slowly against a fence and looked at us with glaring hatred.

"'You're a spy,' I said with solid conviction, holding out the cylinder and chain for her to see. 'We found your secret message in here. You have to come with us to the police. You can't go free.'

"She screamed—God how she screamed—louder than the sirens on the trucks that carried the war criminals—and the sound brought her uncle running from the deli waving a large knife and shouting something in a language we didn't understand. I tried to draw the pistol from my pants, but the hammer hung up somewhere inside my trousers and I couldn't get it out. Doors began to slam in apartments whose back porches bordered the alley, and loud adult voices wanted to know what was happening. Despite the compelling patriotism of our mission, we ran like hell. We were good at running, and good at vanishing into the warrens of a half-dozen city blocks; running in different directions, we quickly disappeared. In the rush of being chased by a mad spy with a knife, I kept the pistol from slipping down my pants leg and managed to hang on to the gold cylinder and its secrets. I slipped into the house, unnoticed by my grandmother, and returned my weapon to its hiding place among the underwear.

"A cop rang the bell of our apartment shortly after I had gone to bed, and I heard him talking with my grandmother in the kitchen. I was torn between the emotions of having escaped from a bad situation and harboring information that would make me a hero to my grandmother and the cop. Feeling safe in my own home, I crawled from my bed and walked into the kitchen with the necklace in my hand, ready to receive a hero's welcome. The cop took it from me, and without showing the least concern for the German secrets that I knew were burning inside it, placed it in the top pocket of his blouse and buttoned it.

"'It's a spy message,' I told him. He nodded and smiled.

"'Thank you very much for coming, Officer, but I'd like to take it from here,' Grandmother said, and she proceeded to show the cop out. I got that sinking feeling that it wasn't going to go the way I had planned when she sat down beside me and reached over to hold my hand. I had the feeling like I was going to get a lecture about sex or something else I didn't want to hear. She explained to me that the girl was a refugee from a concentration camp in Poland, that her mother and father had been killed, and that she had been freed and nursed to health by soldiers like my grandfather and sent on to live with her uncle here. She wasn't a spy, she was a Jewish victim of a Nazi concentration camp; the little cylinder around her neck was a *mezuzah*, and it contained a scroll of her religious belief in a language called Hebrew, not German or Japanese, and she was just getting over the sickness of being held in the camp. When I had held the mezuzah up to her and shouted at her in a language she didn't fully understand, she thought I was threatening her and going to hurt her because she was a Jew. 'She is distraught,' Grandmother explained, 'out of her mind, and they have taken her to the hospital.'

"I didn't understand what a Jew was other than those mentioned in the Bible, or how they were different or why she would have a mezuzah, but I knew that I had done something very wrong, and I remember that my grandmother spent several hours at the side of my bed explaining it to me until her voice lulled me to sleep. The next morning, she took me to the uncle's deli where she told him what had happened and apologized for my terrible behavior and stupidity. Afterwards, I apologized and asked him how I could make it up, but he glared hatefully at me,

"'Please leave store,' he said, and ushered us out. I didn't see the girl again until after the summer vacation. When school started again, we once more occupied adjoining seats in a similar classroom. She had gotten slightly taller than me over the summer and seemed less timid of her surroundings and her circumstances. She walked around with a new confidence and had become more fluent in the language.

"I tried on several occasions to apologize, but when we came face to face, she looked away and avoided contact with me. I watched her when I could. I caught myself staring at her, and found myself putting her in my daydreams. Finally, late that year, I wrote a note, folded it over several times and bent it to fit my rubber band and shot it across the aisle where it hit her arm and fell into her lap. She didn't move until class was over. She unwound the note and smoothed it on her desk and smiled. All I had written was 'I love you.' That was the beginning and the end of my first serious love affair, with a girl with hair on her chest and with whom I have had a love affair all my life."

"Why didn't you marry her instead of me?" Leigh asked.

"She was not my lover but a person whom I loved. And besides, she later left the country. And what kind of question is that anyhow? I married you because I wanted you to be the lover in my life and the mother of my children, the song in my heart, the sweet potato in my pie, the sugar in my tea, the dumpling in my wonton soup, the...."

"Stop! Enough already. You are turning me into food. I get the point. It was just a dumb question. By the way, have you talked with Rose Caine yet about her story?"

"No, not yet. I'll do it tomorrow night after the seminar."

"Going for the old warm-cookies-in-the-kitchen trick again, huh?"

19

Rose's Confession

Carrying his leather writing pouch, Charles approached the parsonage to find Rose when his attention was drawn to Jesse's voice singing an Italian aria. Thinking he might say hello, Charles followed the sound into a wing of the old church, which held Jesse's office. He had no intention of interrupting Jesse if he were rehearsing, but as he approached the open door, he saw him singing vigorously in front of a full-length mirror, gesticulating as though he were performing for an audience. Charles stopped in the open doorway, his mouth agape, intrigued by Jesse's antics. Jesse saw him and stopped singing. He saw the confused expression on Charles's face and laughed.

"Think nothing of it, Charles. I am not Narcissus; I'm just tidying up my presence and practicing my performing image. It's one of the routines that a lot of people forget until they have to pay a coach big money to teach it to them."

"Oh, yes," Charles said, still taken aback and slightly embarrassed as though he had caught Jesse naked in the shower.

"Rose is in the kitchen, I think."

"Okay. I'll find her," Charles said, walking away quickly. Despite Jesse's rational explanation of the exercise before the mirror, there was something puzzling about it. Charles had never watched himself speak before a full-length mirror, and he wondered what impression he made and whether or not he could be critical of his own image. He had always assumed that his image would be impressed on the listener by what was being said rather than how he said it. In the scene he had just witnessed, it struck him that Jesse was the "I" standing in the nominative case, arranging his adjectives before the mirror.

Before reaching the kitchen, Charles smelled the cookies. Rose was taking the hot water kettle from the stove.

"Coffee or tea or neither?" she asked.

"I'll have coffee."

"Good. I was about to make a fresh pot."

When they had arranged themselves comfortably around the kitchen table, Charles slid the large brown envelope from his leather pouch and pushed it toward Rose.

"Was it better or worse this time?"

"Rose, I really want to apologize again for my behavior the last time. I am slightly out of practice giving editorial advice to students; you can be assured that it won't happen again. Yes. It was very much better this time. At first I didn't think it could be improved, but I made a few notes that you should consider before you put it in final form."

Rose broke into a big smile, then lowered her head for a second as if to pray.

"Wow. That's great," she said, finally. "That's super. Can we talk about it?"

"Oh, I want to talk about it with you so I can better understand; I would really like to know how much of this is autobiographical."

"That's difficult sometimes, isn't it—knowing the difference between the truth and the fantasy when you're the root of both of them?"

"I don't mean to pry, but the ending is remarkable. Can you enlighten me a little bit without divulging personal secrets?"

"Where do I start?" She rose from the table as if to find the answer to her question and, instead, took a bottle of Bailey's Irish Cream from the cabinet and poured it into her coffee. She held it out to his cup, and he nodded for her to pour.

"With the accident, I guess. Less than two years ago, I was in a car wreck that, except for the grace of God and the miracles of medicine, would have taken my life. My face went through the dashboard, both of my ankles were broken as well as my pelvis and some other small bones. The bones of my face were crushed, the roof of my mouth split in two, and the doctors feared I would lose an eye and never speak again should I regain consciousness. The surgeons went into my head, wired and molded my bones back together, wired my jaws and, when my skull had been realigned, they began restoring my teeth.

"Of course, I lost some memory, which was the most frightening aspect of the entire experience. When I healed, finally, and started taking a few college classes, I didn't know if I could learn or retain, or remember enough to make the links necessary to understand complex ideas. It was terrible at first and then it improved, and I found that hard work and study was helping with memory as well as my ability to think.

"My husband, Jesse, is a wonderful man, and I would have undoubtedly not survived without him. He is a mathematical genius who can add four columns of numbers in his head, has the voice of an angel, speaks poetry from his sermons, but he's always been a little rabbity in bed. I began to have some erotic dreams about him, and I suppose that was the trigger that made me want to start a new life with him."

"Look Rose, this is private stuff that I really don't need to know. I mean, you don't have to tell me. I didn't mean that I wanted to know...."

"Relax, Charles, don't be the president now, nor my teacher. What I need most is a friend. Is that permissible?"

"Yes, I suppose, up to a point."

"Okay. Have another cookie and relax." She poured some more coffee into their cups and added another dollop of Bailey's Irish Cream.

"When I was so smashed after the accident, Jesse fell apart. I think my ugliness frightened him. He prayed for me not to die, but he couldn't heal me. He saw me day after day as damaged flesh, and he knew I would never be right again. His prayer for healing had no visible effect on me and I think he began to lose faith in himself. His patience ran out. It was as if the magic of his God had abandoned him. Finally, he gave up that religious bravado, love everybody, lay on hands, and 'we can cure the ills of the world and make it a better place' kind of stuff. He couldn't face the fact that he didn't have the miraculous touch—that God's healing didn't slide from his fingers when he wanted it to, so he consulted the stars and looked and plotted birthdates and backgrounds and tried to foretell the future with the same religious fervor that fueled his preaching. Finally, he discovered that the reason he was no longer in love with me lay in the stars. He found proof in his astrological chart that we were star-crossed lovers.

"He reasoned that my fate had been cast in his bad driving and my ugliness would not repair itself under his touch. His new science made him look away from me. Conversely, I began to look inside to understand who I really was, and what I found was a woman different than the one who had married the preacher. It didn't matter if my face wasn't the same, wasn't beautiful—that wasn't where the good feelings were going to come from. I felt like I was being reborn."

"I understood all of that very well from what you wrote."

"Of course, the story drew out the gradual revelation that my husband no longer loved me. What I omitted, of course, was the fact that he would like to screw every good-looking woman on this island by Friday and then start again on Monday. Pardon my language, but that's how it is. At one point I fantasized being reborn as Salome and dancing with veils and loving someone throughout the night, but I couldn't be promiscuous, even to spite him, although I'm beginning to think it might be worth a try...," she said and winked at Charles. He blushed.

"I just can't get myself to do it—to give myself like that to someone else for the sheer pleasure of it. Although you make a pretty good reason to try, if you'd like to know. That's not a proposition. It's a statement about how far I've come these few months."

"Let's stick to the story. I already know more than I should, Rose."

"Oh, it's not so devastating and I am not going to lay down and die because I am no longer the person that he hurt. I stay with him because I don't feel secure yet in striking out on my own, and because he needs me for a while, until he finds the track, or the 'star' to his destiny." She laughed as if she had made a joke. "However, at the end of the summer, I think Jesse will go his way and I will go mine. I love taking your seminar and interacting with you. I'm not immune to your charm. When I'm around you I have to keep saying, 'Get thee behind me, Satan!' and I slip into a dream of another life—I couldn't do that before the accident—I couldn't imagine another life than the one I have been mandated to live with Jesse. Now I can. Now I am more of a realist, and I try to face things squarely as they are. Life is precious to me. There is much to live for, and I don't want to waste time on the trivial."

"Will you write more?"

"Oh, yes. I want to write lots of things. I'm working on the rewrite of Maestro's play, and I'm loving it."

"Good. When will I see a script?"

"Maybe a week, maybe two. We'll see."

"Where will you go after the summer, if not to New York with Jesse?"

"I may go back to the university for more classes."

"When I came in, I saw Jesse practicing in front of a mirror. Does he do that a lot?"

"Very often. It's curious the way he always leaves the door open. It reminds me of someone practicing to be a flasher." Charles laughed at her joke, a small tint of embarrassment rising in his neck and ears.

"Well, Rose, I had better get across the bridge," he said, rising from the table. She reached up and took his hand.

"I'm glad we've become good friends and nothing more, Charles. I think I wanted a man to know that I simply wasn't a dried-up preacher's wife—that Salome's inside here somewhere, dancing her heart out. I hope you don't mind my spilling my feelings to you."

"Hell, Rose," Charles said, "I've learned to accommodate my editorial criticism to cookies in the kitchen. And for what's it worth, I think your new persona suits you. I shall enjoy your acquaintance."

20

Andromeda

Luke had finished the first draft of a short story that was based on a childhood experience of one of Andora's artist friends. It was written from a female child's point of view and he wondered if he had maintained that perspective throughout the story. He wrote a note to himself to check for it when he starting rewriting, and then he began to tidy up the waste paper and soda cans that had been the result of his four-hour writing session. Although he preferred to wait until the morning to clean up his messes from the night before, his association with Andora had rearranged the few personal habits he maintained on the island. He now prepared his room in the evening, in anticipation of Andora's arrival at dawn, to make their morning liaison more pleasant. It never required much. A subliminal thought of wanting a love bower made him more fastidious. His few years in the military had taught him not to be slovenly, and, to his morning's assignation, he was simply trying to add charm: clean sheets, a tidy room, and a few stolen flowers in a mason jar. His attempts at making a nest were subtle intimations to Andora that love on land was certainly more pleasant than love in the hold of a boat. He checked the room again and then went to sleep.

In the morning, instead of lying, as usual, content in the afterglow of lovemaking, Luke rose from the bed, put on shorts and T-shirt, and padded down to the kitchen to look for coffee. The pot was empty, and by the time he made the coffee and brought two steaming cups back to the room, Andora was drying herself after her shower. She was still wet in places, her red hair darkly plastered against her face. He put the coffee down, took the towel and dried the drops of water that still lay in the small of her back.

"My God, you are beautiful. You are like that painting by Gustav Dore of Andromeda chained to the rocks, and I am Perseus, the lover who will marry you and create a great lineage, and you, the mother of gods, shall remain immortal among the stars." He kissed her and would have continued but she wiggled from his grasp and made for the cup of coffee.

"You sound like Jesse talking about stars."

"Not so. I'm talking about Greek mythology and the fact that Andromeda is a constellation in the northern sky. According to her mother, she was more beautiful than the sea nymphs just as you are more beautiful than any river nymph on Trinity Island. The difference is that you are chained to a boat instead of rocks." He did not mean the remark to be sarcastic or insensitive, but it changed the mood of their playful conversation as though a curtain had been brought down.

"We need to talk about that," she said. "Don't forget that I know all about constellations from living on a boat and I've had enough of searching for a fair harbor among the stars."

"Okay," he said, and waited for her to continue. It burst from her awkwardly as though the thoughts had been under pressure.

"I want to build my life on my love for you and make a home and children together—warm, rich, creative, for the both of us. I admitted as much to Will the other night. You know what he said? That he understood living on a boat was not the life I wanted, and as soon as he finished the overhaul, we would go back to New York and live again in the city.

"It was like he didn't hear your name or what I said about wanting to be with you. I remember one time we were in a little French sea town, anchored next to a brightly painted old fishing boat. We were on deck having wine one evening when I pointed to the boat and made the simple remark that it was a pretty boat. He said, 'What do you mean,' and I said, 'It's very pleasing to the eye.' He laughed at me and remarked that it wasn't very seaworthy. He didn't understand my pleasure of viewing the simple lines and colors of the boat and the attitude it presented on the water. He only saw the things that made the boat work. There was no beauty in it for him. It made me sad and I started to cry, and he just looked at me dumbfounded. I can't make him understand."

"But he loved the little girl. He loved Tilley?" Luke questioned tentatively.

"I'm not sure he loved her because of the beauty that a child brings or because she was his possession. He mourned her death deeply as though she was the most precious thing in his life, but he never coveted her that way when she was alive. Of course, she really wasn't his, but I never told him.

Regardless, I don't want to have Will's baby. A child of his will be a child of sorrow."

"Then, after you told him about me, he said he wanted you to stay with him and raise a family?"

"Yes. He completely ignored my wanting to be with you as though it were someone else's problem, as though it had no effect on his future. On some level he understands we have not had any of the emotional or spiritual experiences that people normally have in a close marriage. He thinks he understands it now and wants to work it out, but I'm not convinced he can sustain a relationship."

"How did you leave it with him?"

"I told him I owed it to him to think about it, but I wasn't sure that the problem was just his. It's mine, too. I know it's mine." She clinched her fists. "Since you and I have been together I have felt what it is to be free for the first time. I know that a life with you would give me a chance of making me the person that I want to be. I've opened myself to you more than anyone else in my life, and it's becoming my spiritual salvation, but still, it's a leap of faith.

"Life with him will be full of spiritual drudgery and a constant sacrifice of the things I love. I can't free him from what he is; I'm not sure that it would help to even try. Can I be more selfish than that?" The question hung in the air, and then she continued, "You are magnificent in so many ways; could I be less so if I were living with you? For the first time in my life, I have begun to feel that my cup of joy is filling up. How can I not want the full measure?" Her voice broke with a croak and she tried hard to clear it. "I'm beginning to understand what makes me feel like a victim. It's not those forces of nature over which I have some control, it's my incompleteness and lack of resolve that keep me from creating the life I want. If I remain in this relationship with you—I can hardly fail. The prospects for failure for Will and me are strong and they'll keep the sails full. We'll never bury that dreaded box of our memories. He hasn't renamed the boat—said it could wait until the work was finished—but I know he's going to name it *Tilley* after her."

She coughed and drank from her coffee cup. "I'm sorry, I didn't mean to lecture."

"You weren't. You just feel passionately about it. You know I don't have any special magic, don't you, and that life with me wouldn't always be good?"

"I'm not that stupid," she said, losing clarity in her voice again. "Life with you is always full; it's not trying to run on empty."

She stopped. With no more coffee in her cup, she went into the bathroom and filled it with tap water and drank it down. "Don't be angry with me," she said from the sink.

"I'm not, but I don't know how to make it any easier for you. We all want to be loved, and he wants to be loved as much as we do, but he sounds as if he can't give love to another person. He can't show love to you, and you doubt that he ever felt love for his child. You want to give him a second chance because he says he knows what it takes to make a marriage, and yet, down deep, you don't believe he is capable of it. Aren't you just ignoring the evidence? It doesn't sound like a human condition that is fixable."

"After he said he wanted me back and would try hard to listen to my needs and understand me, I said okay, I would consider moving back in with him as soon as possible and we could start the dialogue, but then he began backing off because he wanted to spend more time repairing the boat. My attempt to give myself back to him at that moment interfered with his plans for the damned boat. It made me get a glimpse of my value to him after all. What a sin it would be to set our love aside for the trim of a boat. I won't let him take that from me."

"Then tell him that. You can't keep doing this dance with him. You're going to have to resolve it, and you know I can't help you."

"I know, but maybe Jesse can. He's been spending a lot of time with Will on the boat lately. Maybe Jesse can make Will understand that he really doesn't want me and I'm a part of the past he can never have again. Anyhow, I'm not spending another night down there with him—Jesse can keep him company. You and I need more time together. I'll get Will to understand, you'll see. Be patient with me. I need your friendship, your love, and your inspiration now, more than ever." She pressed herself into him and clung to him as though she were trying to enter his body, and he held her there for a very long time. His mind turned slowly from the warmth of her to the iniquitous thought that there was more in Will's lack of intimacy with his wife than they understood, something diabolical waiting to be grasped, but it slipped away from him, chased by the pleasure of holding her.

21

The Crab Feast

The traditional crab feast was scheduled to begin at 6 p.m. at the firehouse. The arts consortium sponsored it for participants in the arts camp, many of whom had never eaten a blue crab cooked Southern Maryland style. Island residents were invited as a gesture of appreciation for their forbearance and assistance in making the summer camp a success. The fire engines, pulled from their normal places inside, rested outside like medieval beasts on a concrete pad in front of the station, leaving an enormous indoor space inside for tables and folding chairs. Brown kraft paper covered the tables and each place setting was equipped with a cheap, dull-edged paring knife and a small wooden hammer resembling a child's toy. In the center of each table stood small paper cups for crab meat or vinegar and a large shaker in which extra seasoning was kept. Two gallon buckets, white and plastic, were placed at the end of each table to facilitate the removal of crab offal by the servers without interrupting the rhythm and flow of the crab pickers. Rolls of paper towels stood in readiness next to the buckets for cleaning crab muck from the pickers' hands.

The crabs, *Callinectes sapidus,* red, rosy, and steaming hot from the kettle, were brought on trays, a dozen or so at a time, and dumped in the center of the table within reach of the diners. Veteran crab-eaters become engaged in a rhythm of movement not unlike that of an expert crocheter, barely aware of the fingers nimbly set in a repetitive task. Thus, the feaster's mouth, when not receiving pieces of crab, is free to talk to a tablemate in a voice loud enough to be heard above the din of pounding hammers and ripping shells. Background music is rarely played at a crab feast or in a crab house for fear that it will destroy the ambience.

A happy and a noisy activity, eating crabs may take several hours because the process of picking is slow and the meat is not particularly filling. Those characteristics are the excuse that non-crab lovers give when they order fried chicken or a hamburger instead of eating crabs. Or they are simply put off by the fact that it is a very messy aboriginal meal eaten with fingers that require frequent cleaning and an occasional dip in vinegar to restore their grip.

The drink of choice at a crab feast is beer—ice cold beer. It marries with the salt, red pepper, and Old Bay seasoning and clears the palate without becoming dull even when consuming at least a dozen crabs. Bottled beer is preferred, because it can be handled with a slippery crooked forefinger with more precision than a can of soda or a glass of tea. Properly steamed Southern Maryland crab may be listed among the earth's gastronomic treasures, and eating them is one of the most amusing social pastimes ever invented.

It was in this milieu that artists from the camp sat with enthusiasm...if not total conviction that a crab was a creature edible and harmless to their health and welfare. Volunteer firemen steamed the crabs in large stainless steel pots made especially for the purpose. A few crabbers who had been preparing feasts since they were old enough to catch crabs stood around picking through the baskets, making certain that no dead ones were cooked. Through the steam and bustle of the kitchen the men moved like shadows in a scene from hell.

At ten o'clock, when the last of the eaters had finished, male volunteers divested each table of its condiments and rolled the shells and internal mess of the crabs into the kraft paper and stuffed it into a small dumpster. Tables were wiped down, folded and stored. When the floor was swept clean of the last evidence of crab shell, the fire engines were started and moved back to their place of readiness inside the firehouse garage.

The clean-up crew migrated over to the cooler and drew from it their last beers of the evening before closing down. Sitting in the lounge, they recalled the significant events of the evening—the dancer who spilled vinegar over the table and herself and had to be cleaned up; the writer who tried to eat the crab whole, shell attached, and cut his lip and gums until they bled; and the fire call they had answered with efficiency and dispatch that turned out to be a false alarm.

Among those men slouched over the chairs and couch was one Elvis "Possum" Gravis, one of the oldest members of the Trinity Island Rescue Squad, but one who no longer deployed during routine emergencies. In fact, no one currently active on the squad could remember ever having seen Possum at a fire other than the one he had made in his own backyard once when the wind upset a charcoal grill and ignited a pile of brush along his property line that burned about six feet of his newly painted pine fence before being controlled. Possum helped his son do a little crabbing but, more importantly, he was the self-appointed liaison with the art folk and was currently helping the dance crew produce a stage set.

Possum Gravis came from a long line of Charles County folks who were hard workers, good of heart, and outstanding citizens. Unfortunately, they were not blessed with good looks. Family characteristics passed down for generations included a nose too large, accompanied by fleshy lips that, in Possum's case, were equipped with a perpetual toothpick rolling from side to side. His pendulous ears swung loosely when he moved. But Possum's most distinguishing feature, not always found in other family members, were his eyes. Foggy blue and dimly opaque, they were nearly obscured by several layers of undisciplined skin resting on his eyelids, forcing them to a nearly closed position. On his head sat a too-small baseball cap at a rakish angle. When under the influence of his beloved whiskey, Jack Daniels, and with his body in an extremely relaxed posture, his eyelids assumed an imponderable weight that bore down and formed tiny slits out from which Possum peered inscrutably. On important occasions he had been known to improve his eyesight by taping his eyelids to his very prominent brow.

Possum limped heavily in a rolling gait from an injury he received as a child when a tornado hit the La Plata schoolhouse in 1928, and the injury had prompted him to develop his mental acuity more than the brute strength required in manual labor. His body movement and the slow smile that frequently crept over his face reminded his friends of the furry woodland animal they frequently chased and seldom caught, so they nicknamed him "Possum." Those who knew him carried a grudging respect for the name and frequently warned others that, "He may look like he's asleep but don't let that fool you."

Possum came from folks who practiced the storytelling tradition and he became a very successful practitioner. He could always add glamour, fear, knowledge, speculation, and contradiction in telling a story or anecdote in any situation. Despite looking more like the slow village dimwit than the island sage, he drew other men to him in anticipation of a good story or a snappy witticism or pleasant and intelligent conversation that could brighten an uneventful evening.

Possum reached into a cabinet behind his chair and drew out a fifth of Jack Daniels. He broke the seal, unscrewed the cap and took a swig, then he passed the bottle to the man sitting at his left. The next man, leg-weary from working the crab feast, took a swallow, chased it with beer, and passed the bottle around. Possum looked sadly at the empty bottle that returned and asked the fellow sitting close to the cooler to pass him a Coke. Catching the can thrown gently to him, he threw back his head and admired the label.

"This reminds me of one of my finest hours," he said. "Did I ever tell you all about my entrepreneurial experiences when I was associated with the Coca-Cola Company?" he asked of no one in particular and, receiving no response, he began talking to the tired and inattentive volunteers.

"You should listen up, because things like this don't come along every day, and when they do, they can change your life.

It was when they were building the bridge across the river, and the Coca-Cola Company needed someone to supply the workers with drinks and I got the job to do it. I'd load the bed of my old pickup truck with twenty-pound blocks of ice, chop them up, and then go to the Coke plant and stuff as many bottles in it as I could, and by the time I made the trip down there, the drinks were cold. Everything I sold was in those itty-bitty green glass bottles, and those workers were thirsty enough to empty the truck before the ice had melted, so I had to hire me some help. They paid me a nickel a case, so I gave an old boy from North Carolina a penny a case to help me load and sell them right off the back of the truck. I never did know what his full name was but they called him Jimmyup, and it fit his job very well.

"Well, Jimmyup was as poor as dirt, lived in a little house in the woods down in Nanjemoy, and had to hitchhike everywhere he went when I wasn't picking him up in my truck. I was living in La Plata at the time so it wasn't a problem. He was always grateful to me for the job and begged me to take him back to North Carolina sometime in my old truck to spend a day or two and meet his sister. By that time I was flush with money from selling Coke, so I drove down to North Carolina with Jimmyup to visit his folks. When we got there, the first thing he did was open a half pint of crystal-clear home-made whiskey and pour some into a glass with some Coca-Cola. I had been there long enough to drink a couple of glasses when in walks Jimmyup's sister who evidently had been somewhere tending the still because she had a gunny sack over her shoulder with two-quart jars of whiskey in it. I took a good look at her, and boys, she was 'ravenous.' She was so 'ravenous' that I couldn't keep my eyes off her. She sat right down and had a drink with us and, presently, she announced that she needed to gather the eggs from the henhouse, so I volunteered immediately to help her.

"On the way to the henhouse we passed a little shed that held the straw she used to plump up the nest and make it soft for the chickens. So I started putting straw into a bushel basket, but I never got to fill it up. We took a look at each other and went into a clutch that lasted until sundown, sleeping a little, lovin' a lot, sleeping a little—you know. Then, in the pale light of dawn, I saw the door of the shed open and a hand reached in with a bacon sandwich, a half-pint of that whiskey, and a bottle of Coke. Since we had been resupplied, I didn't see much sense in leaving the shed right then, so we stayed a while. It was during the third morning of this spiritual retreat that I first became aware of the symptoms of what is now known in medical circles as 'Lover's Colic.'

"Take note of the symptoms: first, your male apparatus is swollen and sore, not unusual given its extended use without the aid of any lubricating oil or grease; then, there is the pervasive smell of a feral woman. Everything in and about that shed, the straw, the whiskey, the feathered air coming from the chicken house, my clothes, all of it was full of the pungent odor of sexual ardor. On top of it, so to speak, the colic makes you dizzy and incomprehensible as if a blanket is covering your brain making it hard to think, making it hard to determine the relationship between cause and effect. Finally, the disease completely exhausts you. When I got enough strength to put my clothes back on, I left Jimmyup's ravenous sister sleeping in the straw and I grabbed Jimmyup from the house, jumped in the truck, and came back to Maryland as fast as we could. I thought the bouquet of the colic would wash off in a hot bath, a good scrub with lye soap, and a hot gargle with salt and soda, but it was just as bad the next day as it was the first. I could tell from the people around me that they couldn't smell a thing different in me, but I tell you boys, I couldn't smell or taste anything but the ardor of love until I thought I would suffocate. I knew this problem had to be cured, and I was the only one to do it.

"Well, I was loading up the truck a few days later in the hot sun, and I guess I was a little rough on those cases of Coke because a couple of them bottles started exploding, and before you know it, I was covered all over with Coke and itty-bitty bits of glass. Well, I picked out the glass—it wasn't much—and when I changed my clothes, I noticed that the 'eau de love' had left in those places where the Coke had soaked me. It was gone. It was like finding a cure for a skunked dog. I was so happy that I sat down and wrote a long letter to the Coke-Cola Company telling them about the experience and suggested that I had found a valuable cure in their drink for an embarrassing medical condition and hinted that it might be worth a reward. Well, they wrote me a short, sassy letter back strongly suggesting that their product would no longer be available for sale through me and that they recommended abstinence to be a better cure for the disease. At first it made me mad, and then I begin to think it wasn't such bad advice."

The men, who by now were alert and listening carefully, laughed and scoffed at the story. "Pure Possum scat!" one of them said, dismissing the story.

"Wait a minute, wait a minute," Possum protested. "It's true—swear to God—it's true. I even had an advertising slogan for it: 'If you cannot abstain, just wash it down the drain. Things go better with Coke.'" The men laughed and hooted at Possum as the light switches began to click somewhere in the building and one by one the lights of the firehouse shut down. As the volunteers of Stationhouse 6 ended the evening with "goodnights" and "see you tomorrows," Possum could be heard remarking to a small group walking toward Scuttlebutt's bar, "She was the most ravenous woman I have ever seen, from the toes to the top of her head, and every time I drink a Coke I can't help but think of her and...."

22

Pila's Skull

Sunday evening, Ward and some members of the string section were playing music that had been scored for the dance ensemble's show. They finished and packed their instruments, storing them in the kitchen closet, when Pila walked in carrying a black cloth book sack like the ones sometimes carried by professors in the tonier Eastern colleges. She was smiling from ear to ear. Rather than talk immediately to Luke, who was sitting adjacent to Andora, she sought out Jesse, who was helping the string ensemble with their instruments. He listened to her, and then went to the piano and asked Ward to grab the attention of the group with a few well-struck chords. The room quieted.

"You remember Pila, who gave us the 'Legend of Santasay' last week? Well, the archeologists have had a good week at the dig and she says she has a surprise for us." Ward struck a few more chords that would have been appropriate for the introduction of a circus act as Pila stepped forward.

"I'm sorry to disappoint you, but we didn't find the ring. What we did find doesn't glitter, but it may be more interesting." She reached into the bag and pulled out a stained light brown object that looked like a rock, but when she turned to face those seated, they could see it was a human skull minus its mandible. A collective intake of air could be heard throughout the room.

"We discovered this artifact a few days ago, but we don't believe that it was in a grave or burial ground. When we finish excavating, we'll know more, but for now it appears to have been tossed into a shallow well. I thought I would bring it along as a kind of mascot since the yacht club is putting on that Crystal Skull celebration in a week or two. We can let them see what the real thing looks like." She turned and presented it to Jesse, who received it as if it were the Holy Grail. He paused to gather his thoughts.

"The human skull," he said, pausing again, "is one of the strongest symbols in Christianity." Turning the skull slowly in his hand, he ran a forefinger over the knitted joints. "It was attributed to Origen, around 200 A.D., that Christ was crucified above the grave of Adam at Golgotha and, therefore, man was redeemed by His blood both physically and psychologically. The bloodstained skull is said to have been dug from its grave and kept in the vault where Jesus was entombed. It was one of the enabling sources in the Resurrection." Jesse smiled gently and looked around the quiet room. Finding everyone attentive, he continued.

"The skull of Adam is the symbol of eternal life, representing time past, present, and future—representing the Father, the Son, and the Holy Ghost. Some who have contemplated the skull speak of having shed their earthly existence for the feeling of ecstasy in the unity of the Trinity. It is also said that through contemplation of the skull we may foresee our future on earth." His voice had grown soft and mesmerizing, his eyes bright and focused on his finger tracing the skull fault lines.

"As our spirit is drawn in by the skull, we may begin to understand the mysteries of life that have eluded us; all may become clear to us as the curtain of time is pulled away and we are drawn to the blinding light of truth as it was in Tolstoy's *Death of Ivan Ilyich*." He turned back to Pila.

"I'll just keep this safely in the office until you need it back at the dig, if that's alright."

"Sure. For the time being, it's our mascot. I call it 'Yorick.'"

Jesse winced at her offhanded remark, "If there is nothing more for this evening, you are free to go," Jesse said, and turned back to the skull. He was soon surrounded by several students, including Andora, who wanted to examine it.

"Can we get out of here?" Pila asked Luke.

"Sure, follow me," and they made their way to the porch.

"Can I take you to one of our finer nightclubs for an after-sermon drink?" Luke asked Pila as they skipped down the steps and onto the lawn.

"I insist, but only if you carry me to a beer joint and buy me a beer."

"Easy enough," Luke said, taking her arm and walking her down the road toward the marina.

They sat at a high table on the deck and took long chugs of beer.

"What did you think of Jesse's performance?" Luke asked.

"Is he for real? He's got that preacher thing down pat, and my God, the voice is wicked. He made that skull into a sacred relic before our very eyes. It was genuinely erotic."

"That's Jesse. Always on the easy make, even if he has to use a dirty skull. But his ambitions are higher than hypnotizing a small audience sitting around on futons. He's headed for the big top, or so he thinks: New York, the Met, the lights on Broadway—all of that stuff swims in his head. It's in the stars."

"Well, it's nice to hear that someone has ambition around here."

"Was that cruel and insensitive remark meant to slander me?"

"Can we just walk a little?" Pila said. "I don't want to discuss your career path in a bar because if I start screaming at you, someone might take it seriously and start a fight or something. So, let's walk." They walked arm in arm up the road, past the parsonage and theater and on toward the Fessenden road sign. Finally, Pila unhitched her arm from his and stopped.

"You know I want you to go to Israel with me and work in a kibbutz. I have always wanted to do this since I was young, and I can't imagine anyone else I would rather do it with than you. This time, I need you, Shake. It will be a good experience for both of us."

"Oh, Pila," he said, protesting mildly. "I don't have the passion for Israel that you have. It doesn't run in my blood as warmly as it does yours. I'm not even Jewish."

"But you have been circumcised."

"How do you know that?" he exploded. "Anyhow, that doesn't always determine who's Jewish and who's not."

"But you have been circumcised, so there must be a Jewish inclination somewhere in your family."

"Nevertheless, it does not make me Jewish. It was my grandfather. He insisted that to be circumcised was to be a true follower of the Old Testament, but he was Irish so that doesn't mean anything. It doesn't."

"It does, it does. I couldn't possibly go to Israel with someone who didn't have a Jewish schwanz. It would be unacceptable at the kibbutz. You would not be authentic." She thought for a moment. "Maybe it's not so bad with you. You've got a Jewish-looking schwanz so maybe if we get married, the rest of the Protestant in you we can overlook," she smiled at him.

"Is that a proposal?"

"It is if you want it to be."

"Can we be serious?"

"Haven't we been serious in one way or another since we met?" she asked.

"Pila, I can't remember the time when I haven't loved you more than anybody. It's been forever. But I don't think I'm what you want and need. You need a 'mensch,' somebody with the balls and integrity equal to your own. You need to pull someone down from the ceiling of the Sistine Chapel," and he flexed his muscles into knots and puffed his cheeks. "I'm working on it, but I'm not there yet. I can't commit a scarecrow to you, of all people. I'm too empty. I would disappoint you. You are on a quest to accomplish something, and I look for a name tag on my shorts to see who I am each morning."

They had reached the Fessenden sign at the end of the road and he stopped beneath the dim street lamp and faced her. He slipped his shorts down to his ankles and stood in front of her, naked.

"You may have all of my Jewish schwanz that you want, but I don't think it will be enough for you. It's the least important part of me that you could have."

She looked at him and snickered.

"What's wrong," he said.

"I didn't realize how small you were. You know, I think I exaggerated how good you might be in bed. Oh well, such a disappointment."

He reached down and pulled up his pants. She reached for his hand, and they stood facing each other. He smiled and kissed her fully on the lips, and then he unbuttoned the top button of her blouse and held the next button and flipped it, too, from its hole. He parted the open blouse and kissed her at the beginning of the cleft between her breasts.

"Pila, are we sharing prenuptial intimacies, or just fooling around?"

She grabbed him in her arms and squeezed him upward in a bear hug that began to make him red in the face.

"I've got you now, Mr. Big-time Spy-Catcher."

"Pila," he gasped helplessly. "You're so easy to love. Put me down." Then she burst out laughing, dropped him in front of her, grabbed his face and kissed him.

"I don't know why I love you so much, you goy—you, who hurt my feelings and trampled my religion, and sent me into despair—I should still want revenge for what you did to me. It seems to me that when you write a suicide note and send it to your dearest friend, you are obligated to commit suicide. Nobody in Shakespeare would have reneged on a suicide obligation. I should have come to this island and found you dead so that I could throw myself on your grave and weep, and go to the Wall in Israel and weep. You have deprived a Jewish woman of her strongest instinct, you incompetent putz. You have deprived me of a proper wailing."

"Oh, Pila, you wanted me dead because I hurt you, and now you want me alive because I love you. You want me, Pila, because I gave myself to you. You know I will love you forever in payment for what I have done to you—I owe you that—and yet you don't want me on those terms because you don't want my shame. You cannot accept it, and I cannot stop giving it to you. How do we resolve that?"

"Such things are not for resolution, Shake, only for understanding, and if you thought you could help me, I would take you—don't worry—do you think that a Jew can't love and appreciate a little more guilt? There are times when I can't stand what you write, but I am in love with your guilt. I think you are probably right. You don't know who you are, and I can't do what I have to do in Israel with someone in disguise. Don't worry, there will be someone else, not lean and starved like you, but a guy who ruts around with legs like telephone poles and a chest like a barrel who will work from dawn to dark and have enough Jewish schwanz left to drive nails."

"Thank God. As much as I want to help you, I don't want to leave now. Pila, you know I will never break my covenant with you. If you insist, I will go to Israel to build the kibbutz, but I have to tell you that this is where I belong because this woman Andora is the one I will marry."

"Are you in love with that man's wife? The guy on the boat?"

"That man's wife?" Shake asked quizzically. "That's funny. I don't think of her as being married. I never see her with him. I can't connect them enough to see a relationship between them. He's always on the boat, and I am with her as much as I can be. I don't know if it's love, but I am enthralled, captivated, and I can't get enough of her."

"That's too bad," Pila said. "You aren't fit to take the wagon train to Israel, anyhow. You can't do the hard stuff."

"Like what hard stuff?" he asked, slightly offended.

"Like letting her go because she's another man's wife—that simple—that hard."

Shake felt as though he had been hit with a physical blow that knocked him down, but nothing moved in his slouching figure. He looked at her.

"You want me to make that choice?"

"You would have to make that choice if you came with me," she said.

"You mean I couldn't make that choice simply for my love of you?" He stubbed his toe in the ground, moving the gravel around as though he were playing chess. Finally, he turned quickly away from her. He kicked out viciously at the air in front of him, sending pebbles skittering down the road like his own inadequacies and walked away from her, down the darkening street toward Maestro's cottage.

He was twisting inside. The thought of losing Pila wound tightly around the frailness of his courage, crushing it painfully in his mind. He needed someone—he wanted someone who would understand—someone who could lead him out of the pain. Maestro's cottage was dark, but he tried the door and found it open. Maestro had told him that he was welcome anytime, so he stumbled in the dark until he found the lamp by the chair and turned it on. Going to the cabinet in the kitchen where Maestro kept the whiskey, he took down a bottle of Jameson, poured himself half a jelly glass, and, rather than drink it down, he sipped it. By the time he reached the bottom of the glass his emotions had almost returned to normal. He poured another. Oh, Pila, he pined, every time we move apart, I feel like shit. Will I ever get it right? Losing Pila was like watching his life's blood drain away and he could feel it run warmly across his emotions. Andora notwithstanding, he would terribly suffer the hurt of losing Pila. He went to the extra bedroom, lay down without undressing and quickly fell into a deep whiskey sleep.

On his way home from the theater, Maestro passed Pila headed in the opposite direction. She was whistling what sounded like a marching song to which she was keeping a steady pace.

"Evening," Maestro said, as he passed and wondered why she was wandering around the dark streets at night.

When he reached the cottage, Maestro noticed several lights burning within, and he entered expecting to find a visitor. He saw the whiskey bottle on the kitchen sideboard, and when he looked into the small bedroom, he found Luke, sprawled and sleeping soundly. He recovered the whiskey bottle from the kitchen, rinsed the glass and wiped it dry, and took them both into the living room and sat down at the writing table.

There was a light tapping at the door. When he looked up through the glare of light from the inside, he saw Lonnie standing there, smiling.

"Come in, come in," he said, beckoning her with his hand. "What brings you out in the dark of night to visit your old director? Please sit down. I was about to have a drink of whiskey, but I think that I'll change that now to a swig of Cremant. Will you join me?"

"I don't know what that is."

"Oh, it's just champagne that is not made in the Champagne area of France so we must call it by another name. I'll fetch it from the fridge." He brought back the bottle with two small glasses and opened it, twisting the cork until it released with a sigh.

"If you let it pop when you open it, you're showing off," Maestro explained. "When you ease the cork out slowly, you preserve the gas and the bubbling essence of the drink." They lifted their glasses to each other and drank.

"Is this a social visit or are you here to talk show biz?"

"Can it be both?"

"Sure. But just remember that Jesse is the certified shrink."

"Oh, I don't need that. I need to know more about Ruby, like what would she be like if she wasn't half-crazed by something."

"Probably more like you: stuffed with life and willing to love it. But she can't, of course. She sees her life in a series of fractured events—like looking through a kaleidoscope—bright colors swirling around, changing shapes, nothing to hold onto and then Luke destroys her little squirrel rifle, her only possession. Her life isn't an orderly series of events so much as unexpected explosions over which she has little control. She cannot keep her fuses from burning and igniting at the most critical moments. She may have a soul, but it is a vacant lot that holds no memory of human habitation. Do you remember the line she says to Luke about making love?"

"Yes, she says, 'I never saw my mother and father make a kiss. Mama kissed the babies once in a while, but when she finished nursing, we never got kissed again.'"

"Doesn't that say that Ruby's soul is empty of kisses? The Irish playwright, Synge, once described a woman saying that 'she's lonesome in her mind.' Ruby is lonesome in her soul, and that's a bad place to be."

"I don't feel that yet."

"I know. You aren't quite edgy enough. If you don't mind my giving you a little advice, why don't you try hating Luke more. Luke is your nemesis. For you, he's what's wrong with the center of your universe. You've got to hate him more. Roll up all of your pain and despair and aim it at Luke. Show him no consideration. Cut him when you can. Make him bleed."

"I've never been that way with anybody in my life."

"Because you've never done it doesn't mean that you can't. That's what acting is: being able to do the thing you most likely wouldn't do in front of people who don't expect you to do it. Learn to hate Luke. Do it with restrained passion."

"He's such a nice guy, though."

"That's what you think. I know better."

"Tell me."

"Don't worry, you'll find out. Take my word for it." She stood up. "Won't you have more?" he said.

"No thanks. It was very nice, that Cremant."

"You are welcome any time."

As she prepared to exit she turned back to Maestro, "Hate him, huh?"

"Right to the core."

23

Crab Dance

Jesse saw a bit of commotion at the theater as a pickup truck pulling a crabbing boat on a trailer backed up to the front door. At second glance, the trailer was carrying only the shell of a crabbing boat and not much of that. He went from his office to the backstage entrance of the theater and gathered up Luke, who was making a doorframe, and proceeded to the front entrance where two men were waiting for someone to open the doors.

"This is my son, Hank. I'm Elvis Gravis," the more elderly of the two men said. "The boys call me 'Possum,' so you can too, I reckon. This is part of the set for the dance show on Sunday night. Hank and I made it for Miss Antonia and her dancers out of an old crabbing boat we had sitting in the backyard. We took it apart, then we put it back together in pieces so you could move it around. When you put it together, I swear it looks like a real boat. Miss Antonia needs it on stage today because she starts dress rehearsal, and Hank and me get to be on stage as the crabbers in the boat. Ain't that something?"

Jesse shook the men's hands. "I'm Jesse, this is Luke. We don't have an official crew to help you, but we'll give you a hand unloading if that's what you need." As they moved to the rear of the truck and were about to unload the cargo, a small, trim, energetic middle-aged woman followed by a troupe of a dozen dancers, male and female in working shorts and T-shirts, trotted up to the truck.

"Hey, Possum, the *Pequod* sails again!" she said, referring to the name of Ahab's famous whaling ship whose letters were fading on the bow of what was left of Possum's boat.

"It does, it does, Miss Antonia," Possum said, greeting her and shaking her hand. The dancers moved forward and Possum began to disassemble and unload parts of the boat from the truck. Throughout the day, Possum and his son, together with Luke and the dancers, worked on the stage creating the set for the show. All three scenes, "Crabbin' the Pots," "Trollin' for a Rockfish," and "Oysterin' on the Bar," made use of the boat as their principal stage set. When the basic work was completed, Andora and a fellow painter began closing unsightly seams and touching up places on the river façade so it resembled water. For the next several days, the theater bustled with dance rehearsals.

Hank Gravis, fishing fifty pots twice a day between Woodland Point and the Swan Point Bar, would unload his catch at Captain John's Restaurant, then dock his boat at the marina on the Wicomico side of the bridge and meet his father, Possum, on the Tiki deck at Scuttlebutt's. Together they would scuff up the road in their stained, white rubber boots to rehearse their crabbing scene at the theater. When Sunday evening came, the crabbers and the dancers were ready. Flyers had been distributed to doorsteps earlier in the week inviting island residents to the show, free of charge. At 7 p.m., a half-hour prior to the opening curtain, the theater was nearly filled. Despite additional chairs brought from the firehouse, there was standing room only.

At 7:30, the curtain parted and an audible sigh arose from the audience in appreciation of the unique stage set. The show began with dancers wearing white crabbing boots, tossing and juggling colorful cork floats. Next, they passed half-sized crab pots, made of yellow, green, and red vinyl wire, and formed geometrical shapes with them on stage. The dancing crabbers simulated hauling, winding, emptying, and tossing back the pots—in rhythm with the music and each other. Then, dancers dressed as birds with diaphanous wings circled the boats like seagulls, dipping into the river where the old bait from the pots had been emptied until the stage seemed to be one continuous animation of the energy expended in catching crabs. Finally, the smallest dancers collected themselves in the boat and were tossed back and forth, signifying the culling process. After stacking the crab pots on the cabin roof, Possum took a handkerchief from his pocket and wiped his brow in an exaggerated symbol that the day's crabbing had been completed. The curtain closed to long applause. The scene had been choreographed expertly around the crabbing theme, and the audience eagerly waited to see what would happen in "Trollin' for Rockfish."

The scene opened with a single fisherman tending several rods bristling from the stern of the boat. Six dancers in masks and costumes resembling rockfish performed a swimming dance in and around the boat, periodically plucking shiny, jeweled, imitation baitfish from the floor in rhythm. One of the baitfish, picked by a dancing rockfish, was attached to a rod in the boat that suddenly bent. The fisherman heaved on the rod while the fish pulled and danced in a whirling, squirming frenzy revealing its agony at having been caught—hook dangling from its mouth. As the dance progressed and the music became more tortuous, a stream of blood ran out of the fish's gills. The more the fisherman pulled, the more the fish resisted in a thrashing, twisting dance. A man in the audience rose quickly from his seat and yelled, "Cut the line, cut the line, you're killing her!" As though directed by the shout, the actor-fisherman on stage drew a knife from his belt, made a quick cutting movement of his hand, and dropped the line into the water. The fish stopped its frenetic dance, regained its equilibrium and danced and swam elegantly from the stage. Reeling in the line, the fisherman looked disappointed as the lights dimmed and the curtain closed.

Backstage, the dancers clasped each other in amazement. The shout from the audience member to "cut the line" could have stopped them dead in their tracks, but the actor had cut the line and continued to act as though the scene had been rehearsed. They had all been spontaneous—reacting to an audience in a way they had never experienced, and it thrilled them. Miss Antonia hugged them and hurried them into changes of costume for the next scene.

When the curtain rose again, two dancers appeared from the wings carrying sixteen-foot-long oystering tongs. Dancing with surprising grace around the tongs, they vaulted to the boat's deck effortlessly and exaggerated the motions of tonging for oysters from the make-believe river. Although isolated on the boat with the unwieldy long shafts of the tongs, the dancers used their space to perform a dance within a dance—requiring more gymnastic ability than grace—and the audience applauded each difficult movement as though watching a troupe of Chinese acrobats. Finally the scene was successfully concluded, the house lights went on, and the audience rose, applauding thunderously. The dancers made two curtain calls and then Possum and Hank Gravis appeared with Miss Antonia perched on their shoulders—the crowd erupted again in appreciation. It had been a new experience for dancers and audience alike. The citizens of the island had watched symbols of their livelihood lifted by artistic expression into new experience and meaning and, for the first time, some of them understood the purpose and the promise of art.

The crowd dispersed to their homes on the island, and Leigh and Charles walked slowly over the bridge and back to Chigger City.
"That was an extraordinary performance," Leigh remarked. "That director or choreographer or whoever is very talented."
"I believe she's on loan from a dance company in New York," Charles said. "Would you like to stop in Captain John's for a snack?" he asked, but Leigh declined so they walked silently, hand in hand, the remaining distance to their rented house.
"Before you came tonight, the archeologist brought in an old skull they had excavated from the dig at Wollaston. Jesse went into a positive ecstasy over it and frightened the troops out of their wits. Jesse brings a new angle to things—an element of discovery and animation—I can see how Rose might want to continue to be his wife, but I don't think she has a chance even if she wanted to stick with it. By the way,

her story was very autobiographical, although she isn't about to commit suicide. Her will to live is very strong and her lust for life is growing."

"How do you know that?"

"We talked."

"Did she say lusty things?"

"Only that she has this Salome image building in her psyche."

"Aren't you supposed to stay out of her psyche?"

"I thought it was her bedroom you wanted me to stay out of. You get the psyche with the warm oatmeal cookies and a glass of milk."

"Just make sure you can tell the difference," Leigh said and poked him in the ribs as they climbed the steps to the house. "What is it about summer camps or the beach that makes everybody horny?" she asked indifferently.

"Nobody wears clothes. Everybody tries to get naked to beat the heat."

"Is that your theory?"

"No, my theory is that everybody is horny to begin with and hot weather exaggerates it. Speaking of horny, Jesse wants to have a session with you and his astrological charts for his research. So give him a call, if you're interested."

Leigh looked at him askance. "Have you lost your mind?" she asked.

"Hasn't everybody?" he answered, wiggling his eyebrows and leering at her suggestively.

24

Ruby Breaks Bad

Luke was late meeting Lonnie at the theater for rehearsal. He had lingered in bed with Andora and then dozed off again when she left. When he finally reached the theater, Maestro was sitting in the director's chair reading the morning paper. Lonnie was walking aimlessly on stage whacking a paddle ball and counting aloud: "eighty-nine—ninety—one—two—three—four—five—six." Then she missed the next one and, in one motion, threw the toy at Luke as he approached, narrowly missing his head.

"And that's probably how many times you bopped your easel-toting honey to make you late, isn't it?" she taunted.

Luke picked up the paddle and handed it over to Maestro, who wore a smug look on his face. Incredulously, Luke looked at Maestro, but before he could say anything,

Maestro suggested they make up for lost time by reviewing the blocking of the scene.

Lonnie quickly read her line, then moved effortlessly, while Luke missed his next cue and froze like a deer caught in headlights.

"Well, move!" she exclaimed, and he responded with a little jump. As she moved around the stage reading her lines, he continued to be late with his responses and completely uncoordinated in his movement.

"You can't be there," she shouted at him. "I can't talk to you with the back of my head," she yelled and moved him into his proper place. Finally, Luke's attention focused on his script and the stage, and they finished the scene without interruption.

"Take a break," Maestro said, "and when we come back, we'll do it again."

"At this rate, you might do better if you replaced me with a dummy," Luke said, watching Lonnie walk off the stage. Her strident reading of the script and her abrupt answers had put him in a quandary.

"What's going on? What's wrong with her?" he asked Maestro. "Is she nuts?"

"Don't forget, she's supposed to be."

"Can't you get her to back off a little?"

"Are you kidding? She's electric. If she can do that on the stage, she will steal every scene she's in. The only one that has control over her is you. What are you going to do about it?"

"Do you mean what would Luke do about it? He won't tolerate it. He'll throw her out of the cabin."

"Well, then?"

"I don't want to start a fight between us."

"You don't have to. Just be Luke: confused, angry, finally fed-up."

When Lonnie returned, they rehearsed the scene again, this time with more precision and less distraction created by her feisty attitude. They went through it again with more intensity until Maestro could feel Ruby's hate in his own bones.

"Keep all of that," he instructed his actors, "and don't let it go. That's enough for today. I think you have it."

Neither actor showed pleasure at the director's remarks. Lonnie marched from the stage and Luke went to the backstage area where he thought Andora might be working. Maestro shuffled his script into his pouch and walked off the stage, encountering a man seated in a chair close by the door.

"I think we met the other day," Possum said, by way of introduction.

"It's Mr. Possum, isn't it?" Maestro asked.

"Just plain Possum will do."

"You'll have to pardon me. I get in the habit of calling my students by the title of Mister when we first meet since I believe it makes them more comfortable."

"I enjoyed listening to your rehearsal. Reminds me of a few rounds that I had with my first wife," Possum said.

"You're welcome to sit in anytime. We only ask that there be no interruptions of the rehearsal."

"That's okay. I just thought I'd drop in since the door was open. You know, I was one of the crabbers onstage with the dancers the other night. That was an experience I never had before, and it wasn't bad, either."

"Good. Well, Possum, I'm going down to Linda's for a coffee. Care to join me?"

"Sure, I will. Need one myself, hot, black, and strong."

On their way to the coffee shop, the two men chatted aimlessly, stopping to watch an osprey fly into a nest on top a power pole at the ramp to the bridge.

"Know much about the osprey?" Possum asked.

"Hardly anything," Maestro answered. "Only that they're beautiful to watch."

"They have two chicks up there, and the whole time they're growing in that nest the parents are building the nest higher and higher. They don't want those babies to fall out, and they're also teaching them how to live. The chicks watch the old birds place a new stick inside the nest, weaving it between the others, day after day—and in about thirty days, they have a pattern of nest-making in their little brains that will last a lifetime. Same way with fishing. When the chicks are young, the parents like to dive and fish nearby so the chicks can watch and learn how to do it. Chicks might not know it then, but they've got to be able to get their own supper in a few weeks. Same way with leaving for the summer. You can watch them join up and circle, soaring higher and higher until they catch a big airflow heading south that will take them to their wintering quarters. You can lay on your back and watch them through binoculars sometimes until they go out of sight. They've probably been doing that for centuries. They get in here about St. Patrick's Day and leave in September around Labor Day. In six months or so, them chicks gotta be hatched, fed, flown, taught to hunt and build a house before they ever leave here for their winter grounds in Argentina or wherever. Pity we can't do that well with our own ain't it? We have a tough time knowing when our own are ready to fly."

Maestro looked at him without comment and they continued their way over to the coffee shop. When she saw

Possum coming, Linda poured him a large cup of steaming black coffee and passed it over the counter. Maestro ordered a mocha and then he and Possum took a seat at a table.

"I take it you are a native of the island?" Maestro asked.

"Used to vacation here when I was young, and then I moved here to raise a family."

"Then you would know about the Legend of Santasay that was told to us by one of the archeologists up at the Wollaston dig."

"Heard of the name Santasay, but I don't know of any legend about it. Can't be much of a legend down here if I haven't heard about it, can it?"

"I wouldn't think so. Let me tell you the short version and see if it rings any bells." Maestro sketched the story out for Possum, who laughed a few times and shook his head.

"We don't call our bait 'Tom's Body,' at least we haven't for as long as I've been here. She's making all that stuff up."

"I thought as much, but I thought I would ask someone who might know."

"Haven't seen any lights underwater lately, either. Come to think of it, I never seen any lights underwater." The siren signaling a call to the firehouse went off with a shrill blast and Possum rose from his chair and headed for the door.

"Got to go see what's happening," he shouted at Maestro, closed the door and was gone down the steps in an old man's trot toward the firehouse. A few minutes later, a truck and an ambulance roared across the bridge and up the road toward Swan Point.

"Wow, what a racket," Maestro said to Linda.

"Yeah. I use to keep a shortwave scanner in here, but it was such a disruption with all that static and chatter that I took it out. Let them run to the siren. You can't think in your head with that scanner going all the time."

Luke left the theater and walked the short distance to the parsonage where his MG was parked. He was still upset about the rehearsal, and frequently, when things became a little stressful, a top-down ride through the countryside calmed him. He jumped over the driver's door into the seat, turned the key, and started down the street toward the bridge. As he passed the firehouse, a hard object suddenly came flying from behind a large oak tree and fell on the hood, making a sizable dent and removing some paint before it skittered away to the road's shoulder. It took him a moment to realize someone had thrown a rock at him. Glancing back quickly, he saw no one, so he turned the car around and raced back to the firehouse, coming to a sliding stop in the rear. No one was to be seen. Hurrying through the back door, he saw Possum in a chair reading the newspaper.

"Did you see that?" Luke blurted out.

"See what?"

"See who threw a rock and dented the hood of my car!"

"Well, it wasn't me and I'm the only man who's been here until you come in, so I reckon I didn't see anybody throw no rocks."

"Damn, damn, damn!" Luke said. He looked around angrily, then turned back to the parking lot and got into his car. Possum waited for a minute before going over to a clothes locker and opening the door. Lonnie slid out easily and looked around.

"Wow, he was really angry, wasn't he?"

"Probably had a right to be."

"Naw. He deserved it, the arrogant bastard—thinks he's king of the hill."

"He can't think that. Old Possum's king of the hill."

Luke drove as hard as he could the short distance to Linda's and slid to a halt in the gravel parking lot. Taking the steps two at a time, he yanked open the door and faced Maestro engaged in conversation with Linda.

"You've got to do something about that bitch," he yelled, "or she's gonna get it!"

25

Shabbats

Pila's old pickup rattled into the firehouse parking lot late Friday afternoon. She made her way to the theater in search of Luke and found him there alone, gluing the legs of a kitchen chair.

"Luke," she shouted at him, "let's go. We've worked enough for one day. Come on!"

He shoved the rung into the hole of the leg and hit it with a rubber hammer, then wiped away the glue that had been forced out of the hole.

"Where are we going?"

"Let's go for a boat ride."

"I don't have a boat."

"Come on, we'll rent one from Captain John's." Luke grabbed an old baseball cap with *J's Cars* on the front, and they walked across the bridge to the restaurant/marina/ship's store and rented a twelve-foot boat powered by a fifteen-horsepower motor. Pila grabbed a six-pack of ten-ounce cans of Budweiser from the cooler and paid the clerk in cash.

"We got paid today, so everybody took off early," she said, scooping up her change.

They were instructed about the gasoline and the life preservers, and after a few hearty pulls on the starter chord, the engine sputtered and they launched from the dock.

"Which way do you want to go? East or west?"

"Let's go to the west. I want to see the dig from the water."

The little outboard motor labored behind the fiberglass boat, pushing it out of Neale Sound and into the Potomac, heading in the direction of Swan Point where the sun lay low on the horizon. Skirting the shoreline past Woodland Point to the entrance of Weir Creek, a large bowl of water surrounded by marshland and a few fairways of a golf course, Luke found himself in shallows and was forced to back away from the entrance and abandon any thoughts of seeing the archeological dig from the water. He headed the boat toward Swan Point where there was at least a vantage point for watching the sun go down. There were layers of clouds in the sky through which the sun slipped behind the horizon of the Virginia shore, spreading vibrant yellows and reds as far as the eye could see. They floated, drinking the beer in the rented boat and watched the colors change gradually, the afterglow spreading subtly across the sky.

"Ain't that somethin'," Luke said.

"Very poetic description of a dynamite sunset, very poetic," Pila responded.

"Don't belabor me, Pila, because I've had my fill of feisty women today," Luke fussed in mock anger.

They were silent, swaying gently with the tide, watching the afterglow disappear into the blue night sky. "We should get back while I can still see the tree line," Luke said. "Besides, this is the last beer." He turned the boat and lined it up with a point downriver, then took a long swig of beer. Pila, turned toward the stern to face him, asked curiously, "What's that?"

Luke turned and as he looked over his shoulder, the little boat veered from its course.

"Where? I don't see anything."

"About a hundred yards off the wood line. I thought I saw a light in the water."

Luke regained his course and increased the throttle of the motor to add speed.

"Turn around, Luke, let's see what it was."

"No, you're not gonna fool me over lights in the water and good old Santasay looking for her children. Don't scam me, Pila."

"I'm not. I'm serious. Honest. I saw a light beneath the water."

"I knew you were a cheap date, but these hallucinations after three little beers is a bit over the top, isn't it? We've really got to get this boat back before they send the Coast Guard looking for us. Besides, you made all that stuff up about Santasay, didn't you? Are you beginning to believe your own tales, now?"

"Don't be stupid. I saw something. I wouldn't tell you I saw something if I hadn't really seen something because I know you would make fun of me just like you did."

"Look, we'll rent another boat next Friday at sundown and tell them we're keeping it for the evening and I'll chase Santasay around the river until the oil in her lamp runs out, if you like, but right now I'm going back to the marina."

"Ach," she blurted. "I just remembered when you said sundown and Friday. Today is Shabbat, and I'm supposed to be in prayer and not here in this boat with you anyhow. I forgot about it. The sky was so beautiful. Damn!" she wailed.

"What do you want to do now?" Luke asked, concerned with her dilemma.

"We can't get to my camp by water. By the time we get back to the marina, it will be too late to drive back. I'll just have to find a place to stay on the island."

"You can stay with me, I've got room."

"I don't want to cramp your style," she said.

They returned the boat to the marina and walked back to the parsonage where they found Rose and Jesse sitting at the kitchen table eating hot dogs and roasted ears of corn.

"Sit down and eat something," Jesse offered. "The hot dogs are vintage kosher half-smokes and the corn is sweet and delicious."

After getting plates from the cabinet, Luke and Pila joined them. While they were eating, Pila described seeing the light in the water. In response to her curiosity, Jesse, who had no explanation for the phenomenon, said he would ask Possum the next time he saw him. Perhaps Possum, the island's repository of things known and unknown, could explain it.

"The Navy is always testing missiles and weapons up and down the river, so maybe it was a bit of fluorescence floating about from one of their experiments."

When the talk turned to sleeping arrangements, Rose ignored the recommendation that Pila sleep in Luke's bed and Luke sleep on the floor. Instead, she announced that Pila could sleep with her since her bed was king-size, and Jesse could either sleep in his office or on the boat with Will, as he had done frequently this summer. With the problem resolved, Luke and Jesse said good evening to the ladies and went off to their respective sleeping places. Luke was a bit relieved over the arrangements because there was no way to let Andora know of Pila's presence in his room until she slipped into his bed and found Pila, and Pila wouldn't have known Andora was coming...the scenario grew funnier as he thought about it and he went upstairs to make some notes about it for a possible short story.

After clearing away the dishes, the women sat down again at the kitchen table to nibble cookies, drinking the iced tea that remained in their glasses.

"I really hate to put your husband out of his bed," Pila remarked.

"Think nothing of it. It's a chore for him to be there anyway."

"Oh, sorry, didn't mean to...."

"Oh, I don't think it's much of a secret," Rose said, interrupting Pila's apology. "There isn't much left in our marriage and certainly nothing that would require a bed."

"Sorry to hear it. What happened? If I may ask."

"It's a long story."

"You can tell me. I'm a good listener."

"I met Jesse at a revival in Texas—we were young—he was trying to make rain in a dry-gulch county one night during a revival. We got married in his last year of school and then were sent to a Methodist church in City Island, New York. That's when we met Andora and Will. City Island didn't work out so we went to a small church out on Long Island, a very conservative little town, a grey town down to its soul. We settled there and preached God's love with enthusiasm and tried, as much as we could, to stir the pot of Christianity in a place that needed spiritual sustenance. But the folks there would rather talk about religion than experience it, and when Jesse started counseling teenage girls who were pregnant and youngsters who had difficulty with drugs, the community thought his behavior unbecoming of their religious leader. An 'unseemly' bunch of kids were going in and out of the parsonage and the congregation kept muttering and gossiping about it. Then, Jesse went into the black community and talked to some people and held some meetings on how they might help themselves, or how the church could help them, and that upset the parishioners a little more.

"He used to have coffee once a week for the other ministers and the rabbi in town so they could let their hair down or share problems and discuss how they might better work with the state and town social systems—but that upset some of the ministers who thought he was proselytizing and attempting to disrupt their ministries. Jesse didn't much care what your religious affiliation was if you were in trouble. If a bum came to the door for help and said he was a Baptist or Catholic, Jesse would try to help with his problem and then he would refer him to the minister of his faith—sometimes he would drive them over there after giving them a couple of bucks to tide them over. Most of the other ministers hated to see him coming because there wasn't much they could do for homeless people except give them money, listen to the stories, maybe keep them over if they thought they might place them in a job. But, for the most part, they resented Jesse for delivering the needy to them."

"It sounds like Jesse's a good man."

"He was, and he seemed to have energy and powers that none of the others had. Two young ladies from Jehovah's

Witnesses came to the door one day and they talked with Jesse for about two hours, and when I came back from shopping, they were on their knees in the living room praying. The next Sunday they came to our church and converted. Jesse can be very convincing. He was particularly attentive to young girls who were pregnant, without a husband, and no place to go. To him they represented the Madonna—the expectant mother who could find no place in the inn. He would send them to a clinic in the city where their babies would be delivered with the help of midwives and a volunteer physician, and afterwards, they would receive postpartum rest and education on infant care. He tried to hide the cost associated with that practice under building and maintenance, or missionary contributions, but in the end he was chastised for spending church money inappropriately, for purposes the congregation thought of as illicit. The congregation reported his irregular financial activities to the bishop who carried out an investigation and suggested several remedies by which Jesse might pay back the church for its unapproved use of funds, and that obligation has kept us constantly in the poorhouse.

"Then we had the accident that almost killed me, and, eventually, they just relieved him of his duty and sent him down here to stay out of trouble. By the time I recuperated from the accident, I had changed and Jesse had changed, and he doesn't love me anymore." She shrugged her shoulders. "What's a body to do?"

It was not a question Rose expected Pila to answer, but unwilling to let it pass, Pila responded, "Get on with it."

"What?"

"Just get on with it. Look at yourself: you're strong, attractive, smart, and make great cookies—a dynamite combination—take 'em all with you and make a new life.

Hell, better than that, I'll give you a place to do it in. You can come with me to the kibbutz in Israel and have a great adventure."

"You're kidding?"

"Not in the least," Pila said, rising from the table. Rose also stood up and carried her cup to the sink.

"I couldn't leave him. I couldn't do that even though I know he doesn't love me. I'm his wife. I have an obligation."

Pila walked over to Rose, put her arms around her gently and held her.

"You're the one I need. You are the one who will make a difference. You are the one that I want in my kibbutz. Will he leave you when the summer is over?"

"I haven't really thought about it, but he has already left me in so many ways that I suppose he will finally make it intolerable for me to live with him. I will have to leave."

"When you find that is true, call me. I will come get you and hold you tight and give you the love that you need—the love that will make you whole again."

"Are you intimating that we should have an adult relationship—you and I—like two women in love?"

"No, certainly not! When you are rid of the residue of Jesse, you will live again and you will see with whom you want to express your love and your sexual desires. Shall we go to bed now? You on one side, me on the other, and I will tell you about life in the kibbutz. If it interests you, we'll take a little trip Sunday morning and I will show you something that I think you will enjoy."

26

Mikya

The peninsula of Cobb Neck rises from the flat Potomac River basin to form a ridge that separates the Potomac and Wicomico rivers. Pila and Rose took the right fork from Route 257 at Tompkinsville to the Mt. Victoria Road and up the spine of the ridge, changing gears in the old Ford pickup, zigging and zagging around sharp turns until they turned onto a graveled road. In another two hundred yards, they wheeled carefully into a dirt track and then onto a soft carpet of leaves and pine needles where they stopped and got out of the truck. Pila slung the day pack over her shoulder and led the way down a hillside on a winding path to the bottom of the ridge. The path opened to a meadow covered in grass, in the middle of which shimmered a pool of water the size of an automobile. The color of the pool from a distance appeared black, but when they came closer, they could see that it was crystal clear, the darkness caused by moss on the rocks at the bottom. A spring bubbling from the base of the hill trickled through a gravel runway and into the pond. Although the pool was surrounded by oak trees whose branches overarched the area, enough sun shone through to let rich, spring-fed grass grow lushly around the pool. Anyone not knowing it was there would have easily missed it.

"What a beautiful place," Rose said.

"Yes, a beautiful and secret place, Rose, that we want to keep for ourselves" Pila said. "It is the place of my *mikva*. Remember I told you that I was from a family of reformed Jews who held onto some traditions but abandoned others because they weren't compatible with modern life? This is one of the traditions that I truly love. It belongs to all Jews, men and women, but it seems that women take it more seriously than men. It has become more of a woman's secret rite."

"Don't spook me, Pila."

"Don't worry, it's a very practical ritual. When a Jewish woman finishes her monthly period, she is supposed to wait for five days in what is called *niddah* or separateness, and then go to mikva to cleanse and purify herself of tainted blood before she reunites with her husband. It is a rite of purification. There are many ways of doing it, but the point of the whole thing is that it provides the woman with a rebirth, and reuniting with herself before she is coupled again with a male. It can mean many different things to people who perform it as a religious obligation so don't think that you are abrogating a religious tradition by coming here. In a real mikva that is built by a rabbi, a Gentile would not be allowed to bathe. The only requirement, other than those established by the rabbi, is that the water come from a natural source, so that you can't have mikva in a hot tub or swimming pool. This place does not meet strict rabbinical requirements, but the water is natural, and the pool seems as though it is held in God's hand." She paused and then said, "Take off your clothes."

Rose looked askance and the blood rose in her cheeks.

"Don't worry, I won't be looking at your body. Turn your back to me and slip off your things. I'll hold this towel over you. When you're naked, sit on that grassy bank and then slide into the water."

Doing as she was instructed, Rose squeaked at the sudden coolness of the water's temperature and that of the moss-covered rocks and leaves at the bottom. She then settled down to her neck without difficulty.

"You must dip and cover your head and make sure that the water touches every crevice of your body. The water must completely infuse the spirit."

Rose lowered her body, then raised her dripping head, exposing it to the slanting rays of the sun, tasting the dribbling water on her lips.

"Now I'm going to read in Hebrew, and you won't understand it, but I want you to clear your mind. You should think of nothing and let the water wash into your soul and mix with the words: '*Barukh ata Adonai Elo-henu Melekh Ha-olam, asher kid'shanu b'mitzvotar v'tzivanu alha-t'vila.*'"

Pila put her hand on Rose's head and pushed down gently. When Rose came back to the surface, she sputtered. Pila ordered, "Now go under again, and say your own silent prayer."

When Rose came up again, Pila whispered "Kosher" and put her hand atop Rose's head. "Now stay under water and I will read the next prayer." Rose sank beneath the surface.

"'*Barukh ata Adonai Elo-henu Melekh Ha'olam shecheyanu v'kiymanu v' higyanu lazman haseh.*'"

Seeing Rose rise for the third time, Pila said "Kosher" quietly. "You are now pure in spirit, Rose," she said. "If you choose to submerge a fourth time it shall be for the building of your future. It will help you gather hope and guidance for the construction of your individual temple."

Rose rested, saying nothing, and then she sank slowly into the pool and stayed submerged for a much longer time. As Pila was about to reach down and pull her up by the hair, Rose bubbled to the surface and breathed deeply. She stood up and faced Pila, unafraid and uncaring that she was naked, and reached out her hand. Pila took it and pulled her gently from the water.

Turning Rose toward the pool, Pila wrapped the towel around her completely, put her arms around her and held her tightly. Finally, Pila dropped her arms, and Rose turned to face her. Tears welled in Rose's eyes and rolled gently down her cheek. She breathed deeply, pulled the towel more tightly around her, and sat down on a large rock.

"Are you going in?" she asked Pila.

"Not today. Only one person should bathe in any one day. We must wait for twenty-four hours until the water in the pool is exchanged for new water from the spring. Each time, the water must be as pure as a prayer in our heart. How do you feel?" Pila asked.

"I've never had a feeling like this, and it still surrounds me. May we sit here for a while?"

"As long as you want."

"Have you ever gotten the feeling of being completely accepted? Of being totally yourself, relaxed and confident in your skin?" Rose asked.

"Something of the sort, in my first mikva."

"When was that?

"When I was very young. It also involves a very good friend that you know. You call him Luke, but he was known to us kids as Shake. No one calls him that anymore. His real name is Charles Shakespeare Abell, but we just called him Shake."

Pila told Rose how Shake had devastated her as a young child. Then she told a part of the story she had never revealed to Shake, despite their close relationship.

"After I received that wadded little note that said, 'I love you,' I begged my aunt to take me to my first mikva, although I had not yet come into my period. But she said no, it would be improper unless I had shown signs of menstruating. About a week later, after a lot of prayers and rubbing of my stomach, I began to show signs of bleeding—like I had willed it. When it stopped, she took me into the mystery of mikva. When I walked into the pool, I was a frightened little girl recovering from trauma. When I came out, I felt strong and confident as though the water had filled me up—brought me to a place within myself where there was no fear of my past and only an eagerness and joy for the future. I felt as though I were coming into adulthood and a new love of life. If that's what you feel now, it's what I felt as well. I was brought up with the ritual, and I hold onto it because it is still comforting."

"This is kinda what Christians are supposed to feel when they embrace the life of Jesus Christ, but I've never felt this way. How did you find this place?"

"A friend who lives at Banks O' Dee—a Jewish girlfriend who married a Catholic guy—found it. She still comes here once in a while when she feels she needs to be renewed. It's our little spa for the soul in this piece of meadow where the clear spring runs. I've never seen another person here."

"I feel as though I've been put back together, finally, after being torn apart by the accident and my feckless husband. I feel like I did in the dream world I inhabited while I was comatose."

"Good. Come with me to Israel and we will explore a new world together and have fun, and I will teach you the secrets of the Jews. We will walk back into a time and a place where men and women were created equal in the eyes of God. We shall observe the laws of niddah and the mystery of Jewish womanhood and purify ourselves in mikva. We shall have men who are loyal and strong and who will treat us like goddesses." Pila grabbed Rose and hugged her tightly, and they laughed and giggled with happiness as they walked back up the ridge where they had parked the truck.

27

On the Rocks

When Luke awoke on Monday morning, instead of Andora, he found a note on the pillow beside him:

> *I have borrowed your car and gone to town to talk to a lawyer.*
> *See you tomorrow.*
> *Love, Andora.*

He thought about it for a moment and reached the conclusion that she was becoming serious about divorcing Will and needed some legal advice. He felt unhinged, as though his future had been put in motion without him, and he had better run to catch it. He went down to the kitchen for coffee and found Rose wiping a few dishes.

"What are you guys up to?" he asked.

"It's only me. I don't know where Ward is and I believe Jesse may be in his office. He has a session with Lonnie this morning," she said, scrunching her eyebrows at him. "I hope Ward doesn't play any of that atonal stuff until late this afternoon so I can have the morning to work. I'm punching around that final scene for the play. What are you up to?"

"Another short story, and then I have to help Maestro with some stage stuff. If you see Jesse, tell him I'll be upstairs. He wanted to give me the horoscope he's been working on."

Each went about their daily work and it wasn't until evening that Ward's piano grew silent downstairs. Luke drew on a clean T-shirt and padded down the stairs and found Ward making notations in a notebook.

"You hungry?"

"And thirsty," Ward said. "Do you have money?"

"Enough for us. Let's go to Captain John's." The two men walked to the waterside restaurant and, after a modest meal of fish and chips, lingered over their beer and the French fries.

"I have a capital idea," Ward said after Luke paid the check. "Let's get a bottle of vodka, a couple of Cokes, and watch the moon rise down on the river."

"You are a genius, Ward," Luke said, and they walked through the rear of the restaurant into the ship's store where they purchased the cheapest fifth of vodka on the shelf with two cans of Coke, nearly exhausting their common supply of money for the remainder of the week.

They walked down Potomac River Road to a small access at the eastern tip of the island where they could climb out on the rocks. The seawall had been built of large stones meticulously placed, flat side up, providing a comfortable place to sit. A wooden dock extended into the water some fifty feet. The evening had fallen warm and gentle with few mosquitoes to bother them. They uncapped the vodka, and each of them took a large drink from the bottle and chased it with Coke.

"It's beautiful, isn't it?" Luke said. "Makes you want to write poetry, if you could write poetry, instead of lying here swilling cheap booze."

"Don't get moody on me. I've a confession to make."

"Let's drink to confession," Luke said, raising the bottle to his lips, taking a swallow, and handing it to Ward. "Well, when was your last confession, my son?" Luke said, mocking the seriousness of a priest.

"I don't think my sin, Father, is very high in the hierarchy of sins—more of a youthful indiscretion, if you will."

"Well, this will certainly not require much of a dose of penance, will it? We aren't too good at handling indiscretions. Hardly worth the time anymore. Give me a good venality, a healthy two-page penance, and I'm your collar."

"Cut the crap," Ward said jokingly. "I had a visitor to my room last night looking for company, which I grudgingly gave her."

"How was she after all the grudge?"

"Hungry," Ward said. "Very hungry."

"Then you have made her a very happy woman."

"She's a loving person," Ward said, "but I just don't have time for a liaison. I sometimes wish that I did, but I need the sleep. She pinned me," he said, taking a piece of jewelry shaped as a red rose from his pocket and pinning it to his T shirt. Luke laughed. "You mean like you made a donation and received a Buddy Poppy?"

"You obviously don't understand the full obligation that a guest needs to render unto the hostess upon an occasion of expressed need. It cannot be ignored. She wanted to dance for me," Ward said.

"Well, you may not be the only guy that she's deflowered," Luke said, laughing at his own pun.

"I think not. I am probably special, and I shall wear her token like a badge of honor," Ward said.

"Maybe if there are enough of you, you can have a secret handshake in honor of Rose. You know, meet each other on the street, smile, engage the secret handshake, say nothing and move on through the crowds, smiling enigmatically. Is that why we're out here with a bottle of vodka watching shooting stars?"

"I had to unload, you know. The situation has become too heavy for me; it makes me feel closed in, but this is good—this place. Rose made me ponder my future and I thought you might lament over it with me, you being a professional lamenter. I couldn't study all day—played a few chords and gave it up in a fit of remorse. The guilt, oh God! What did I do? How about you? How do you write in that den of guilt that you're making upstairs?"

"How, indeed? A word, a worthless line—after one morning of not seeing her, my head is full of Andora—she inhabits me like another soul. I hold her inside me—I am pregnant with her—feeling her, thinking of her, smelling her, wanting her, not getting enough of her. I am totally saturated with Andora, yet my thirst is insatiable. I am overcome like I've never been before, and I can't begin to ask whether or not it's good for me—can't even think about it. I sit down to write and can't finish the sentence, or what does come out is drivel, pure emotional slop. So I've stopped for a while. The theater is taking up my time—we're working on the set for the next scene together and she's helping me learn lines. I can hardly get any work done. There's her husband working at the dock on their boat and being the nice guy that everybody likes, and here I am, totally in love with his wife whom I make love with at every opportunity. The outside of me moves around in a shroud of expectation and the inside of me is completely immersed in ecstasy. Our bodies together are the sum of a night like this with starlight and the rapturous feeling like I am eternally traveling through space, joyously hoping it will never end."

"But has she given you a pin?"

"You shit! You half-assed Venteuil-playing piece of shit! Make fun of me, will you, you F-flat turd with your midnight assignations with a minister's wife."

"I didn't pin her. She pinned me. And Venteuil doesn't exist; he's a character out of Proust, you illiterate! To have refused would have been gauche and unkind and I'm too polite to refuse. Anyhow, it was a one-night stand. She's probably gotten me out of her system and moved on. After tonight, I'll forget it. You, on the other hand, are cooked. Obviously, Andora's husband doesn't care about your affair; or, he knows and probably approves because it keeps her away from the damned boat and out of his hair. He'd rather work on the boat than her. And so there you are. Free for the first time in your life. Free to choose and be chosen, and you have fallen down the great wishing well of male libido. No wonder you haven't written anything. What could you possibly write that would give you the same thrill as being with Andora? Have another drink. Try to think about it. What word or line of poetry can you make that will create in you the ecstasy you feel with Andora? Not John Donne or Shakespeare or Milton or any creator of the language could keep you satisfied with words that adequately described your state of being. Give it up, for God's sake, man. Bite your pencils in half, take down the marquee that says 'writer' and buy a golden jockstrap to carry your soul in, because, Lukey my boy, at the apex of your apogean ride, the sun has become dangerously warm and your protection from it tragically fragile—you know the old Icarus myth. I don't wonder that you can't write, your wings are already singed. I wonder that you can walk and talk."

"Isn't that a bit much," Luke said. "Don't you think you're overdoing it?"

"How could I possibly exaggerate when it's so conspicuous. You're the only one having trouble seeing. Luke, how much of yourself do you plan to give away?"

"What? That's what Maestro asked, but there is no plan."

"That's what you think. Where was she today?"

"Seeing a lawyer."

"What's that if it isn't a plan? You don't go to a lawyer if you don't want a plan. Lawyers are the most planning sons of bitches on earth. All the more reason to give serious thought to your situation. How much of yourself are you willing to give to a beautiful relationship with an exquisite female and how much are you willing to give to your art, because while they are not mutually exclusive, they are mutually demanding. My carnal indulgences have never found a completely dedicated outlet, not because of any moral virtue, but because of musical preoccupation. I know that the more I give to a lasting relationship with a woman, the less I have for my music. And so I choose. Art is such a singular expression that it is difficult to include someone else in its making. I can't say to her, 'Come help me play this sonata,' that's obvious—someone in a close relationship is always on the outside pushing in, trying to get in there with you when there's only room for one, and that's where the whole thing doesn't work. I think it's probably better for an artist to collect an occasional pin and wear it on the outside of his shirt than fill his soul with a woman's hot breath and take the forever trip to the moon."

Luke looked over at him, took the bottle, put it to his lips, and didn't drink. He handed it back. "Maybe I'll just take the summer off from writing. You know, if my love for Andora is unmatched by anybody's art, greater than the sum of my past experience, why should I not encourage it? Why not just dive in?"

"I can see that this conversation is going to move from stupid to stupider, but I guess we are licensed by vodka to insult each other without recompense, are we not?"

"Sure."

"Ok, then, listen to me. When the good screwing is over, there you'll be—you and the exquisite Andora—making stage sets in an amateur theater someplace. Don't forget, Andora hasn't been to college, which is probably a good thing. From what I know, she had a kid right out of high school and she's been sailing around the world with a rich guy on a schooner for a couple of years—no social or civilizing experience to speak of, and now she touches land and you become the rock in her growing adulthood. Man, she doesn't know anything about anything. She's a painter, for God's sake! And you don't seem to know much—although in mid-process of knowing a little—and together, in five years if you're lucky, you'll end up in a line someplace in New Jersey waiting for food stamps. Try that image in your horoscope. Talk about your rapture! Go right ahead. Take the summer off from writing and studying! Just remember, it's not a yo-yo. You don't get that time back."

He paused and looked at Luke thoughtfully. "Have you ever seen yourself screwing in a mirror? It's pretty ugly, you know. It's a lot uglier than the image that you create in your head when you're doing it. I always thought that if we knew what we looked like when we were making love, we wouldn't do it at all. I can tell you that it doesn't come up to the beauty of a rose pin the next day," and he reached to his chest and stroked the rose pin.

"Damn! We are almost to the bottom of the bottle."

"Maybe at the end of this subject, too. If you want my advice, my diddling friend, wear it out, turn a page, and get on with your life. Get off this time-warped island and go back to the world. Kick the love narcotic; you will find that you can write better without it."

Luke handed the bottle to Ward, who drained its remains. Finally, Luke broke the long silence.

"What is this life we're living here on this crazy island?" he asked. "Each day seems like a fantasy filled with the promise of good things—it's a fantasy we're living—even when I don't write a word, each day is full and I can't wait for the next one. Is this what heaven is like?"

"Stupid question!" Ward muttered. "Just remember that, at some point, the bill will have to be paid. We will have to run like thieves in the night from our obligations or commit ourselves to them. Right now, I don't owe anybody. You, on the other hand, are deeply in debt."

They sat in silence, then fell into an alcohol-induced sleep lasting until the light crept over the horizon and glazed the river in brightness, finally waking them with the rising sun. They roused themselves and sat looking at the river, heads throbbing from the overuse of vodka.

"Wow. Do you think that the Mrs. Rose Caine will be kind enough to give us breakfast if we stumble into her kitchen, hung over from prowling the dark corners of our souls in the starlight?" Ward asked.

"Breakfast and a hug or two to make us feel better, if we're lucky. A cookie might be good," Luke answered.

"I always seem to have a hangover of spiritual starvation after a binge of physical intoxication," Ward lamented. "Perhaps she and I might kneel and pray together."

"I thought that was against your artistic principles?" Luke said.

"It is, but there is always the denouement to be worked out."

They climbed sluggishly back over the rocks and onto the road and walked back toward the parsonage.

When they entered, Rose was sitting at the table in a pink chiffon wrap, drinking a cup of coffee. Her hair had been cut short and swept back, her face scrubbed, her lips dabbed with the slightest suggestion of lipstick. Her altered visage caught Ward's breath, and Luke's only comment was "Wow."

"I'll just grab a cup of coffee and go upstairs," Luke said, leaving Ward and Rose frozen in the aftermath of passion. Luke kicked off his shoes and fell on the bed, feeling the need for a nap before he could start the day. He was almost asleep before he realized that no piano was playing downstairs. He smiled at the silence being created by the denouement.

28

Thou Shall Not Commit Tomfoolery

Jesse had been practicing to Ward's accompaniment for several hours. Ward stumbled over several chords in a passage and pounded the piano as if to correct his error. Jesse stopped singing and put his hand on Ward's shoulder.

"We've been at it all morning. Let's stop. I don't want to tire my voice now when I have to practice this afternoon and rehearse the play tonight."

Ward gathered some sheets of music and moved them to a growing pile on the side of the piano.

"You seemed nervous and unsure of yourself today. Anything I should know about?" Jesse asked.

"Nothing more serious than a bit of a hangover. Luke and I had a long philosophical discussion on the rocks last night. You could call it vodka on the rocks," he chuckled. "He is smitten with Andora—deeply overboard with Andora—and

I tried to caution him to slow down a bit. He needs to work his talent, not his love life; he needs to write, not screw his life away."

"Sometimes, it can't be helped. Sometimes, the screwer visits the screwee in the dark of night when he is unawares, and she is hungry. Isn't that how it goes? Wouldn't you say?"

Ward blushed immediately, his ears turning red—he knew that Jesse was not referring to Luke, but to him and Rose. He sat more stiffly at the piano, pretending to read a sheet of music.

"A parishioner once confided in me that he was impotent and couldn't perform for his wife, and he wanted my advice. I didn't have much biblical knowledge to give him and simply advised him to have pity on her since she was being denied the physical love of her husband."

"Look, Jesse…," but Jesse smothered Ward's protestation and went on.

"I know he felt the pain, but I advised him to pray over it because, in a way, it was God's will, and her seeking satisfaction elsewhere might help to maintain an otherwise loving relationship with her. I know the feeling. I believe that, in some way, I love my wife, but I have to tell you that I do not desire her either physically or spiritually. I harbor no jealousy. It is as though we are in a strange and lifeless place together. I have prayed hard for it to change, but I reach the conclusion every day that it will not. I have even entertained the argument that in some cases of clear destiny, murder is an acceptable—perhaps more honorable—form of dissolution of an unproductive and burdensome relationship, but I don't think I have the stomach or the patience for it. I have consulted my charts over and over, and they tell me that my future is first in my voice and second with another person, a new spirit of freedom and adoration. I read in them that I am destined to follow in the footsteps of the prophet Elijah, the prophet reborn to bring the message of God in a new way, a pathway made by stars."

"Whoa, Jesse," Ward said. "Listen to me. The other night was a mistake. It was just a mindless indiscretion that I probably encouraged somehow, although I can't think how at the moment, and I can assure you that although she is a beautiful woman and lovely person, I have no long-term interest in your wife. I like her very much, but I really can't afford any more entanglements than I already have. No, really, it's over before it has a chance to get started. You need to pay her more attention, that's all."

"But I can't. I believe strongly in the message from the astrological charts. I will be ordinary in this existence unless I find a gemstone that is destined to be mine—unless I possess a gem that will add value and meaning to my life, I am doomed to mediocrity. It is obvious that the gem is my voice—my destiny—I don't even understand what it fully means."

"Jesse, you should stop it. You can't think about murder or destiny if you're going to be a singer. Stop all of this bullshit. Wake up! If you're going to be a singer, concentrate on training your voice. You don't need to spin your gyroscope in the planets and examine mysterious signs or try to find God's message in the Zodiac. Sing if you must, but for Christ's sake, don't pretend that there is meaning in all that palm-reading drivel. It isn't prophecy. It isn't religion. It isn't a search for God. It is your false aspiration and crooked thinking. You've been taken out of your church and you resent it. Your voice is who you are now. If you want to call it a gem, that's fine with me and everybody else, but stick with that. Take it from old

Ward, Chapter 1, verse 7, 'Thou shall not commit tomfoolery in public places. It is far worse than adultery.'"

Jesse laughed. "You make it sound as though I'm going to quit the church."

"Let me put it to you straight, Jesse. They threw you out. They got tired of you, and they don't want you anymore. You are being strung along until they find the right words to cut you permanently from the fold."

"That isn't so. They didn't throw me out. They denied me trial and crucifixion. I wanted to face them and answer the charges, but they didn't want the publicity. You know that I'm waiting for a reassignment in New York by the bishops. Churches don't come so easily in the city."

"You made it clear to them that you would only accept a position under certain conditions, didn't you?"

"Well, I did have some conditions. I have to have more time to study voice."

"And you haven't heard from them since, right? Face it."

"Oh, ye of little faith. If I don't hear from them by the time the summer is over, I'll go to New York and start my own church. It's a godless city that will support a man of vision with a new message. The ancient scribes simply reported what happened. It is far more important to be capable of interpreting God's will in the stars than it is to translate an ancient text written years after it faded from accurate memory."

"What? Jesse...."

"There is not a man alive who does not want a peek at the larger vision—a look beyond the present into the near future before the end of his time—a vision in reality instead of the vague promises of a Christian heaven. I believe I can tell a man his destiny, and people will listen, Ward, and they will believe."

"Jesse, have you lost your bearings?"

"Not nearly, Ward. If our born-again Christians rely on texts that have been overwritten and misinterpreted for centuries, what can they find in the living testament of the universe...the first witness and the final memory of man's existence?"

"Aw, shit!" Ward said. He slammed the piano closed and stormed from the room.

29

The Barn Burner

Easels cluttered the porch of the parsonage and spilled onto the lawn, each holding the work of a camp artist. Finished pictures leaned against the building for viewing and received comments from students and islanders who stopped to look at them. Sitting on a chair surrounded by several paintings, Andora continued to work on a large canvas propped on an easel. The art display, taking the place of the usual Sunday evening meeting, would be followed by another scene from the play after sundown. Luke was sitting in the grass watching Andora paint.

"You make it look so damned easy."

"That's because I've gained more confidence. I can mix colors without hesitation and my hand is driven by the idea in my head of what I want it to be. Of course, the more successful the painting becomes, then the more creativity flows through the brush, and the more it stretches beyond my own imagination and becomes a thing of its own. You told me once that there are times when your characters take on a life of their own and so can a painting. Not always, but more frequently than you think. When you look at several paintings by a single artist and you see one that strikes you as more accomplished or exciting than the others, chances are that at some point in its creation it began to have an independence from the imagination of the artist, a life of its own."

"I've never thought of it that way, but I can understand what you're saying."

"Artists rarely talk about it because we like to take all of the credit."

"There's some wine on the porch, a gallon of white and a gallon of red—good stuff. Probably made up fresh yesterday. Can I get you a cup?" Luke asked.

"If you can wait, I'm almost finished here, then you can help me carry these canvases into the house before nightfall. Aren't you acting tonight?"

"Yes, it's my last scene. I'm anxious to be through with it."

"You go ahead then. Carry these other canvases up to your room and I'll take care of the easel and paints. I'll see you after the show."

As the art show began to break up, people moved toward the theater, some carrying an unfinished cup of wine or beer. The evening was warm; the doors and windows were thrown open to circulate the air and eliminate the lassitude, assisted by wine and the aesthetic contemplation of art, that had settled on the art show attendees. When the house lights in the theater dimmed, the scene on stage depicted winter, the complete opposite of the weather outside the theater.

{Ruby is in a rocking chair, sewing by a fireplace. Luke enters carrying an armload of wood that he stoops to place in a potbellied stove. He shakes the cold air from his coat and sits down facing Ruby.}

LUKE. You're gonna stay here tonight, and I'm going to sleep in the barn again, but Mama wants you to come to the big house tomorrow so she can look after you better. She says you're due anytime now. Besides, there are only three days till Christmas. It'll be warmer and more comfortable for you over there.

RUBY. I don't have to do that. I'm okay here.

LUKE. Just do what I'm telling you, Ruby. You pack up your things tonight, and I'll come to get you in the morning. It's better for you to be with the family when you're having the baby. Just pack your things.

RUBY. I ain't got nothin' to take.

LUKE. I'm gonna spend tonight in the barn—my last night in the barn sleeping with the animals instead of my wife—I'll pick you up in the morning. *{Luke rises from the table, takes a whiskey bottle from the shelf and takes a swig. He puts the cork back in the bottle, walks out the door and closes it behind him. Ruby continues to darn his sock. Then she goes to a music box, winds it, and it plays, 'Blessed Be the Ties That Bind.' She sits down, darns for a minute, then rises again and takes a kerosene lantern from the shelf and lights it. She adjusts the wick, throws a shawl over her shoulders and starts to leave but hesitates, grabbing the whiskey bottle from the shelf before leaving the cabin. In a few minutes she returns without the lantern or the bottle, blows out the candle and* *goes to bed. Lights dim. Several minutes pass and a red glow begins to grow through the cabin window. Outside there are faint shouts of 'Fire! Fire!,' then suddenly the cabin door opens and a young girl runs in shouting.}*

LIZZIE. Fire in the barn! Fire in the barn! *{Ruby puts on slippers, throws the shawl around her shoulders and walks slowly out the door amidst the general excitement of the burning barn. The stage darkens. When the lights come up again, the family is looking out at the audience, faces dirty from fighting the fire. They stand there in the smell of smoke and puffs that cross the stage while friends and neighbors gather behind them. There are buckets, wet grain sacks, and rakes and shovels being held by those who have been fighting the fire.}*

BROADUS. Where is Luke, Ruby?

RUBY. In the barn. He was sleeping in the barn.

BROADUS. Oh, my God! my God!

MOTHER. *{Drops to her knees.}* Oh dear God, take me now, but stop it! stop it! stop it! *{She screams and wails and is finally taken into the house by Broadus. The minister arrives and falls on his knees in prayer. Tears fall on his cheeks. Ruby stands silently with others, turns, and walks into the house. A few men continue to rake through the smoldering rubble.}*

SHERIFF. *{Putting his arm around Broadus.}* We found what's left of him, Broadus: a skull and a few bones. We put him in one of those apple boxes Ezra found in the shed. I already sent for the doctor. Soon as he gets here we can have an inquest and get this night over with.

BROADUS. Much obliged, Sheriff. There doesn't seem much to talk about.

SHERIFF. You know it's the law. I gotta hold an inquest regardless of who it is. *{There is the sound of a wagon outside.}*

I guess that's him now. I'll just have him look at the remains before he comes in. *{Sheriff leaves, returns with the doctor (carrying small bag), Ezra Gandy, and a few men who have been fighting the fire.}*

DOCTOR. Just pull up chairs around the table here so I can conduct the inquest. Sheriff, swear in the jury. *{The sheriff takes a Bible and six men put their hands on it and swear allegiance to the laws of the State of Maryland. When they are finished they take seats around the table.}*

DOCTOR. Sheriff, get Ruby in here, will you? We'll start with her so she can get some rest. *{Ruby enters from offstage, followed by the sheriff. She stands at one end of the table and puts her hand on the Bible.}* Do you swear to tell the truth, Ruby? *{She nods her head.}* Then why don't you just tell us how this thing happened.

RUBY. Luke came in way after suppertime with a load of wood for the fire and said he was sleeping in the barn like he's been doing since I've been big. He told me to pack up my things because the next day I was gonna move over here to the big house where I could be more comfortable. He said Christmas was coming and I could be looked after over here better. I said okay, I'd see him in the morning. Then he took his whiskey bottle and left.

DOCTOR. That was the last time you seen him?

RUBY. Yes, and then Lizzie came running in yelling about a fire in the barn and woke me up.

DOCTOR. What did you think?

RUBY. By the time I got there, I didn't think that anything that was in that barn would survive. I thought I heard the colt whinny once, but then there was only the sound of flames.

DOCTOR. Thank you. Broadus, who saw the fire first?

BROADUS. I reckon I did. Do you want me to swear? *(Doctor nods, Broadus puts hand on the Bible and is sworn in.)* I got up before midnight to use the chamber pot, and I saw a strange reflection on the wall, and when I looked, the barn was burning hot and bright. I woke up Lizzie and told her to fetch Luke from the cabin. Then we wet down gunnysacks and tried to beat out all the little fires that were starting around the house. There wasn't anything we could do about the barn. I heard the horse or the colt whinny once and that was all. Then we just watched it burn. Ruby told us Luke went to sleep in there, and I knew he was dead in the fire.

DOCTOR. Does anyone else have anything to tell us different than what we've heard? Well, they found the charred remains of the horses, and I identified the skull of a human as being Luke from where the gold was in his teeth before it half melted away. We have what's left of the lantern and a broken whiskey bottle nearby, so Sheriff, it looks as though Luke emptied that bottle then had some sort of accident with the lantern and burned himself up in the hay. What do you think?

SHERIFF. That's what I'm thinking too. It wasn't suicide, because he would have put the animals out before he set the fire. If he was going to kill himself, he wouldn't have killed the animals too, so the only reasonable conclusion is that it was an accidental death.

DOCTOR. Does the jury agree? *(Men sitting around the table nod their heads or raise their hands in agreement.)* That being the case, my report will show that Luke Adams died an accidental death from a barn fire at Elysium on December 23, 1896. Now, if you will excuse me, I'll go see how the women are faring, especially Ruby. *(Men leave the table. They return with two small trestles and boards to make a table. One man follows behind carrying an apple box in both hands that he places on the boards. Faintly written on the side are the words, 'Elysium Orchards'. They step back and circle the box. Ephraim, the minister, steps forward and asks people to bow their heads.}*

EPHRAIM. Lord, you move in mysterious ways that are unknown to us, Your servants. You have taken the best of our youth for reasons we cannot fathom. As we ponder the events of this night, let us remember that Luke Adams was taken from us in the mystery of Thy love and shall rest in Your arms forever. We pray that the child he leaves behind will grow strong and healthy in the glory of Your goodness and in the name of Jesus Christ. Amen. *{The doctor reappears and speaks to Broadus.}*

DOCTOR. She's very close to her time and something like this could make her have the baby regardless, so you all watch her close, and at the first sign, come get me. I don't think there will be a rush—it's her first child—but come for me anyhow. We've had enough disaster around here.

BROADUS. We won't be coming for you. Our horses burned in the barn.

EPHRAIM. You can use a rig of mine. I'll go now and get it. I'll have some of the boys make room in that tool shed. You can keep it there.

BROADUS. If you don't mind, go by Mamie Jackson's and ask her to come over and help out here. You can give her the rig to use, otherwise she'll have to walk. Tell her to bring a bag, we'll be needing her for a few days, I think.

EPHRAIM. I'll tell her. Anything else?

BROADUS. No. I guess we've done all we can do now.

The scene ended, and there was light applause as the house lights came up and people headed for the exit. Andora waited for Luke. When he came to greet her, the patrons had cleared out and were heading for their homes or one of the restaurants on the island.

"They didn't seem to like this one as much," Luke said.

"The ending wasn't as dynamic. It left them holding the bag, so to speak, or the apple box, if you prefer. You gave them a funeral to attend without a wake to put things back in order. No wonder they were a little glum."

"I suppose you're right, but I know that Maestro will be thinking of how it can be rewritten, so I suppose I'll need to talk with him as soon as I can. When I wrote it the first time, I didn't expect that kind of audience reaction. I was just building up to the final scene, but I know he'll want to talk about it." They walked slowly down the street without a particular destination in mind. Finally, Luke asked the question he had been holding back since he had found the note on his pillow. "How was your trip?"

"Alright, I suppose. It's shattering when you think you understand something and then someone more expert than yourself recasts the facts and produces an entirely different scenario. Lawyers do that very well. At least this one did, just as though he had heard the story a thousand times, and he laid it out to me in the hardest, simplest terms. Basically, I haven't established irreconcilable differences between us enough to satisfy a judge. He will see this as my having a summer fling to distance myself from Tilley's death while Will remains in deep grief and mourning. Of course, I could leave him anyhow, and that would make me a blatant Jezebel incapable of loving my grieving husband and indulging myself in licentiousness of the most scarlet variety. He advised me to talk more directly to Will about leaving him, and try to get him to accept the reasons for my actions. Evidently, the worthiness of the lover or the future needs of the wife are not important at this stage. It's like taking on a building-block mentality, devoid of emotion and spiritual necessity: clunk, mortar, clunk, mortar, one block at a time until you have enough defense to stand behind and wage war. I hate it."

"I'm sorry."

"I know. Suddenly it has nothing to do with us and our love, and everything to do with Will and his civil rights."

"What will you do?"

"For now, I'll talk to Will. You know that I'm not good at talking these things out, but if it's talk he needs, I'm gonna give him an endless stream."

When they reached the side street to her cottage, Andora stopped and kissed Luke deliciously on the mouth.

"I'll go home without you, and I probably won't see you tomorrow. I need time to think about this," she said.

"Okay," he said, kissing her hand, "I'll be waiting for you." She turned abruptly from him to the right and walked down the street toward her cottage. He stood watching her walk in the dim light. In need of a talk with Maestro, he took the road to the left, toward Maestro's cottage. About to knock on the door, Luke peaked into the window and saw the older man writing at the table. Since Maestro looked as though he was absorbed, Luke hesitated, backed away from the window, and went back down the driveway.

Inside, Maestro was writing another letter to his wife:

I make up my days and nights with talk—of ideas or reality and of things that never were and never shall be. We pretend to be philosophers. The boy, Luke, is wildly poetic and may be a writer some day. Charles, our president-in-residence, is cautious yet inventive, a decent chap, but nonetheless driven by all those things that we thought important in our earlier career and kept us from doing the things that we really loved. The attention to duty for the public welfare has little personal reward in the end; the constituency doesn't understand when you make something out of nothing. Then, here I am. sagacious and outrageous in my opinions just enough to frighten the undergraduates. We are time, we three, future, present, and past, put together in this bubbling milieu that is more art than living, more soul than mind, more freedom than duty. A few weeks from now will be our time of dissolution, and I have a foreboding about how it will end. I fear we will have a less than graceful winding down of our studies and our fun, but while I sense the movement of the players, I cannot see them beneath the surface. It is a feeling that impending destinies will be tried on and fitted amidst the smell of a freshening river breeze, and like Callinectes Sapidus, some will fill a new shell as others wash away in the outgoing tide.

The play goes well, although tonight's scene by Luke will need some work before it is finished. The final scene has made the boards amid a growing fever of anticipation. The author of it is still a mystery to the troupe and we are rehearsing it in sections, purposefully confusing the actors over the sequence of events. What fun!

Yesterday, my neighbor brought me two nice soft-shell crabs that I sautéed in butter and washed down with Pouilly Fuisse. How I wish you were here with me to enjoy it. You are ever in my thoughts, Maestro.

He finished the letter, folded it, slipped it into an envelope, and placed it on top of a growing pile at the corner of the table.

30

In the Stars

Lonnie had been receiving a voice lesson from Jesse in his office where they worked on her development of a controlled scream in the play's last scene. When they were both pleased with her progress, she thought she might go to the theater and talk with Maestro who was rehearsing lines with other actors. She thanked Jesse for the time, and turned to leave.

"I finished charting your future last night," Jesse said.

"Oh, super. What did it say?"

"It really isn't that simple and there are lots of things that you should consider. It's not like getting a prize in a Cracker Jack box. You have to understand that it's a map of possibilities based on your life thus far, your talent, and your potential."

"Well, aren't you going to tell me about it?"

"Sure, but you really have to understand that you're hearing about the possibilities in the future, not exactly what will happen to you. You may learn some things that surprise you. I'll go over the broad points, and we can talk about details later."

"It's okay, Jesse, honest. I'm ready for it. I really am."

"Some people reject my study of astrology as unimportant in the development of Christian faith, but so was Christ rejected when he foretold the future. It just can't be dismissed."

"Well, tell me about it. I'm anxious to hear."

"The more I worked on your chart, the more it became familiar to me in some ways, and then I realized that it was possible our destinies were on a similar track. I went back to my chart and found the crossing of another star and certain planetary motion, which at first I identified as a gem-star and thought it meant the voice I had been given by God. After I finished your chart, I discovered it was your star that crossed my path, meaning you are the gem in my destiny—you, Lonnie, you are the light and love of my future."

"You mean it said that you and I would have a future together?"

"It was not a certainty, but there is a strong pull of our destinies in a single direction that eventually coincide. It appears that you are destined to be the gem-star of my future."

"What about your voice?"

"That, too, but I had not fully understood the influences until I finished your chart."

"What did it tell you about already being married?"

"It mentions nothing about Rose and there is no indication in my chart or hers that we will continue to spend our lives together. Already, she and I know this is true. Someday, you'll see me 'floatin' in the sunshine,'" Jesse said, quoting a line from the song in *South Pacific* and then he sang a verse for her. Lonnie blushed.

"Oh, Jesse, that's so corny."

"That's what the truth is, Lonnie. The truth is simple and corny. That's how I see our future. We are happy and together. I don't know precisely how that is going to happen, but we will get there, for sure, because it's in the heavens." Jesse took her hands in his and kneeled in front of her.

"Let us pray for it, Lonnie, shall we?" he asked. Taking her hands, they kneeled together. "Dear God in heaven, where destinies are made, we thank You for the revelation that You have given us in Your love. We worship You and accept Your divine will in directing our lives to the fulfillment of Thy divine purpose. We may not understand Your reason, but we accept the duty of Your revelation and the rewards of life everlasting in Your kingdom of love. Our love will be Your love, forever and ever. Amen." Jesse kissed both her hands and then embraced her.

"And that is done," he said, rising from his knees. "Can I take you home?"

"No, I think I'll walk and think for a while. I love you, Jesse, as a friend and teacher, but my destiny has kind of snuck up on me. There are a lot of questions I need you to answer. Will you answer one now?"

"You know that I'll try."

"What made you leave the church, before you came here this summer?"

"That could take a lifetime to answer, but I'll try. First, I feel it is my obligation to a congregation to love them and lead them into an experience of love—for God, from God, and with each other. It should be a church of love. You preach to them from the heart, pray with them when they are ill, visit them in their homes, and tend to their problems, and after a while, a few of them get to know you on a deep personal level. But eventually, you find there are very few who can live and express themselves on that creative and spiritual level and the rest ignore you and revert to the comfort of a system of morality that is cold, judgmental, and bound by what it disapproves rather than what it loves. I simply cannot function around people who do not love me, and so the more I reject them, the more the feeling becomes one of mutual disaffection. The simple solution is to move on, and that is what I did."

"Thank you," she said. "It was very honest." She turned and walked from the office.

Jesse watched her go. Smiling, he tidied his small desk and left the office, heading to the parsonage kitchen.

Rose was there rubbing salt into a pork roast. She rubbed it hard, then slapped it a couple of times.

"Jesse, you really should be more careful how and where you carry on. These students are not all as horny as Texas toads. We should keep a little propriety in the parsonage, especially in your office."

"I'm a little more discreet about what goes on in my office than the sneaking that you do into Ward's bedroom," he responded tartly.

"Sneaking is an abominable word, Jesse. I believe I was cautious of your feelings, sympathetic to them. I'm sorry you found out, but I'm not sorry I did it. Ward is a sweet young man—a kind lover. It was only on an impulse—no—a need—a burning desire that you couldn't satisfy. At least he's not young enough to be my child. Have you no desire for me any more, Jesse?"

"Forgive me, Rose."

"Forgive you what? The false promise of marriage? The false promises to your parishioners? The false promises to yourself, Jesse, not to mention your God? What promises did you make to Lonnie? What future did you spin for her when you and she looked at the stars? Did you find what position her Virgo was in when it sat on your rising star?"

"It's not what you think, Rose. She is the spirit of life rejoicing in my voice. I am the song maker in her heart. I am destined to be with her. She and I will have a future together, a future that you and I lost somewhere, Rose."

"Oh, Jesse, don't debase the girl with that slime. She is by far the most wondrous-looking female on this island, and if you could add her affection to your whoresome voice, it would make you king of the knights, wouldn't it? It would be the conquest that would ultimately justify your leaving of me, wouldn't it? Don't answer because I suddenly realize that you probably don't even know. You move in such 'creative' ways to satisfy your pathetic ego that you really aren't aware of what you're doing."

"Forgive me, Rose."

"Does forgiveness help, Jesse? You gave me up for dead, and when I didn't die and you couldn't heal me, you walked away from me. You lost faith in yourself, Jesse. You ceased to believe in the resurrection. I finally understand that you don't want me in your future life, but if you are destined to be with her, why are you spending so much time on the boat with Will? Have you found a lonesomeness greater than mine?"

31

Old Souls

Lonnie had stayed to talk with Maestro following rehearsal. He wanted her to show a more visible transition from the rigid body posture that normally characterized Ruby to a completely relaxed state without muscle tone. They had finished their technical conversation and were sitting at the table, stage center, when she asked him a question. "What will happen when this summer ends?"

"You are not the first person who has asked me that." He paused before answering. "I think that some of us will be amused, and others will meet themselves in circumstances that I don't envy. Perhaps I have the best ending for the play—perhaps I don't. Perhaps I'll keep searching for it; perhaps we will all keep searching for something. There is a speech by Prospero in Shakespeare's play, *The Tempest*, that is very apropos. You should learn it. Let me see...." He rummaged through several books of Shakespeare's plays, riffling through the pages until he found Act 4, Scene 1, of *The Tempest*, from which he read aloud:

> Our revels now are ended. These our actors,
> As I foretold you, were all spirits and
> Are melted into air, into thin air;
> And, like the baseless fabric of this vision,
> The cloud-capped towers, the gorgeous palaces,
> The solemn temples, the great globe itself,
> Ye all which it inherit, shall dissolve,
> And like this insubstantial pageant faded,
> Leave not a rack behind. We are such stuff
> As dreams are made on, and our little life
> Is rounded with a sleep.

He smiled at Lonnie. During his lifetime, Maestro had known only a few women whose physical ripeness lay quivering in the nanosecond before exploding—every limb filled firmly with flesh, symmetrical, neither hard nor soft but accentuating movement with a music of its own, a splendid movement of form—a grape, luscious and fragrant, about to burst in ripeness, tight within its skin wanting to be picked before the others—demanding attention and wanting to be consumed. That's what Lonnie was, here, with him in the theater, talking, asking innocently about dramatic tension, the absent line, the unthroated word that gives more pleasure from its silence than a stanza of poesy. She created in him an unwelcomed restlessness that spun through his bones—and like a falling celestial body, she was delivered to him now in his old age. He listened to her breathe. He knew it was one moment, one thing, one play— this life and death and joy and pain. He sighed. Her presence silently consumed him as gravity consumed the apple. And he, the apple, could not help himself, could not leave her or drive her away any more than the fallen fruit could reattach itself to the tree; he could only reach into the darkness of his desire and savor the moment—the ecstasy of being held in suspense the instant before liberation—of being held in anticipation of the release that never comes—the never-ending promise of eternal joy and the fulfillment of eternal agony that gathers in the bones and will not leave.

"The mind is the sexiest part of the body. Thinking is the sexiest part of living," he pronounced, totally out of context with the conversation he was having with her—a subscript running in his mind like a subtitle in a foreign movie.

"That's not what Jesse thinks," she responded, switching subjects as easily as he. "He believes that sex is a kind of secondary union with God—a romantic ritual of love as much as religion—he thinks there is a kind of parallel."

"May I tell you something, Lonnie? With all my heart, because I really care for you? Jesse is a fraud. All he cares about is getting into your pants as you fall at his feet in adoration. He is a first-class heretical villain."

"That isn't nice to say, but I know it's true. Although it's funny—he hasn't made a real move on me. He hasn't put his hands on me in that way. He's talked a lot about it, but that's all. He's married, you know."

"Yes, but I understand that he has no physical relationship with his wife. Did you know that he was once smitten with Andora when she was your age?"

"He seduces with his voice. It unties me."

"That's why he romances you with song. His voice is his manhood and you are left mesmerized and wondering when he's going to act. It's a great romantic notion," Maestro said.

"There's nothing wrong with that. It seems to me that we can use a little more romance in our lives. Romance is the stuff a woman builds her dreams on."

"Perhaps, but romance occurs when a man is wrapped in forgetfulness of who he is and what he's about."

"But romance is the poetry of life," she said, with the fervor of a true believer.

"Romantic love is sex adorned, dressed up in a story or a fairy tale. It is the dance of seduction. When a man loves a woman for her character—truly loves her and admires her—it's not romantic. That kind of love brings with it too many things that are real and incapable of being romanced. When the emotional response, the prelude to the sexual dance, gradually disappears and a man's sexual well runs dry, what's left to him in the cold night is to snuggle up with character, and it is either there or it ain't. That's what a man my age is left with when all of the uncertainty of romantic love fades and the certainty of life is snoring next to him, dreaming of grandchildren—and you, my dear, have not yet gotten around the corner.

"Too often character is smothered by the blanket of romance and it breeds grasping little habits and gestures that are meaningless and tedious like dung beetles, rolling away, uphill and down, and although their load grows larger, it is still only the shit of another animal and not their character. When you drop the toiling dance of romance, the sweating, semantic, grunting dance, you may pick up the good stuff that requires only that you take it as it is—unadorned with notions of propriety—the warmth, humor, honesty, and kiss of life, the striking note and clanging bell of character. You come to understand that there is nothing wrong with sex without the mask of romance: it's funny, practical, healing, and it feels so damned good. It is what it is; a spasm of joy. Dress it up in romance and it speaks with forked tongue. It lies to you; the Devil is in romance. Eve romanced the apple down Adam, and look what poor John suffered at the romantic, demented hands of Salome and her mother—his head resting on a plate.

"When romance loses its form, when it adds a little roll of fat and sag and there is no attempt to deceive—no pretense of beauty—then you may see the remainder of all the little calculations that life has given and the sums it has taken, and the thing you are left with is character and you thank God that death is a part of this life—not an extension—the climax of life without romance. I have been devoted to romance all my life—raised in it—sweated by it—listened to others cry over it, and now, it has vanished from me like fog before the rising sun. Stop the dance and get down to the work of building character and you will succeed in filling the cup of an otherwise empty future. And don't ever forget that the mind is the sexiest organ of the body. Choose it and you will never be without." He paused and chuckled to himself.

"Sorry, I didn't mean to make a speech. You have a perfect right to think as you like about romance. My experiences are not infallible rules of spiritual bliss—quite the opposite."

"You needn't apologize. It seems as though we've been friends a long time, beyond the few weeks that I have known you here—that we were friends before I ever knew you."

"Perhaps it's what they call an old souls' relationship, where people feel a kinship that is without time and place."

"I am here on this island because of you—not only to be taught and coached by you, but to feel a deep affection for you inside—as if we have been lovers in another time. It's a good feeling."

"The more that I live, the more I feel that memory is a shifting thing, quicksand of the mind that is not so much a defect of who we are, but more a gift of life, another experience," he said.

"Whenever it was—back in time somewhere—in another life, I would have taken you for a lover then as I wish I could now. But that's a romantic notion too, isn't it? To sacrifice my virginity on the altar of an ancient god."

"Whoa, now, Miss Lonnie. Careful what you do with your dramatic license. Because an old man appears impotent, ancient, and benign doesn't mean that he is not dangerous. I look at you and savor you and would like nothing better than to make love to you until the sun came up, but that is the wolf in me, howling. I know that I would make a mess of it and your beautiful notions of love would become thorns in your imagination, and I would have sacrificed your virginity to an indignity where nothing I say would ever be honest again."

"Is that a compliment?"

"It is recognition of your beauty. Consider yourself ravished."

"Wow. That's cool. But if you have such a strong feeling for me, why couldn't it happen?"

"It is not in the stars, my dear, as Jesse might say. I am much too sensible a man to want you for dark memories."

"It might not be that way, you know. It requires two of us, and maybe...."

"Hush! Despite our fondness for each other, it would end up being a very stupid thing."

"I guess I haven't reached the point in my life where I can see the consequences of strong emotions."

"If you have not already, you will tomorrow. It comes with maturity and the skill to separate dreams from reality."

"See. This is the kind of stuff that makes me want to be with you. It's not that I'm an old soul; it's the fun and the love of life in you that is eternally young."

"Thank you. It's the nicest thing you might have said. Shall we get back to the business of creating this character, Ruby? You can do more with it, you know."

32

The Night of the Crystal Skulls

The weekend of the Crystal Skulls began on Friday evening with a welcoming address from the commodore of the Trinity Island Yacht Club to visitors from other yacht clubs up and down the Potomac River who had floated in for the occasion. Students and boaters met in the theater for introductions and explanations of the day's activities. After addressing all of the questions, the commodore announced that the event would start with a torch-light march down Wicomico River Drive to a spot where the opening ceremony would be held. Then he introduced Jesse Cain as the master of ceremonies, who appeared from the stage wings awash in colorful silks and satins resembling an eastern potentate of the sixth century, carrying a golden staff wrapped round with a snake and topped with a small skull. The effect was dazzling.

Jesse advised the followers to either light a candle, available at the door, or carry a flashlight as they marched toward their destination. With appropriate theatrical pomp, Jesse descended the stage and led his followers east toward the place where the Wicomico and Potomac rivers joined. The flashlight parade walked down the narrowing end of the island and came upon a large swale in the road whose bottom tilted toward the river. At the riverside, a small plot of ground, obviously unbuildable because of its vulnerability to high tides, was overgrown with marsh grasses on the perimeter. In the dry center of the lot, where the grass had been mown, stakes placed in the ground supported plastic skulls with lighted candles on their domes. Jesse walked to the center of the illuminated skulls and faced the crowd gathering in the road. As the crowd increased and occupied the slopes on both sides of the saddle, it waited for something to happen.

Charles and Leigh had gained an elevated view of the little plot of marshland and the skulls on sticks. The young people in the hollow, who were once laughing and animated, had begun to move arm in arm from side to side in a slow rhythmic swaying. A low humming sound began to rise from the crowd but quieted again as Jesse raised his arms for attention.

"Welcome to the celebration of the Crystal Skulls," he said, his voice rich and pleasant. "For these next few days, we should relax and enjoy events that will bring us fun and pleasure and deep satisfaction as we search for the Crystal Skull in the hope that all of this will add meaning to our human existence." He reached into the bag he was carrying and withdrew the human skull that Pila had excavated from the site at Wollaston. He held it out for everyone to see.

"This could very well be the skull of Santasay, the beautiful concubine of Captain Neale who still wanders our waterway at night looking for her children. We think of her as a distant story of the dead, but now and then we see her lonely light and are reminded that she lives. We believe the skull is a symbol of death, but from its antecedents on Golgotha we have come to realize, instead, that it is a symbol that illuminates the cycle of human understanding. The skull points us to a way of introspection, a path to self-realization. As the receptor of your contemplation, the skull may draw you into another world of ideas and understanding. It is the grim reaper of old ideas and the symbol of a new life to come. The skull represents the going under of man and his deep submersion into eternal life in order to rise and be reborn to a creative life in this world."

The crowd began to sway and hum as Jesse continued. "It is not the fear of death we find in the skull, but the symbol of life and love— the spirit of Santasay," he said, holding the skull high for all to see. The crowd directly in front of Jesse began a low chant repeating Jesse's words: "The skull is life, the skull is love, the skull is life, the skull is love...." The chant became louder and more intense until the words became an indistinguishable outpouring of human sound. A young woman in the front row joined Jesse within the ring of skulls and began dancing back and forth from the crowd to Jesse as if she were trying to entice others to join the circle. Charles and Leigh, standing on the higher ground, looked at each other in amazement.

"What the hell is going on?" Charles asked Leigh. "What kind of ceremony is this?"

"I think it's left over from a Halloween party," Leigh joked. "I don't think it's anybody's show."

The girl, now dancing around Jesse, jumped and twirled and threw her arms into the air and then fell limply, seductively, to the ground in front of him. As if on cue, several persons in the front row also slumped to the ground, and the crowd began to murmur excitedly. Those closest to Jesse seemed to be in some stage of losing consciousness. The chanting intensified and the crowd split itself between the active participants in the front several rows and those who were spectators leaning for a closer look from behind. As Charles pressed closer to see what was happening, he heard the siren blast a call from the firehouse a quarter of a mile away. Someone had summoned rescuers. Before the siren finished its sobering wail, several more bodies crumpled silently to the ground. Charles thought he could see at least a dozen people lying about on the macadam road and the grassy shoulder of the little plot. Others tried to revive them with fanning and propping them into sitting positions, but in order to get a better look at the spectacle, the crowd shuffled closer, hemming them in. "The skull is life, the skull is love, the skull is life, the skull is love...." continued to reverberate until it was drowned by the approaching rescue squad.

Charles watched as the boxy trucks barreled down the street, all lights blazing, sirens and horns searing the atmosphere. The crowd parted slowly to allow the trucks to the bottom of the swale, and to allow rescuers access. By the time the scene had sufficiently cleared, a few of the fallen had begun to rise and stagger toward consciousness, but the medical technicians convinced them to quickly lie down again while administering smelling salts and applying blood pressure cuffs. One fallen celebrant was placed on a gurney and rolled to the rear of a rescue wagon, where Charles supposed a more serious injury was being attended to. A fire engine came roaring down from the opposite direction, throwing a burst of light on the rescue operation, followed by another, and together they illuminated a scene that had the shape and feeling of an animated Brueghel painting. Bodies lay about, people walked in a variety of directions, and the crystal skulls on white posts reflected incidental light in the chaotic flow of the crowd that milled around in the shadows. Most of the fallen began sitting up, ready to resume the evening's festivities, except for one who had scraped her head when she tumbled and was being patched with an oversized bandage.

The crowd began laughing and reliving the event, wandering around, then breaking up and heading slowly back toward the parsonage and the bars and restaurants where they would finish the evening's festivities. Students pulled the stakes crowned with crystal skulls from the ground and hoisted them aloft, which could be seen bobbing periodically among the crowd. Jesse, still the figure of a majestic eastern potentate, walked slowly through the crowd, trailing a thin group of followers toward the parsonage. When they passed, Charles thought he observed a beatific look emanating from Jesse that encircled him and set him apart from his followers.

Possum Gravis, who had been a quiet observer standing next to Leigh and Charles said, "Wow, wasn't that something. Ain't seen nothin' like that before. Gotta be a trick in it somewhere," and then he attached himself to the procession as it passed.

Leigh mentioned to Charles that all of those who had fainted appeared to be female. "Wow, a mass 'falling down of the sisterhood' in a state of euphoria. I think they've seen too many weird movies," she remarked.

"Pity they can't do that over a math equation or an English paper."

"They probably could if they had Jesse teaching them. Do you have any idea what Jesse's up to?"

"I think he's acting out his need for attention," Charles remarked drily.

"Well, he's certainly gotten it tonight. It's hard to tell whether or not he wants to be Billy Graham, Falstaff, or the Wizard of Oz."

"Oh, I think that's easy. He'd be Billy Graham, because Possum is already Falstaff and Maestro is the Wizard."

Charles and Leigh walked slowly along with the crowd, which began to disperse at the bridge. He felt disturbed by the scene of student hysteria despite the fact that it had been in the spirit of carnival. Jesse had gone a bit over the top by attaching religious significance and ceremonial deference to the skull, which Charles was sure the yacht club had no intention of doing. However, the summer was coming to a close, and the youthful enthusiasms suppressed in long hours of study, rehearsal, and practice needed an outlet, an expression of freedom from diligence. Well, Jesse had put on a show, like it or not, and if the undertones of occult celebration stopped there, perhaps it wasn't such a bad thing. Tomorrow there would be performances and a great deal of physical activity, Charles reasoned. And perhaps once was enough for that kind of woozy behavior. These were not freshmen, after all.

When they reached the house in Chigger City, Charles was restless. He poured himself two fingers of John Jameson, added an ice cube, and carried it to the rocking chair on the front porch. Leigh came out and sat in the chair beside him, rattling the ice cubes cooling her glass of Coke. The night was still warm, the view of "Marseille" across the Potomac was hazy in the moisture-laden atmosphere, and his thoughts turned inward as they had not done since his arrival on the island several weeks ago.

"Will you be sorry when it's over?" Leigh asked.

"In a way. After all, it's a break from what I do for a living, although I'm beginning to wonder if what I do is really as important as the value I place on it."

"Are you beginning to doubt yourself? Why? Look at all you have done."

"It's what anyone with a half a brain and an ounce of energy could do."

He thought of having to go back to the role of being president and it was difficult for him to imagine how he would feel. Here, he spent hours in contemplation and conversation, teaching and learning, and prying the imagination of his students from the lethargy of youth and the stasis of common thought. He wanted them to reach and stretch until the flab of conventional thinking burned away, replaced with new intellectual vigor.

As college president, the excitement of accomplishing things fueled his motor, but he rarely savored completion of the finished project. Always another, more demanding objective in the planning scheme was ahead, driving him to more difficult and complicated tasks, one after another, until the rhythm of his heartbeat was counted in square feet of masonry, or equipment, or landscaping—he was measured off in lengths and cut to the pattern of educational cloth that he had designed and created with others for the next semester and semesters to come. He wondered if the corduroy was wearing thin around the shoulders of his resolve—reduced by the need to assemble money and support to maintain the vitality of the college. There was perhaps a stiffness developing in his intellectual athleticism, a loss of dexterity in his thought that once enabled him to walk unmindful through the brambles of public administration. He didn't feel as though a depression had overtaken him without his knowledge—not a lonesomeness or emptiness or lack of love for the job. It was something else—a loss of life's rhythm created by music and the beauty of words, and relationships with others that beget love and laughter, where free-flying imagination is unencumbered by someone else's need. Perhaps he had compressed too much of the time that was needed for the college to grow, had made it muscle up too fast in the effort to lose the sense of past failure and squandered opportunity.

"Are you feeling burned out?" Leigh asked unexpectedly.

"I don't know what that feels like," Charles said, "but I don't think so." He was at the apex of his work—the height of his skill—his achievements were public knowledge. Perhaps those very successes were creating a sense of futility.

"I feel helpless for you," she said.

"You needn't worry. It's a minor funk. Maybe I'm just tired of the dance. Perhaps I need a rest from the conjugation of doing, doing, doing, done. Perhaps I should just let it go, glide away from it."

If he were empty, would he be thinking of the problem, conscious of his feelings in this way? Or would he be thrashing about like a hooked fish, unable to disgorge the lure that would ultimately be his demise? He was here, on this island, intact, with love for his wife and family and his position as president, but lately he seemed to have lost the music in his soul—the rhythm in his life. And yet, he couldn't just walk back into a classroom and flip off a lecture or discussion of any value, or if he could, he didn't feel as though he could both teach and administer the college effectively. It seemed impossible to alter the direction of his trajectory after the trigger of presidential expectations had been pulled.

What was it he was trying to get back that was more important than what he was doing? It was difficult for him to even frame the question. He had accomplished for the college what he had set out to do—more, in fact—but he could not shake the feeling that in some way it was taking a larger share of him and giving less substance in return. Ah, well, he thought, tomorrow is another fun-filled day of hunting treasure on Trinity Island. He raised his glass and sucked down the last sliver of ice.

"Listen," Leigh said, as the sound of strings floated softly to them through the clotted air. "Some of them have survived Jesse's séance enough to play through the night."

"What is it about this place that makes writers work all night, or musicians play and sing you to sleep, or painters work in dimly lit garages until all hours, and dancers morph into crabs and seagulls? Listen! It's ethereal—it's a magical island where art consumes time—neutralizes it, weakens it, overcomes it, and destroys it. There doesn't seem to be a rational moment in our time here that's not pregnant with meaning."

"Maybe when we leave, it will all disappear and Trinity Island will become Cobb Island again," Leigh said.

"'We are such stuff as dreams are made on and our little life is rounded with a sleep.'" Charles sleepily quoted. "And I am going now to get mine. Will you join me?"

"Will we sleep?"

"Only after a fashion."

Their lovemaking had been fitful, dispassionate, as it sometimes is for couples long married, and Leigh lay back unable to sleep because of Charles's snoring. He didn't mind if she shook him out of it, but she decided not to bother him. The string musicians had stopped their serenade from across Neale Sound and her mind wandered.

She had married a successful man, but the prizes won in his career were not her prizes. His success was not her success. She could appreciate and admire it, but she could not own nor feel it as deeply as he did. She could love him for his accomplishments, and she understood how much of his success was because of her. He had always acknowledged her gifts of wifery as the elixir of his success, but he was only one part of her accomplishment, for she had poured her energy and her love into their children as in a cauldron of creation with sparks and fire and the forging of their talents and urging them into their unique shapes and forms.

She had to admit there were times when she considered Charles more troublesome than the children, but the pleasure she took from them growing up gave her the strength and resiliency to suffer Charles and his peckish character. She understood more completely what kind of people her children might become, but Charles was less predictable, less tractable, and more difficult to surround with her love and devotion. She had come to this place in her understanding after thirty years of living with him, and still she could not put in words what he meant to her.

She loved him, but seeing this summer how other woman were affectionate toward him, she began to change her understanding of their relationship. With curiosity, she began to look in the nooks and crannies of him as though she might have missed something, and she was beginning to find new shapes of shadow and light in his personality. More surprising, she found a darkness in him that had eluded her in their ordinary life: she found a deepening sadness that he carried hidden in his walk and talk—a growing irritation of his own inability to succeed that showed itself in sarcasm and self-deprecating remarks belying his normal positive outlook. He was growing more pessimistic about the willingness of the community to support the efforts of the college as each project became more difficult to accomplish. He had begun to sound as though he was building a case for divorce with an unfaithful wife. His disaffection with either the college or himself, she couldn't tell which, was growing, and unlike her sense about her children, she didn't have a premonition of where it was headed. Her first instinct was to help, but to help what? And so she worried, by default, for not knowing what stick was stirring, creating the swirl of stuff inside him.

33

Carnival

The treasure hunt began from the steps of Linda's Gallery. The commodore of the Trinity Island Yacht Club, replete in blue blazer, white trousers, and a white hat whose black brim was encrusted with scrambled eggs, raised his arms for attention from the crowd. His gestures being largely ineffectual, he finally pulled the rope on a brass ship's bell mounted on a wooden stand that quickly rang up the group's attention.

"This is the beginning of the Treasure Hunt for the Crystal Skull," he said loudly. "There is a miniature crystal skull encrusted with precious jewels hidden inside a small treasure box somewhere on the island. As you go from one event to the other, be on the lookout for it. The finder of the treasure can redeem it for a keg of ale at Scuttlebutt's.

"After you attend one of the Treasure Hunt performances, you will be given a small bead or token to thread on a string representing the event. We will also give you spacer beads to complete the necklace. For instance, if you attend the beekeeper's lecture, you will receive a handmade charm resembling a bee with a hole through it for threading on the necklace string, or if you watch the lecture on oyster farming, your prize will be a bead resembling an oyster. Pretty simple. At the end of the day, the person who has successfully attended the most events will be the recipient of another grand prize. When you come in this evening for the performance in the theater, this is what your necklace should resemble." He held up a rather large piece of string containing beads and tokens and charms and placed it around his neck. The crowd cheered. String and spacer beads were passed among the crowd. The bell shattered the air again, demanding everyone's attention.

"Don't forget to look at your schedule because some of these events will occur only once at a given time and will not be repeated. That's all, and good luck." He stroked the bell one last time for emphasis. As the crowd dispersed, Maestro, who had no intention of walking the island collecting beads, found himself face to face with Andora.

"Aren't you going treasure hunting?" he asked her.

"No, I'm going to the theater in a minute for a last walk-through of the props and set. Can I buy you a coffee?"

"Yes, you can," he replied. "I haven't had a more exciting invitation from a beautiful woman since the last time you treated me to a mocha." They went inside and sat on an old leather sofa while the coffee was being drawn.

"I haven't seen you since we finished the set a few days ago. How've you been?"

"To tell the truth, Maestro, a little confused—a little up or a little down. I can't seem to maintain my keel. I suppose it's no secret that I am seriously in love with Luke and we want to make a life together?"

"No, not a secret, because I don't think you ever intended it to be."

"It couldn't be helped. We went up like a flare, and truthfully, I don't want it put out. I'm talking to Will now about separating and going on with Luke."

"I take it he's not warm to the idea."

"No he isn't, because he wants me to have his child. I don't think he cares about my love affair with Luke. I think he condones it because he thinks if I'm happy, I'll continue to be his wife—or his shipmate—whatever. In the meantime, he has more frequent conversations and periods of relaxation with Jesse than he does with me."

"Is Jesse helping him?"

"In some way, I think he is. Will told me the other day that Jesse had made him aware of his shortcomings as a husband and that he wanted to try to be the kind of person that I could love. How do I teach him that? He doesn't seem unhappy enough to change—that is, if he knew how to change." Linda brought their coffees and placed them on the table in front of them. Maestro sipped his, licked the whipped cream from his upper lip, and sat back.

"What do you want in your life?"

"I want a sense of ordinary well-being. I want to be able to express my creativity, free of all the neurotic baggage that I carry, half of which isn't mine. I want to love and be loved by a man who will look me in the eye and tell me that I am beautiful or bitchy or self-indulgent, and on top of all that, I want smart friends, and a safe and wholesome place to raise my kids, and it wouldn't hurt if, instead of an analyst on Park Avenue, I had a stock broker in the financial district of Wall Street. I don't want to worry about making a living. Is that too much?"

"No. It's rather a common list, really. I wonder why it is that very few people have gotten it?

"Oh, I'm sorry Maestro. I didn't mean to unload on you"

"It's alright. I can listen if you don't expect brilliant advice."

"Why do you hesitate?" she asked.

"I simply don't know if Luke can give you all of that. He will be a writer, you know."

"I don't know what that means."

"Well, you are not only a woman who will fill a man's living hours, you will also crowd his dreams. I'm not sure that Luke, the writer, can give you the life you want without giving up his own. On the other hand, Will needs you to fill him up, make him whole, make him the man he has never been. Knowing what you want is not necessarily a sure bet that you will get it. But I'm being pessimistic and overly abstract, I'm sure. 'You have to play the music that has been measured,' some witty musician once said."

She looked at Maestro and then grew silent. She sipped at her coffee. "Maestro," she said, hesitating. "What about after?"

"After what? After the summer finishes, after this balloon we are living in pops? This luscious balloon. What will become of the world we have built here with our close relationships, our conversations, and sharing of deep feeling and commitment?" He scratched his grey head. "It will come crashing down and it will be hurtful. It will come to an end as all romances do—brought down by the weight of their own reality. There will be a great wearing, and we will be swept away in an apocalypse," he said, throwing out his arms in dramatic emphasis, "or some such rubbish like that." He laughed heartily. "It makes good drama, does it not? I may eventually be able to use some of the stuff we have created here for another play or a short story. It's powerful material. On the other hand, didn't T.S. Eliot say it would end, 'not with a bang but a whimper'? Take your choice. If you're finished, I'll walk you to the theater."

Upon arrival at the theater they saw Jesse setting up his "astrologer" station on the front porch of the parsonage. On the walls behind him were astrological charts, signs of the zodiac, and various maps of the sky. A large sign hanging from the portico contained an arrow pointing to Jesse with "Astrologer" written on it while another arrow pointed inside in the direction of the "Fortune Teller." The venue was perfect for Jesse, who needed fresh clientele to help him continue his research.

Leigh and Charles had been down to the dock to witness the operation of Fireboat 6 attached to Fire Company 6. It threw an impressive stream of water at least three hundred feet to a small island in the middle of Neale Sound. After watching and listening to a fifteen-minute demonstration and lecture of the fireboat's prowess, they walked up the road toward the parsonage and found the astrologer and fortuneteller open for business. Jesse, dressed in bright robe and pointed hat, was engrossed in his charts—Charles sought out the fortuneteller, leaving Leigh to visit with Jesse the astrological wizard.

Charles found Rose in the kitchen, dressed more like a veiled image of Salome than a gypsy fortuneteller. The room had been darkened and, on the table, a crystal ball mounted on a base (from which ran an electric cord), provided much of the room's illumination. Symbols of the occult were placed around the room, accompanied by aromatic candles. The amateurish attempt to create a den of mystery and seduction might have been laughable had not Rose looked at him with serious affection.

"I have come to have my fortune told, O wise woman of the island."

"Then you must cross my palm with pieces of silver before I call on this exotic crystal ball, whose insides consist of snow flying around the Washington Monument, to tell me all that this very phallic symbol knows about you."

Charles dug deeply into his pockets and withdrew two quarters and placed them in front of her.

"Is that enough or do I get change?"

"Don't spoil it, buddy, or I'll create a whirlwind and a snowstorm that will make you dizzy for a month. This is magical stuff. Now, let me see. The crystal is not clear with all that Ivory Snow swishing around. It has clouded your future so that it is difficult to read. Let me try the cards." She pushed the ball aside and spread the brightly colored tarot cards in front of him.

"Close your eyes and pick one. We want to narrow the prospects of your future into a single truth."

Charles picked a card and handed it to her. She held it to her forehead, then placed it on the table in front of them. "The 'Temperance' card has chosen you. Were you born under the astrological sign of Sagittarius?"

"As a matter of fact, I was."

"Wow, this could get spooky. Let me have the palm of your hand." She took his hand and ran her finger over its lines gently and with concern. She fondled the calluses and then ran down and around the tips of his fingers as if to trace an outline of his hand.

"You are a man of moderation and self-control, and I am not sure that you are at peace with yourself. You strive to have harmonious relationships, but they are sometimes out of reach and it is difficult for you to compromise your principles for the sake of friendship. They sometime weaken, but never break. You want to create your path without sacrificing self-control, and while that is an admirable trait, it may cause you to lose originality. You are impatient with yourself as well as others, but you are careful to extend a full measure of understanding when needed. You are attracted to women, beautiful women especially, whom you have learned to admire without coveting."

"Women like yourself?"

"But I am not beautiful."

"More than you know."

"You are being kind. I'm not pretty like I was. You should have seen me when I was the active minister's wife and sang that high C in the choir."

Charles looked at her intently in the dim light as if studying a painting, and she held still for him, chin pointed as if she were being painted. He noted the slightly upturned corner of her lips and the lack of muscle tautness in the left cheek that the scar pulled back slightly toward the ear. Another long scar, beneath the surface of the right cheek, almost invisible, piqued Charles's admiration of her imperfections.

A red scar, hidden by her hairline, ran down the temple and over an ear as if the ear might have been severed from her head. It had become noticeable now that she had cut her hair in a more becoming style. She smiled at him, a deep dimple cleaving her chin, her teeth straight and bright, and he blushed slightly. She saw the pinkness rise in his cheeks. He resisted a strong impulse to kiss her—to caress her scars.

"Have you had enough?" she said.

"I don't suppose I'll ever get enough of looking at a beautiful woman. I'm sorry."

"Not at all. Not at all. I thought for a moment I was being ravished—seduction by moderation—and I wasn't about to stop you. It's my new Salome persona."

With that, Charles leaned closer to her.

"I think turnabout is fair play in this game, so I will read the beads on your necklace and tell your future!" He lifted the necklace from her ample bosom and clicked the beads around the string.

"It's not at all as dreary and uneventful as you think. I can base my reading on the ancient belief that the symbol of the skull is synonymous with the soul and that it holds all of the secrets that rest with you eternally. Look, this strand is divided in thirds by two skulls. Hmm? Here is the oyster bead indicating that the pearl of your life is on this island waiting to be shucked. The crab bead indicates that you will scuttle over the bottom of the earth; the sea glass bead, the lighthouse bead, and the Fessenden bead all indicate a renewed ability for you to communicate with other people—whoa, the snake bead indicates the destruction of the Garden of Eden. You must take care that it is placed between two skull beads to modify and contain its effect—and here is the sunshine bead, which signifies your way off this island. Those are the important ones. The other beads represent activities or places that you will visit or discover." He lowered the necklace to her breast again. "There, a professional reading from a genuine doctor of philosophy who majored in bead reading."

"I'm going to consult your cards again, because inside that façade of moderation, I think you're pretty slick."

Leigh poked her head in the door. "Ready to go?" she asked.

"Just finished. Do you want your palms read?" Rose replied.

"No, I've just had my planets and my stars aligned by the mechanic next door and I wouldn't want to mess up the timing."

"That's okay. The snow hasn't quite settled in my crystal ball yet, so I couldn't get clear reception anyhow. I'd have to make it up."

"What!" Charles said. "What you said about me wasn't true?"

"Oh, it was the truth alright. It was just a trifle muddy."

"Let's go," Leigh said, tugging Charles's arm. "I've had enough hocus pocus to last me a lifetime."

Luke ambled down from his lair on the third floor and ran into Jesse on the porch.

"Come on, Luke, I've finished your chart. Come sit down," Jesse called. Luke sat in the chair in front of the minister in the ridiculous costume, and smiled.

"Is it good news?"

"It isn't bad. It's a peek at your future. You know I'm getting to the point in my studies where I can see many things, and sometimes I think I see too much. In your case, it isn't so bad. Your sun is in Sagittarius and your moon is in Leo—a splendid combination that awakens your passionate and your spiritual side.

"Your ascending sign is Virgo and it gives you a sense of practicality—perhaps. Let's put that aside for the moment. You have Neptune rising and that grants inspiration and mysticism to your nature. Your sun and moon are in trine to one another, which is a good sign for your future health, which is also tied to Jupiter in conjunction with the moon. This is all very good now that Jupiter and your moon are in the occult houses, which means that you will benefit greatly from your studies.

"Gemini is also very strong, which means you will have two occupations going on simultaneously. It indicates that part of the ruler of the sign is also in the fourth house, which is your home environment where you will practice one of your occupations, which, by all indications, is writing. Mercury, by the way, conjuncts your sun and a little behind it, which means that your mental processes tend to work a little slower. Incidentally, my Mercury is also behind the sun so that when I am singing I tend to think about what I have just done rather than what is coming up next. When I sing a good note, I tend to dwell on the beauty of the note or the words which can give me an embarrassing lapse. You have a tendency to think in the past and you should discipline yourself to look ahead more.

"Mars is conjuncting your sun also. Mars, Mercury, and the sun are all conjuncting, adding intense activity to you spiritually. You stand to benefit from everything that you do in higher education or other intellectual activities. The ruler of that house is Taurus and it is conjuncting Saturn and the fifth house indicating that your higher education will be concentrated on the study of theater.

"The ruler of your second house, your financial house, and the ruler of your ninth house, the education house, are in conjunction with your Saturn, the fifth house, which has to do with theater and pleasures and so on. You will make money, but your conjunction with Saturn tends to slow down the money-making prospect. It comes and comes big, but it is delayed until later in life. In the meantime, you must be patient. You won't suffer in any way. Your fortune is the same distance from your ascending sign as the sun is from the moon which for you is in the ninth house having to do with clergy, higher education, the law, and more intellectual and sophisticated pursuits. Much of the inspiration for your writing could come from this trove of mystical understanding.

"I looked at your lineage and found that your father is dead—the indications are by accidental drowning or by fire—but there is a mystery as to your mother. You said that you knew only that she disappeared after your father died and was never seen again. There is a weak sign in the eighth house, the death house, that her life has ended tragically. I couldn't be certain.

"My view is that you will have a rewarding life built on strong imaginative and creative capacities. You are going to have great success, but that also will come later in life. A sign of caution in Capricorn warns your success will separate you from your friends with some suffering and disappointment, but, at the same time, you must do what you will do as it is written."

Luke sat before Jesse somewhat mystified. "Jesse, where did you get all that crap?" he asked.

"Not crap. Not crap at all, Luke. I am certain that it will happen. Here, I have written it all down on these sheets that you should take with you. Forget them for now, but pick them up in a year or two and study them. You'll see." Luke took the papers and went back up the stairs to leave them in his room, leaving Jesse smiling in self-satisfaction.

In late afternoon, a small crowd of treasure-hunters came skipping and whistling down Trinity Island Road headed for Linda's, which had become the unofficial headquarters of the event. Leading the pack was Possum. He periodically raised his hand containing a small wooden box over his head and shouted, "Long live the skull! Long live the skull!" By the time he reached the porch, people from inside and out had begun to surround Possum to see what the yelling was about. He opened the box, and, therein, lying on a piece of blue velvet lining, was the Crystal Skull.

"I found it, Linda! It's mine and I'll get all the good luck I can use because I found it. You know where it was? It was up a tree. They said it would be buried to throw you off the scent, and that's where they made their mistake. They shoulda known that a possum always looks up a tree," he said, laughing and stomping his feet.

"Wait a minute, wait a minute, Possum," Linda said. "You either get to keep the skull, which is worth about a dollar and a half, or you get your own keg of beer over at the marina. Which do you want?"

"They really should'na hid the prize where only a possum could see it, so I guess they ain't too smart. I think we'll get more good luck if we take the beer." A cheer went up from the crowd. He handed Linda the box in return for a certificate good for one keg of beer over at Scuttlebutt's, and the crowd members made their way across the street to refresh themselves with Possum's first prize.

34

The Final Act

The last event on Saturday, the final act of the play, *Ruby*, had been advertised in the flyers for an 8:30 p.m. curtain. People started occupying seats a half-hour early, tired from treasure-hunting, wanting to rest before the show started. More seats were brought in to pack the house, and the doors were thrown open to accommodate latecomers. As the house lights dimmed, the stage right corner lit up gradually, and Ezra Gandy, carrying a homemade fiddle case, stepped into the spot. He waited for the crowd to quiet down.

EZRA. It seemed that my head had no more hit the pillow when there was a rap at the door and there stood the Adams girl, Lizzie, asking for Mary because Ruby's baby was comin'. Since I don't keep a horse, Mary carried her bag, and I grabbed my fiddle, and we walked over to Elysium to help with the birthing. When we got there, Mamie Jackson was already boiling water on the stove and making sure there were plenty of sheets and towels. Mary went on upstairs to see if she could help with Ruby. Broadus had already sent for the doctor, so there was nothing much I could do except sit at the kitchen table with Broadus and wait, so I unstrapped my fiddle and played a few Christmas hymns kinda soft and low so as not to disturb anything. Off there in the sitting room, downstairs, was where Luke's remains were resting in an apple box that had been covered with black crepe.

Upstairs they thought it would take a little time for the baby to come since it was Ruby's first one, and she was so thin they were expecting her to have trouble, but just after dawn, Mary came down and said it was over, Ruby had delivered a boy. They both seemed to be healthy, but there was something about it that Mary thought was strange. We kinda marveled at it, but it didn't really seem unusual when she said Ruby didn't show any pain when she was having that baby. She didn't scream or do a lot of gruntin' or anything like women who have babies for the first time are apt to do. No nothin'. She just bore down and had the baby.

Then when they cleaned 'im up and put 'im back with his mother to nurse, he wouldn't nurse her, wouldn't suck her at all. Mary said he didn't do a lot of crying about it, either. So they brought Mamie up to the room and put him up to her, and Mary said it wasn't no more than fifteen minutes before he was gobbling down milk right along out of Mamie. By that time the doctor had come and looked over everything and told us the mother and son were alright despite the fact that he couldn't get the baby to take to the mother, either. Sometimes they rub the mother with a little cream or butter or honey or something good, and it helps the baby to understand where his food is coming from, but not that one. He didn't take to her no how. Doc said as long as Mamie had milk it was alright, so he left and went on to check on somebody further down the road that he thought had appendicitis.

Everybody was tired from waitin' around, so we gathered ourselves up and went home seein's how we would see everybody again at church on Christmas eve.

{Ezra disappears into a dark stage and then the lights come up gradually on a scene in the kitchen with Mamie preparing food and Ruby standing at the table.}

MAMIE. You sure you feel good enough to be up and around?

RUBY. I couldn't lay up in that bed another hour. I had to come downstairs.

MAMIE. Them folks gonna be surprised when they come back from church and you sittin' here big as life dressed up in your clothes, that's all.

RUBY. It don't matter.

MAMIE: You feel good enough to peel some potatoes? Those folks gonna be hungry when they get back from church. *{She sets a bowl of potatoes and a knife in front of Ruby who does not pick it up.}* Hush! Hush now. Ain't that the baby crying? *{She looks at Ruby and expects her to go to the baby, but finally Mamie rises from the table and goes upstairs. Ruby sits at the table and stares. Mamie comes back with the baby in her arms and stoops to give it to Ruby, but Ruby puts up her hands to reject it.}*

RUBY. I don't want him.

MAMIE. You can't jes not want him. He's hongry.

RUBY. Feed him then.

MAMIE. *(Unpins the top of her dress and snuggles the baby to her breast.)* You got to learn to take care of this chil' if you gonna be the mother.

RUBY. You be the mother. He don't want me and I don't want him, so we're square.

MAMIE. You shouldn't talk like that, Miss Ruby. It ain't right. *(Ruby rises and walks slowly from the table into the sitting room where Luke's remains rest between two candles. Mamie turns her chair and watches her.)*

RUBY. *(She runs her finger around the top of the box and then begins speaking to it.)* You should'na done that, Luke. You should'na tried to make me worthless in the fields and shiftless in the house—lovey-dovey and soft. You should'na wanted me to be like them other girls, Luke. You should 'a taken me to the side of you, Luke, not tried to put me under you. I couldn't be under nobody, not ever. Those girls prancing around was weak, and Daddy always said there wasn't room for the weak around a farm, so you have to get rid of the weak, Luke, that's all. They just get in a man's eye and keep him from his work. The weak can't live with the rest of us. You understand that now, don't you, Luke? Ted Cockrel was gonna tell on me at the bridge, he was gonna say my name, Luke. It's better this way. Luke, you should'na crowned me Queen of Love and Beauty when I was none of those things. I didn't want those things. They just brought trouble. I was blood mad at them Dorsey girls and that Cockrel man, and you, Lukey, and the fire took the pain away.... *(Ruby sees that Mamie has been listening at the doorway.)*

MAMIE. He didn't kill them girls, did he? Cockrel didn't kill them girls, and y'all hung him for it! Hung him at the bridge. Den you burnt up Lukey in the barn, didn't you? I know you was an evil person, but I think you be the Devil himself in woman's clothes!

RUBY. *{Ruby erupts angrily at Mamie and we can see that she is indeed crazed—a madwoman.}* Who's gonna punish me? It ain't gonna be no nigger woman, cause there ain't no nigger woman as big as God. *{Ruby rushes to the outside.}*

MAMIE. Where you goin'?

RUBY. I don't know, but I'm goin' where people don't care who you are and what you do. *{Ruby walks out, Mamie watches her out by the well. Mamie hears her screaming down into the well, 'Ma Maaa, Ma Maaaa, Ma Maaa,' and the sound reverberates as though it was from the bowels of the earth, from the hounds of hell. And then she falls on the bench and cries. The baby, in Mamie's arms, screams. Mamie shields the baby from the noise as Ruby screams again. Mamie walks into the kitchen with the baby and sings.}*

> Oh baby, oh baby
> What's gonna keep you safe from harm,
> Oh, my baby, what's gonna keep you safe from harm
> When you mama killed your daddy in the barn
> Oh, my baby, what's gonna keep you safe from harm
> When you blind eyes seen it from the womb.

{Mamie walks around with the baby and settles its crying, then sits in the rocker, humming the song. Finally, in the distance, there is the sound of a Christmas carol being sung by those returning from church. Ephraim is with them. They are in a subdued Christmas spirit. They come in and most of them go into the room where the box is and sing to Luke in the box a song about a baby born. Ephraim

stays behind and looks into the nursery. He sees that Mamie has been crying as she rocks the baby in the chair.}

EPHRAIM. What's wrong Mamie? *{He kneels beside her.}*

MAMIE. The world's mus' gonna come to an end. I done heard such terrible things from Miss Ruby I couldn't stand it.

EPHRAIM. What did she say to upset you like this?

MAMIE. She tol' me she done burned the barn down with Lukey in it...she didn't tell me at my face, but I heard her telling Lukey in that box. She say she done up them Dorsey girls wid a hatchet, too. When I asked her why she did it, she said it took away the pain and weren't nobody gonna punish her for it, neither. *{Ephraim rises, puts his hand on her shoulder.}*

EPHRAIM. Where is she now?

MAMIE. Out lookin' where the barn use to be, screaming at the night.

EPHRAIM. I'll go see if I can help her. *{When Ephraim enters the kitchen, Broadus is sitting at the kitchen table with his head in his hands, reading a newspaper. Ephraim reaches to Broadus and starts to say something, but Broadus interrupts.}*

BROADUS. Say, Ephraim, listen to this....

EPHRAIM. I can't stay, Broadus, there are still some things to do. I'll be going now.

BROADUS. Do you mind if we keep Luke's remains for a few days?

EPHRAIM. No, no, but death has been too much among us—now it's finished. Let's bury him on New Year's Eve and have done with this year. I'll spend a few more minutes with Ruby before I git up the road. If I don't see you before then, you all have a merry Christmas. I'll keep you in my heart and my prayers. *{He picks up a blanket lying over a chair and goes out where Ruby is sitting on the bench next to the well, her head in her hands. He puts the blanket around her shoulders, goes over to the burned remains of the barn and rakes at rubble. He holds up the remainder of a lance consisting of the metal tip and six inches of charred wooden shaft and takes it back to Ruby.}*

EPHRAIM. Broadus will want to put this in the coffin. It's the remains of the lance that Luke used to win the tournament the day he crowned you Queen of Love and Beauty.

RUBY. He should'na done that. He should'a left me alone. *{She pushes the lance away and Ephraim puts it on the well.}*

EPHRAIM. Ruby, you need to save yourself, you need to pray to God for everlasting forgiveness. You need to cleanse the rot from your soul. *{He puts his hand on her shoulder.}* Let me help you seek forgiveness for your sins through Jesus Christ, Ruby. You think the pain is so great that nothing can help you, but He can. Only He can save you now.

RUBY. You mean you want me to tell God that I'm sorry I did it when I'm not? You mean you think those people deserved to live on this earth, smiling happy when they caused me such pain inside? Do you know about pain inside, Ephraim—you that's never been raped by a drunk husband—you that's never been looked down on as trash—I wouldn't give him a baby so he had to make me do it, Preacher. I cooked, I milked cows, I cleaned and scrubbed, I pitched hay and I cut corn in the field—I didn't want no baby, Preacher, and I only knew one way to make that pain go away. Luke didn't want me. He wanted to put it in me and hurt me and dance with the music. That's all those Dorsey girls wanted—to dance with the music. *{Ephraim places his left hand on her shoulder, takes the ladle from the bucket of water, and dribbles some on Ruby's head.}*

EPHRAIM. Bless this child, oh Lord God, for she knows not what she has done. Take from her the knowledge of sin and evil that keeps her from loving You. *(He dribbles more water on her forehead from the ladle.)* Place in her heart the love and forgiveness of the Lord Jesus Christ. *(He puts the ladle back in the bucket.)* Drive Satan from her soul and restore her to the love and beauty of Your bountiful life. Amen. Stand up now, Ruby. *(Ruby looks up at Ephraim and rises slowly.)*

RUBY. I don't want your forgiveness. Luke shouldn't have tried to make me the Queen of Love and Beauty.

EPHRAIM. Ruby, Luke loved you, I love you, this family loves you, and you have to realize that God loves you.

RUBY. He should'a left me where I was—he should'a left me alone. I'm not sorry he's dead, I didn't want his love.

EPHRAIM. Oh Ruby.... *(As quick as an adder's tongue, Ruby picks up the steel point from the top of the well and plunges it through Ephraim into his heart. His body lurches forward, his arms momentarily embrace her knees and then he sags to the ground at her feet. The sound of voices singing "Silent Night" drift from the house. Finally, Ruby looks at the blood on her hands, holds them up and washes them off in the bucket. She looks down on Ephraim.)*

RUBY. I ain't no Queen of Love and Beauty, Ephraim. *(She walks away into the darkness. Lights dim, music fades. Inside the kitchen, Broadus reads from the paper to several gathered at the table.)*

BROADUS. *(Rising from the table. Reading from the paper.)* Listen to this everybody:
'The year 1896 will pass into history within a few days and the close of the year is a fitting time not only for good resolutions as to the future, but for due thankfulness for favors enjoyed in

the past. It is probable that there is no person on earth whose situation is so bad that he can find no cause for gratitude. Life itself, even in the last extremity is deemed a blessing. Let everyone resolve to make an effort to do better during the future than in the past, so that at the close of the present year, we can look with pride upon our every act, and not feel that another year has been wasted.' Amen.

VOICES AROUND TABLE. Amen, amen. *{Curtain closes slowly with the soft sound of Christmas carols being sung.}*

———

The audience sat in silence, trying to regain a sense of reality, reaching and touching each other in the darkened auditorium for reassurance that what they had seen was fantasy. The house lights came up gradually, and the audience began to clap and then applaud wildly. The curtain was drawn and the actors, one by one, made their appearance to bow and receive applause, and when they had all assembled, holding hands in a line, they gestured to the wing for the playwright to come out.

"Author, author!" they shouted, as Maestro walked slowly from the wings and bowed deeply from the waist. He turned to the cast and also bowed to them. "I think we've found an ending," he said, and smiled. He turned and faced the audience.

"Tonight has been the culmination of several weeks of work by all of the students in the creative writing program as well as the actors taking part in the theater. The writers have been in a contest to write an ending to this play entitled *Ruby*, and until tonight, none of them, except one, knew whose ending was chosen for the final presentation. There is much more to do in making the play a contiguous and complete dramatic presentation, but it has served as a valuable learning experience for all of us. I am pleased to introduce the person whom I hope will continue to collaborate with me and whose name will appear with mine as co-author when it is finally finished."

He turned and beckoned to Rose.

"Rose Caine, stand by me and accept my congratulations and appreciation for your work on *Ruby* and especially for your deep, dazzling display of theater in that last scene." He turned and gave her a peck on the right and then on the left cheek. More wild applause and congratulations burst from everyone except Jesse who stood in the middle of the stage, stunned, the stage lance still sticking from his chest, watching her in disbelief. Lonnie ran to Rose to give her a joyful hug as Jesse turned away.

"Don't forget," Maestro said to the players, "Cast party will follow immediately on Will's boat."

35

The Cast Party

They hugged and kissed and congratulated each other excessively in celebration of the end of the play as well as the general drawing down of classes and rehearsals. Luke looked for Andora and found her dismantling the contraption from Jesse's chest that had made the fake stab of the lance look as real as possible. Lonnie was also assisting, and when she saw Luke, she motioned him to help them unstrap the knife board and slip it carefully through Jesse's arms.

"You did a nice job, Jesse. You were very dynamic and convincing," Luke said.

"Thank you," he said, with a little bow. "I'm still a little confused about who wrote that scene. I thought it was you, but my wife? I never once suspected she had done it. I didn't see that coming. It was a bit of a shock."

"I should think it would be—finding out that my wife had written my death in a furious climax like that," Luke said, smiling. " Go down and shake it off at the party. You are going to the party on the boat, aren't you?"

"Oh yes, certainly, wouldn't miss it."

"Come along with me, then. I promised Will I would get ready for it," Andora said, taking Jesse by the arm and leading him toward the the boat dock.

Luke was left standing there, face to face with Lonnie, the woman who had shown him complete animosity over the past two weeks, culminating in denting the hood of his car with a well-thrown rock. They looked at each other and Luke was about to turn away when she said, "I'll get your car fixed, you know."

"You don't have to. I've gotten used to its having been vandalized by an ingénue actress with an explosive temper."

"Will you accept my apology? I was just trying to get into the part."

"You did a hell of a job on me to get into it. If you'll excuse me now, I have to run over to the parsonage, pick up Ward, and then go on to the party."

"May I tag along?" she asked.

"I guess so," he said, with some hesitation. "Let's go out this way," and they went out the right wing of the theater, through the small underground passage and into the parsonage.

Luke left Lonnie standing in the living room while he went to find Ward, but he wasn't in his room. Returning downstairs, Luke discovered the light near the piano had been turned off. He stopped for a moment, feeling his way to the switch when he walked into Lonnie who was standing there waiting for him. She reached up quickly and kissed him, and then, taking a breath, she kissed him again passionately and forcefully until she backed him up against the piano. He was surprised but didn't resist, overtaken by her passion. She felt for the zipper of his shorts and lifted her skirt under which she had no underwear and tried feverishly to place him into her, but the noise of footsteps coming from the porch made them duck, half-dressed, beneath the grand piano. Footsteps came through the door, stopped, and Ward yelled, "Hello." Lonnie clamped her hand over Luke's mouth so that he couldn't respond. Before the footsteps had died away, she was kissing his neck and chest and preparing to mount him beneath the piano.

Torn between sensibility and desire, Luke could do nothing but enjoy the fullness of the moment and the energy and passion of the woman making love to him. She would not stop, and finally, with the caution of a careful lover, he eased her from him and told her there was a better place for making love than beneath a grand piano.

She relaxed, breathed deeply, and pulled him to her for several intense kisses. When she was finished, he crawled from the piano as carefully as he could and stood to repair what little wardrobe he was wearing. She came out and slipped into the downstairs bathroom to straighten her clothes. He stood there in a stupor, not understanding the actions of the woman who had shown her hatred for him, but whose lustiness clung around him now like a well-fitted suit. When she came from the bathroom, she kissed him again, and in her ardor he read the message that she was not yet satisfied. He took her by the hand, and they left from the parsonage as quickly as possible. On their way to the boat, they passed the children's playground; Lonnie climbed swiftly to the floor of the elevated playhouse and beckoned him to follow. He reached the little platform and she was there in the dark, without her clothes on, waiting for him. This time she was more controlled and eager to be sensual, slowly, with determination and enjoyment. He could but dance to her rhythm that he found deeply satisfying. They lingered, holding each other, kissing tenderly, and then finally decided to leave the little hutch by dismounting via the monkey bars. She looked back at the curving slide and the rings dangling from the poles, "That would be fun," she said.

As they came to the dock, she dropped her hand so as not to appear as his date. The party was in full swing to the music of a guitar, an accordion, and two violins. They got a beer from the cooler and looked around for someone to talk to.

Maestro had been sitting in a deck chair on the bow, watching the party and chatting to students and faculty who came to congratulate him. It was she who did it, he told them, referring to the rewrite of the last act by Rose Caine. "She has an exquisite sense of timing. And Mamie's song—Mamie's song ripped your heart right out. Mamie herself was such a strong figure that he might write a play about her next time," he told them. He stood up on the bow and asked Will to ring the bell for attention. The burble of voices diminished.

"Now, after the completion of every successful production, there are hijinks to be played, one actor upon another, one director upon you all, and tonight is no exception. Through all the scenes we have played, I have kept track of the actors who dropped or misspoke the most number of lines. It is my sworn duty to announce that the winner of the award is no other than our own Reverend Jesse Cain, standing there in the back." He pointed to Jesse, who waved his hand and took a deep bow acknowledging the applause.

"Jesse played a heck of a last scene, although he dropped so many lines he might as well have written it himself." The crowd roared and applauded. "As a reward, Jesse will be made to walk the plank conveniently located at the stern, fully clothed, without water wings. Luke, will you and the boys escort Jesse to the plank, please?" There was general applause. The strings began to play something sweetly funereal, but Maestro stopped them.

"Please, musicians, something more robust for the occasion. Jesse is being fed to the fishes today because he ignored the instructions of the director, the words written by the writer, and generally screwed up the cues for his fellow actors. The theater cannot tolerate an actor amok, and so it is with heavy heart that we send Jesse Caine to his great reward in the sky—back to the planet or constellation from which he came. Goodbye, Jesse," Maestro intoned.

Jesse took a step onto the plank that had been extended from the stern and began to sing something in German from *Die Meistersinger*. He took slow, dramatic steps until he reached the end. Finally, he dropped into the water amid great applause. Everyone was so pleased with the fun of the activity that a little time passed before someone realized that Jesse had not yet come back to the surface.

"He can't swim!" Rose screamed, suddenly realizing her husband was facing death in the warm August water. Luke leapt over the railing into the water, followed by Will. The crowd surged to the starboard side, tilting the boat toward the action. Luke came up for air, inhaled deeply, and dove again. Will came to the surface holding Jesse's leg, followed by Luke, who grasped Jesse around the chest and began floundering and paddling toward shore. They floated him, Will in back, Luke under the head and shoulders, until they reached a short ladder at the end of the dock. With the help of several others who had jumped in, they lifted the listless body from the water onto the dock and rolled him over. Several people began administering revival techniques, but within minutes, a volunteer from the firehouse came running down with a medical case in each hand to direct Jesse's recovery—a few chest compressions, an oxygen mask, and Jesse turned over with a groan. Another volunteer joined the first, and Jesse's recovery was in full swing. Among the crowd, Rose hovered over him, waiting and watching. Maestro sidled up to her.

"Why didn't he tell us he couldn't swim?"

"I don't know. He can swim a little—dog paddle—but he didn't do it tonight. Maybe he didn't want to."

"Our criticism of him was all in fun. It's part of the theater game. Surely he wouldn't turn sour over that?"

"No. Not at all. Don't blame yourself. It was probably one of Jesse's little accidents."

Jesse sat up, blinked a few times, and looked around. "Did I miss my cue again?" he asked, and the crowd roared with laughter. They helped him to his feet and, after a few staggering steps, he gained his equilibrium.

"I didn't miss the party, did I?" he asked incredulously, playing into the lines of the buffoon. The medical people stood by his side and helped him toward the firehouse where they wanted him to lie for a few minutes while they monitored his vital signs.

"I'll go up with him," Charles volunteered. "Keep the party going and we'll probably be back in a few minutes."

As they left the dock, Charles saw with some relief that Will was dismantling the plank that had been rigged on the stern. There would not be another accidental drowning tonight.

They made Jesse strip off his wet clothing and lie on an examining table under blankets as they cuffed his arm to monitor blood pressure. The oxygen cupped his nose and a clip on his finger monitored his heart rate. They sat in silence, with the exception of Jesse's heavy breathing, and then the oxygen was taken away and Jesse could talk freely.

"Sorry, Charles. I guess I made a mess of the party."

"Not at all. It will take more than a little water in the lungs to stop that celebration."

"It was worthless. Nothing happened."

"Nothing happened?"

"When I stepped off, I knew I would sink like a rock. I always sink in water, and I had wondered what it would be like to drown once—not forever—but drown once and have one of those out-of-body experiences that people have when they die and become intensely angelic, where they hover over the scene and watch people lament their passing, and then they are resuscitated and return to their life with a sense of purpose and meaning because they have seen the regenerative light of God. That's what I wanted, but what I got was darkness. In the water—darkness—soaking wet on the deck feeling like a fool. That's what I got."

Charles looked at him not knowing how to respond.

Jesse continued, "I'm beginning to feel tired. I think I'll just go back to the office and rest if these guys will let me go."

"I'm sorry, Jesse," Charles said, not knowing what else to say to a man who had just tried to kill himself—almost.

The attending medics advised Jesse to go home and rest, and with the shake of a limp hand, he left Charles standing in the firehouse and walked across the road to his office shrouded in blankets.

"How close do you think he was from dying?" Charles asked one of the young men repacking an equipment bag.

"It's hard to tell. His heart would probably continue to beat although his brain was temporarily deprived of oxygen. A couple of more minutes and he might have been gone; depends on how strong he is."

Charles started walking from the firehouse back to the boat anchorage trying to unravel Jesse's little episode. Jesse was actually trying to visit an afterlife by drowning and being saved again. Or, as he would say in his own vocabulary, he was trying to be physically born again. He was trying to do purposefully what had been done physically to Rose by accident. The complexity of the action dazzled Charles. If the scenario had happened as Jesse wanted it, he would have come away with an overwhelming story to tell, and the elaboration of it would make him special beyond his expectations. He would have become a messenger from God. He would have had his death and resurrection, and it would have vaulted him into fame and recognition, or he would have made it so. Instead, he got blackness, and ignominy.

When Charles reached the boat and everyone inquired of Jesse's well being, he reported that Jesse was well, a little tired, and resting in bed.

"How is he, really?" Rose asked softly, pulling Charles aside.

"Crazy as a loon," he said, and walked toward the cooler for a beer.

As the sun began to lighten the day, the revelers on the boat slipped the wind from their sails and began the slow and tedious job of cleaning up. They cleaned the decks and policed the area around the docks for fifty yards in each direction. They had undoubtedly disturbed the peace of the island until early morning but were careful not to soil the place where they lived and worked. Eventually, they piped themselves from the boat and headed for home. Luke had lost track of Lonnie during the evening and so he didn't see her walking away from the boat with the others. Andora stepped up from the cabin having just said goodbye to Will.

"C'mon," Luke said, "I'll walk you home."

They left the boat, walking easily up the road away from the dock.

"That was successful," he said, trying to fill the silence between them.

"For the exception of Jesse not drowning himself, it all went pretty well." They laughed together.

As they neared the parsonage, Luke asked her abruptly, "My place or yours?"

"Neither, I think," she said solemnly. "I really need to be alone for a few hours," and they walked on.

"Will I see you later?"

"I don't think so. There won't be any Sunday services tonight, so I think I'll just stay in and try to get my stuff together."

"Will you be here," he said, stopping at the gate to her cottage, "or on the boat?"

"I don't know," she said, and walked into her cottage, leaving him standing there waiting for a different answer.

36

Maestro's Letter

Maestro had left the party in the exciting aftermath that followed Jesse's walking the plank, and when he reached his cottage, he decided to sit down and write to her about it while it was still fresh in his mind. He didn't want to characterize the activities of the summer as being bizarre. They were much too authentic to be turned into comedy on the strength of an accident, or stunt, or whatever it was.

> *My Darling Wife:*
>
> *The golden voice went gargling into the river at the cast party and almost didn't return. It is the first time I have come close to killing an actor for dropping his lines, although I have threatened it many times. Everyone behaved very well except for our matinee idol and skirt monger, Jesse, who willingly walked the plank at the stern of the ship without mentioning that he would drop*

to the bottom like an anchor without a rope. The boys dredged him up, much to our relief, and he sputtered alive again seeming not much worse for the experience. It is a bad joke to say that a dunce who cannot remember his lines cannot remember the space between them either, but it seems to be as much a characteristic of his in life as it is the theatric world of make believe. Ah, well, we seemed to have escaped an untidy destiny with the man who would be the Astrologer. Guess he couldn't see it coming.

As we near the close of camp, I have begun to notice the cloth of maturity appearing on our aspiring artists despite an environment that encourages us to maintain a sort of overdrawn adolescence to retard the inevitable clash with reality. Almost all of our students will go back to university, although a few will continue to graduate study while the more mature of them will search for a career. The bell will toll another transition, and off we will go once more. I will lose many good friends. Although I have found some that are worth keeping close to hand because they are interesting and will make a crease in the world somewhere, I will miss them all. There will be a sadness in our parting. There are a couple....

A knock came at the door, timid at first, stronger a second time, and then the door opened and Lonnie stuck her head in and yelled, "Maestro!"

"Over here at the writing table, Lonnie. To what do I owe this surprise?"

"Nothing big. I just wanted to thank you for everything you've done for me. I also wanted to tell you that I'm not angry with Luke anymore. I just couldn't keep it up once the play was finished."

"I didn't think that you would."

"May I invite myself for a drink? Do you have more of that Cremant left?"

"You may certainly have some if there is any. I do hope that I have another bottle." He left the table and went into the kitchen. Lonnie leaned over to see what he was writing. She picked up the letter he had been writing and read it with growing curiosity until Maestro returned with two jelly glasses filled with the sparkling wine.

"I'm sorry," she said, holding up the letter. "I was just curious as to what you were writing. It's not easy to catch a famous writer in the act of writing and I wanted to see it."

"Each week I try to write a letter to my wife and let her know how I'm feeling. It helps to chase the loneliness."

"But you never mail them, do you? Aren't they stacked there in the corner of the table?"

"I suppose I have been a little negligent in mailing them."

"Maestro, hasn't your wife passed away? Didn't Jesse tell me that she died a few years ago?"

Maestro sat at the table and picked up the letter he had been writing. "Yes, she did leave me a few years ago. I don't want you to be spooked by my continuing correspondence with a ghost. It is merely a comforting place to store the memories." She saw a tear form in the corner of his eye.

"Maestro, there will always be someone to love you. You can send your letters to me. I'd love to have them, but I don't want to intrude."

"That's kind of you, but I am not yet a sorrowful old man living in the past. She is still very much alive in my memories and I like to visit them from time to time. Writing a letter is a good way to do it." He reached his arms out to Lonnie, and they hugged. "Thank you for caring, although you did invade my privacy."

Luke's parting with Andora was indecisive and unsettling and it left him without direction. She said she didn't know where she would be—on the boat—at the cottage—but clearly the message that it wouldn't be with him. What had happened between them that would cause a shift in her affection? Was Will convincing her that he could become a loving husband? Was she having second thoughts?

He walked up one side of Trinity Island Road and down the other kicking questions through his mind as stones in the road. Finally, he ended up at the parsonage and walked quietly to his room on the third floor. In a lightning stroke of imagination, he thought he would find Andora there, but the image flashed and burned in the room's emptiness. He turned on the lamp at his writing table and found that someone had been there. There was a note on his yellow writing pad, and he immediately recognized Pila's printed message. To one side of the note was a small white box that rattled slightly when he shook it. He picked up the note and read:

> *Dear Shake, I hunted over the island and couldn't find you, so I suspect that you are lying about somewhere with Andora in a state of Euphoria (ha, ha) not wanting to be found. We heard this afternoon that a rather large weather front is heading up the coast and will undoubtedly bring big rain and winds and close us down for several days, perhaps beyond the time when we are supposed to suspend operations, so we protected the dig as best we could, packed our stuff and are on our way out. I will head to Chevy Chase to visit my parents for a few days before making preparations for the trip to Israel. I am sorry that*

you will not be with me, but Rose is considering going as my writer in residence to record our experiences for a book, perhaps—that is if she can make peace with herself and Jesse. I'll try to call you before I leave.

The head of the archeology project gave each intern a remembrance of the Wollaston dig which I pass to you with my love and affection. You will recognize it as a cheap imitation of the ring that Captain Neal had made for his wife in England (we think). Of course we really don't know what the original looked like, but ours is adorned with pieces of oyster shells rather than pearls and it is made of pewter rather than silver and the cross and skull aren't hidden in a secret compartment, but are carved right in the center.

Remember me when you wear it.

Love, Pila.

Luke lifted the lid from the first box and found another box inside it, from which he lifted a third smaller box and took out the ring. He held it up to examine it, then he tried to put it on, but of course it was made for Pila's finger and too small for his. He held it tightly in his fist trying to keep his emotions in check until finally he let them go and wept silently. He wiped his eyes, went to the mirror over his dresser where he had hung the string of beads gathered during the Crystal Skull celebration, and with considerable deliberation, arranged the beads in order ascending from Pila's ring hanging prominently in the middle. He put it on and looked at it in the mirror and kissed the ring.

The morning appeared bright and clear without portent of the impending storm or the comfort of Andora's presence.

Luke went downstairs for coffee and found a small gathering of people around the table in an impromptu meeting, discussing the storm and the actions that should be taken to avoid it. Of course, the predictions ranged from an inch or two of rain and thirty-mile-an-hour winds to a deluge of over twelve inches and hurricane-force winds that would mother small tornados within its skirts.

Tasks were meted out to those around the table. Charles would order buses for evacuation to Piccowaxen Middle School scheduled for tomorrow morning at ten. Rose and Jesse would check all of the living spaces occupied by students and make sure that no one was left behind.

Luke walked from the kitchen as the tasks were being assigned and trotted down to the dock where Will's boat should have been anchored, but it wasn't there. It was not in the slip where it had been tied the entire summer—it wasn't there. He ran over to the marina office and asked where the little clipper had gone, but the dock master didn't know. The rental and work invoices had been paid in advance so the boat was free to leave anytime it pleased, although it most likely had put out in the darkness, he said. Luke was stunned.

Andora was gone. Without a word, Andora had slipped out of Neale Sound and was gone. He jogged from the marina to the tip of the island where he could get a view of both the Potomac and the Wicomico, but there were no sails in sight. He trotted down to the cottage, but somehow he knew she wouldn't be there. The door and the windows were locked, so he walked slowly down the road toward Maestro's cottage where he found Possum's son loading baggage into the depths of the trunk of an old Lincoln Town Car parked outside. Luke walked into the house where Maestro was checking closets and drawers.

"Hi, Luke," the old man hailed him cheerfully. "Just in time. I was going to finish up the Cremant that Lonnie and I cracked last night. A farewell toast. No sense in throwing good bubbly down the drain."

"She's gone, Maestro."

"Who's gone?"

"Andora."

Maestro poured the remains from the wine bottle into two glasses, held his up, and touched Luke's glass nonchalantly.

"Here's to your loss," Maestro said without emotion.

"What shall I do?"

"Nothing. There is nothing to be done. Drink your wine." They sipped silently, and then, after gathering his thoughts, Maestro spoke again.

"I vividly remember the film *Rouge et Noir* made years ago from Stendhal's novel and directed by Claude Autant-Lara. You might have seen it. This tragic love affair that unwound each day in prison where Julien Sorel was embraced by his lover's arms. He said when he entered prison that there was nothing left for him as he faced his death—no disgrace, no shame, no ambition, no failure—only the two of them entwined in love. It is an old tale, quite romantic for the French, one which caused a million virgin breasts to heave in empathy—but who would dare in his lifetime to live for a minute by such a principle? A life reduced to nothing but love? Who will die for it? Unless...a writer...of course, a hero hiding behind his words. Enough of this. I have been separated from reality too long. I need to go. Good luck in your graduate studies. If you need me, call on me, and don't worry about your writing. It will come or it won't. Don't sit around waiting for it. It will follow you. Remember the lesson in *"La Belle Dame"*? 'And there she lulled me to sleep, and there I dream'd, Ah, woe betide, the latest dream I ever dreamed on the cold hill's side.'

"Don't leave your talent and your dreams on the cold hill's side. Tumble them in the warm meadows of your heart. Andora will sail away from one place to another and you will hear from her from time to time—she will sing to you a siren's song. But I will tell you from the bottom of my heart that you must place Lonnie in your dreams. Lonnie has character. She will crowd your future and dim your past—she will love you until your dying breath. Andora is an artist, inherently selfish, channeling energy into imagination and medium rather than empathy and compassion. Artists make love with the intensity of gerbils—but not Lonnie. She is an artist but it bores her, and that is because she is art herself; art of another creator, to be sure, but an object of aesthetic value, nonetheless. Lonnie walks among ancient mysteries with ease and lack of sophistication. Like the goddess Diana, her aim is true and yet her feet are clay. She is the rare spirit of heaven and earth whose love springs, unbounded, by her freedom. Andora, for all of her reaching for love is bound to a man who cannot give it. Her secret is the sorrow of the world—unrequited love."

Maestro finished his drink and took Luke's hand. *"Courage, mon ami, le diable est mort,"* he said, clutching him tightly before going to the car. "I've always liked that as an exit line to hapless friends when there is nothing more to say." Luke opened and closed the car door without saying anything. Then he stood there watching Maestro's hand waving through the rear window as the car drove away. Luke raised the empty jelly glass in a mock toast as Maestro's car went down the street and over the bridge.

"Here's looking at you kid, or some such thing," he said, and walked toward the parsonage with the empty glass in his hand.

37

Water Spout

The buses had evacuated everyone lacking transportation from the island to Piccowaxen school on the mainland, leaving a crew of volunteer firemen to resolve emergencies. Possum, undaunted by the threat of a storm, was helping Jesse gather a final load of possessions in his pickup truck to take to the evacuation center. Luke's red MG TD sat in front of the parsonage, canvas top up with side screens attached, waiting to be driven away as soon as he packed his portable typewriter and Ward grabbed a portfolio of music.

The weather reports provided by the firehouse crew were improving; the storm was predicted to head back to sea at Norfolk, and be well offshore as it paralleled the Chesapeake Bay toward its dissolution in the northeast. There would be rain, wind, and a few high tides, but the expectation of a catastrophic storm had diminished and taken the first level of tension with it. When the rain came, it was intermittent rather than torrential, and the winds were clocked at twenty-five to forty miles per hour and gusting. They had survived far worse.

Possum and Jesse delivered the load to the evacuation center and, on their return, Possum remarked that he thought the wind had picked up a little and the water had become higher and more roiled. By the time they reached the firehouse, the wind was blowing a gale, nearly taking Jesse's feet from under him as he walked back to the parsonage.

Luke was ready to leave the shaking and rattling third floor of the parsonage when he looked from the window toward the river and saw through the increasing rain a concentration of water and mist that began to form itself into a circular pattern. My God, he realized. It's a water spout! He grabbed his typewriter and scrambled down the stairs yelling for Ward to follow. He stopped briefly at Ward's room and grabbed him by the arm and headed through the parsonage to the small underground passageway that connected them to the theater. The sirens at the firehouse were screaming frantic warnings.

Luke and Ward reached safety below ground just as an overwhelming roar of wind ripped off the wood and glass canopy above them and threw them violently to the ground. They pressed themselves against the asbestos tiles, hands over their heads as protection from the enveloping chaos. Although it seemed an eternity, the wind and rain soon abated enough for them to rise from the floor and look over the remaining cinderblock wall to the scene outside.

What they saw astonished them. In an area approximately one hundred yards wide from the Fessenden sign to the bridge, there was nothing but rubble. It was as though a great machine had cut a clean swath from one side of the island to the other, leaving a bare strip of land littered with wood and metal. Within that relatively small avenue, nothing was left standing. Houses were gone, the parsonage and church were gone, Scuttlebutt's and the marina and its boats were gone. All they could see was a strip of devastation running down the island, across Neale Sound and into Rock Point. They stood in the underground passageway trying to absorb the fact that every structure around them had been swept away. On the other side of Trinity Island Road, the firehouse and cottages, Linda's coffee shop, the post office, and the Trinity Island Market had not been touched. They saw Possum come out of the firehouse and wave at them, and they scrambled out of their cover and ran through the rain to join him.

"Glad you boys made it," Possum said. "That was a real surprise, out of nowhere like that—never seen anything like that before." Luke looked back where the parsonage had been and suddenly realized that the MG was gone.

"My car!" he yelled.

"Yep, that was something to see," Possum said. "When I heard all that noise and wind and looked out the window, I could see that spout coming down the street from Fessenden Point, taking everything with it. Then I saw Jesse run out of the parsonage carrying that skull under his arm like a football and get into your car and try to make a run for it, but he had no more closed the door when the parsonage collapsed behind him and that little red car disappeared into that swirling, screaming mess—'behold, a chariot of fire and horses of fire and Elijah went up by a whirlwind into heaven'—and he was gone and the car was gone with him—never seen nothing like it—cut a swath through the island like a man with a sickle and out the other side and gone up the Wicomico

River somewheres. It even took that damned Fessenden sign with it. I reckon we better go looking for him. You boys want to help?"

They piled into Possum's pickup truck and headed down the path of the twister. At Rock Point, the water spout had miraculously missed several farmhouses before breaching the width of the Wicomico River, which it appeared to have followed toward Allen's Fresh. They looked and searched the variegated terrain as best they could, but no sign of a red car appeared amongst the debris remaining from the devastating wind.

"They're gonna have to search this by helicopter and boat because there are too many little fingers of water and creeks that we can't reach on land," Possum said, turning the truck back to the main road.

"Do you mind taking us up to the school?" Luke asked. "Jesse's wife is up there and she'll want to know what happened to him."

"Be happy to," he said. When they reached the school, they found students and faculty clustered in a rear corner of the auditorium. Some instruments had been unpacked, and were being played to relieve the monotony of people milling about in a large room with relative strangers. Rose and Lonnie saw them coming and ran to embrace them. It was Lonnie who first noticed that Jesse was missing from their company.

"He was caught up in the storm," Luke told them. "He was trying to escape in my car when the twister lifted it off the ground and took it, God knows where, up the Wicomico River. We couldn't find it. There's going to be a more detailed search, I'm sure, but I'm sorry to tell you that I don't expect they will find Jesse alive."

"Oh my God," Rose moaned. "Jesse taken in a maelstrom. Poor man. I hope he didn't suffer." Lonnie, whose eyes began to tear, put her arms around Rose and cried softly.

For the next week, volunteers and emergency workers walked and boated through the path of the storm looking for signs of Jesse amongst the torn and twisted debris. On the second day of the search, they found a chrome headlight from the MG resting in a foot of water in shallow Charleston Creek. Pieces of fiberglass boat hulls were strewn along the land, and pieces of flotation and the crushed wreckage of houses were bobbing down the river in the outgoing tide, but there were no other signs of the MG or Jesse. After dragging grappling hooks over some of the deeper spots in the river and finding nothing, the search was concluded on the fifth day.

Lonnie returned to the university to finish her degree, and, after officially closing the search, Charles and Leigh moved back to their home in the county where Charles resumed the presidency of Southern Maryland College, which he had happily abandoned for seven weeks. Rose decided against having a ceremony honoring Jesse's death on the island since most of those who knew him had scattered around the country to pursue their own artistic interests. She would have a private prayer service for him at the church on City Island or perhaps Setauket, but that could come later.

Rose was having a parting cup of coffee with Luke and Ward at Linda's before the two men headed for New York. Luke's insurance company was slow in replacing the full value of the car based only on an affidavit signed by Possum and a single chrome headlight as evidence of its total destruction. Ward's father had loaned them an old car that sat in front of Linda's, sadly, waiting to be driven to its final destination.

"It will be strange, but I think, refreshing, to go back to the real world after this island summer," Rose intoned. "My God, there has been a sea change in my life and I don't know how I will feel with real people—I don't mean that—you are all real people—but with strangers and new friends, and people you do not entirely trust."

"You'll forget about it when you fly to Israel to join Pila next week. It'll be a new adventure, a new environment, and new work to keep you occupied and forgetful of this summer," Luke said.

"I don't want to forget this summer," Rose said, glancing shyly at Ward. "For the exception of poor Jesse's death, I wish I could have one like it every summer. I say 'poor' Jesse, but the more I envision his last moments—skull clutched in his arm, the deafening sounds of violence and destruction around him, raising him from the earth—the more I think that he probably enjoyed it—thought he was having a revelation of life rather than thinking he was about to lose it. I can imagine that he was happy, perhaps thrilled, in those last moments, that something out of the ordinary was finally happening to him that he would live to tell about."

"I suppose that's possible," Ward said, "but frankly, Luke and I were simply scared shitless. I wanted no part of the end of the world, if that's what it was. You can keep your apocalypses to scare the brethren into redemption, but I prefer a mild and sunny afternoon without meaning and portent and overwrought religiosity, if you please."

"It was not an experience that I want to repeat. I'll look for revelation elsewhere," Luke added. "You have our address on West 88th St. Write to us when you get there. Keep us up to date on the happenings of our marvelous Pila and yourself."

"I will, I will," Rose exclaimed joyfully, and embraced them in turn. She walked to the car with them and waved as they headed over the Trinity Island Bridge on their way to New York.

38

Autumn in New York

He had come out of the entrance to the Flatiron building at Broadway and Fifth Avenue. It was 11:45, a bit early for lunch, but he was headed for the deli two blocks up the West Side, trying to beat the rush at noon before the offices emptied at the Communist newspaper, *The Daily Worker*. It took twenty additional minutes to get a sub after the people's printers and journalists flooded the deli, dressed in T-shirts and jeans, ordering sloppy meatball sandwiches. It was important to order before the crowd. A rush of people changed the gears of the men behind the counter from making your sub the way you wanted it to a frenzied activity of slapping it together without care.

It was the best sub in the world if you gave them time to make it correctly. They split the warm roll, scooped out the doughy insides with two fingers, brushed rather than squirted the olive oil over the inside of the shell into which the medley of tastes were laid: provolone, several of a dozen types of Italian and Greek sausages, or perhaps just the cheese and the cured Spanish Jamón serrano, dressed with lettuce and thinly sliced tomato and onion, sometimes sliced black olives, and a thin coating of mayonnaise spread across the open side, and then only a dab of the homemade chopped peppers, mildly hot and spicy so as to complement the ingredients rather than overwhelm them—all of it built carefully within the torpedo shaped shell of bread crust that crackled when you took the first bite. Shake liked to chase it with a fountain Coke, still handmade so that your first big swallow of it took your breath in a burst of abrasive carbonated sweetness. It was worth getting there early on days when you could leave the copy on the desk and finish it later rather than having to rush it to make-up. Therefore, the well-made sandwich for lunch required that the timing of his work be precise from his entering the office at 7:30 a.m. until the big clock in the hallway ticked 11:40. Since the sources of his work were capricious, he had difficulty in timing his visit to the deli every day. He made it once, maybe twice in an ordinary week, infrequently enough for the quality of the food to remain constant with his expectations.

It was on such a day when the timing was impeccable that Shake emerged from the building into the Broadway foot traffic and headed north at a quick pace. He stopped at the light on 23rd street and looked vacantly over the cars waiting for the light to change. His eye caught a red MG TD idling there with the top down, a young woman behind the wheel in sunglasses with a scarf pulled over her head, tied under the chin. Lonnie, he thought, a girl like Lonnie, and then with a burst he yelled, "Ruby!" and frightened the woman walking next to him.

"Lonnie," he yelled, and ran between the cars until he reached the MG and vaulted into the passenger seat next to the startled girl driving the car. The light changed, and before she could shake off her fright and fully recognize the young man next to her, the cars behind let off a cacophony of horn blasts designed to raise the dead in New Jersey.

"Come on! Move it," he urged, "or they'll kill us." She ground the car into gear and took the first side street open to her three blocks away and slammed on the brakes.

"Luke! Luke! Shake! Shake," she screamed, taking her foot from the clutch in a lurch and choking out the car, still in gear. They put their arms around each other, awkwardly at first, and then began kissing each other fervently over the axis of the handbrake. A horn blew from the truck behind them, and a rough voice called out, "Take it to the house, lady," and pumped the horn twice more for emphasis. She started the car and drove down the street and up another until she found a small spot to park and pulled over. "Where can we talk?" she asked.

"Let me drive," he said, and they quickly switched seats. He circled back and headed for Greenwich Village, cruising the warren of little streets until they found a parking place close to Washington Square. They got out and started walking toward the park and the magnificent marble arch dominating it, inspired by the Arc de Triomphe. They found a bench and sat down, and in a burst of excitement, asked and answered each other's important questions of time and place, hop-scotching minor events until they arrived, finally, in the present on that bench in Washington Square.

"Oh, Shake," she said. "Here we are again. You are just finishing and I am just starting. Are we going to miss each other again? Maestro said you were here, but he didn't know where. I can't believe that you found me."

"Strange things happen in this city," he said, "like it was the navel of the country. We don't have to lose each other again unless we want to. My master's work is almost finished and I'm marking time writing and editing for unimportant magazines until something else shows up, but I fear that even if the magazines were bestsellers, I still wouldn't be satisfied. In the end, I'd still be a hack. Ward wants me to go out and seek my fortune working for a newspaper like the *St. Louis Post Dispatch*, but that doesn't stir me. Maybe I'm just lazy, waiting around for something to happen to me, and today, something did, thank God. I found Lonnie!"

"Oh Shake, I'm not Lonnie anymore. I had it officially changed to just plain Leigh. I'm not 'Lonnie,' I am the Leigh I was always supposed to be."

"Well that takes the mystery out of that pronunciation, thankfully."

"How is Ward?"

"Good. But as much as he pretends otherwise, he's like me: waiting for something to happen. He's afraid he'll fall into that rut of playing for tips in bars and roadhouses on Long Island. There are a ton of guys who play the piano really well, just as there are a plethora of writers who can turn out copy faster than spit in this town. New York gives you a feeling like you're about to get on top, when you can't even find yourself in the pile. The bottom in New York feels like the top in St. Louis."

"Yeah, for me, too. It's one audition after another and taking roles in plays that are produced in church basements, soup kitchens, and little union halls—very far from Broadway—off- and way-off-Broadway. It's grind without glitter. I'm beginning to think it's not in my blood."

He looked over to a cement chess table standing permanently in the sidewalk across from them. Two players were concentrating on the game as were half a dozen old men standing around them. Shake nodded toward them.

"I'll be like them thirty years from now, after having retired from the *St. Louis Post Dispatch* with fifty bucks a month in my pocket—rook to king four." She laughed.

"Do you want to walk up to the White Horse for an expensive beer?" he asked.

"What's the White Horse?"

"The bar where Dylan Thomas used to get drunk out of his mind while committing alcoholic suicide in New York. People go there to drink, because he went there to drink, and they want to soak up the atmosphere of the drunken poet, and try to feel like the drunken poet, conversing in topics that drunken poets would not even think about, especially Dylan Thomas. It's a comedy all its own. It's the best kind of New York shtick."

"Actually, I'm a little hungry."

"Me, too. I know of a little Chinese hole-in-the-wall with four tables and twelve chairs that makes great egg foo yung. It's right up the street. Then, one night for supper, I've got this Italian basement over in the Bowery with four tables and sixteen chairs where the last person in at 6 p.m. locks the door behind them until everyone seated is finished at 7:30. You eat with strangers and there's one item on the menu posted on the chalk board outside that changes daily. We'll have fun. That's the best of New York."

"Sounds great," Lonnie said. "I'm living with two girls over in the Greek section of Astoria because there was space to park the car and not move it every other day, Normally, I come into Manhattan by train, but it was such a nice day, I drove over to pick up a script. I double-parked, jumped out, picked it up and was gone in a second. Was that luck, or what?"

"Where did you find a car like my old chariot?"

"My father gave it to me as a graduation present. He couldn't understand why I wanted it—too small, too slow, not easy to repair, too cold in winter—he didn't understand that it was a piece of you that I wanted and all those other things didn't matter."

"I hope I run as well. Did you ever think we would meet again?" he asked.

"I did, and I wanted to, but I wasn't too sure about you. After the Armageddon of that summer, I didn't stick around. I figured you were off chasing Andora."

"I came here to lick my wounds and cry for myself and become the most boring graduate student you know. Except for having survived it, that summer was a complete disaster. But let's not talk about that now. I'll call Ward and we'll have a little to eat and drink at the apartment, and there may be some surprises for you." They separated at the car, she spinning her way beneath the el to Astoria and he returning to work.

Leigh was bubbling with excitement at having reunited with Shake and could hardly contain her enthusiasm when she arrived at West 88th St., fifteen minutes earlier than the appointed time. She rang the doorbell for the third floor, entitled "Them," and was allowed to enter the small lobby of the brownstone. Taking the steps, two at a time, she arrived as the door was being opened by Ward. She rushed to embrace him. "How good it is to find you after all these months," she said, shedding a light jacket and then falling back into Ward's arms. "Where is everybody? Are you and Shake the only ones who live here?"

"In order of importance," he said, sweeping her toward the front of the house, "the white Steinway, 'Moby Dick,' lives in the front room as you can see. Then, I have a room, Shake has a room, and there is a smaller room that we sublet for a bottle of wine to a roommate whose turn it is to chase the food tonight. It should be here any minute. Let's sit in here," Ward said, pointing to the room containing the piano. He took the stool and immediately began to riff some light jazz phrases that led into "Somewhere Over the Rainbow" and then into "Autumn in New York" when they heard the front door open to a person who went directly into the kitchen.

"I'll introduce you to the cook," Ward said, leaving the piano. He returned within a few minutes and announced: "And now, ladies and gentlemen, coming straight to you from Woo Sam's fine Chinese restaurant and dry cleaners, tattoos upstairs, to entertain us, the incomparable *La Vie en Rose*," and Ward began playing the time-favored one-step music used by strippers making their entrance: da da da, dee da da da, and in walked Rose Caine, step by step, shaking her shoulders suggestively, and holding out a platter of steaming Chinese food. When Leigh finally recognized her, she jumped from the chair and tried to hug her over the tray of food, which Rose placed on the piano top so that the reunion might be completed without a loss of shrimp and snow peas.

"Lonnie!" Rose screamed. They embraced joyfully, hugging and kissing.

"Rose, are you the third roommate?"

"Oh, just for a little while, and it's not what you think."

"That's great. Are you and Ward together?"

"Let's just say that I pinned him some time ago, and I'm trying to get used to the idea that he might eventually turn a hand to some honest work. Actually, I'm moving to Long Island tomorrow to stay with some old friends in Setauket who have an old stable-cum-studio apartment they will let me use. Pila expects me to finish the book and I want to finish the book, and at the rate that I am pleasuring him, I will never finish the book, and he will never learn to play a decent piano. He also has some important auditions coming up and a concert next month. So, tomorrow we part for a while. Did you know that Shake had received a letter from Andora?"

"No. He didn't tell me, although I don't suppose that I had a right to know."

"Of course you do. We all do. When we have to suffer through his flights of fancy and sorrow, we have paid the price of admission to his private life. Read the letter to us, Shake." He was a little embarrassed but retrieved the letter from his room and began to read.

Dear Luke,

I have not lived my life with circumspection, and I can only now look back at the chaos I have caused. It is a trail of pain and ignorance and suffering because I was not free to act responsibly. There is that word again, "Free." We forget that freedom is the glue by which we cement the future, sticking bone to flesh, mind to body, heaven to earth in never-ending praise of ourselves. I have sailed the world and have not come closer to having it than I did with you last summer on the island. You opened the chest that held my secrets, but I could not let them go. I had to cram them back and lock the lid and smother the men who loved me, Will and Jesse and others whose names I have forgotten, like unknown soldiers. You held your hand out to me and said 'be the person you want to be and be that person with me,' and I knew you were right. But freedom is hard. It is an act of violence that I cannot perform. I lack the faith and the courage. I am free to roam the earth and yet I have no compass inside me that will bring me to myself or to you, again—forever. I am sorry.

"Did you write her back?" Leigh asked.

"No, she left no return address. I could probably send a letter to her mother in North Carolina, but what's the point?"

"Suppose she just shows up?" Leigh asked.

"She won't, don't worry," Rose said. "I've known her longer than any of you, and despite all of the talk about freedom and courage, her destiny, and the sorrow of Tilley, and the coldness of Will, in the end, it's all about the money. Her husband, Will, floats her boat in it, and Shake doesn't have enough to buy her paint and canvas. She knew that Shake couldn't support her in the style that would allow her to paint without having to work. It was that simple. And one more thing that perhaps you don't know. Her child, Tilley, wasn't an easy birth; a portion of her reproductive organs had to be removed. She could not have had another child." Shake was shocked at hearing this information from Rose. It was new to him. He had been convinced that Andora wanted his child, but he had been horribly mistaken. He shook his head.

"All this time, I persisted in 'bringing her out,' as Henry James would say. I became enamored of the thought that Andora wanted to be brought out and that I could help her. How foolish was that?" Shake asked rhetorically.

"Don't take all the blame. It was not an honest love affair, although that sounds oxymoronic doesn't it? She opened herself up to you, but the view she gave you wasn't very clear. To put it bluntly, she lied to you," Rose said.

"If I may help cut through the fog of forgetfulness that has blanketed your mind, dear Shake," Ward admonished, "it was the sex that you hoped would save her soul, not the philosophy. Sex or money will trump love or freedom every time."

"Isn't that a bit cynical?" Shake asked.

"Not if you're holding the trumps," he answered and laughed.

"How many trumps do you think you're holding?" Rose asked accusingly.

Ward pulled a subway token from his pocket and tossed it on the piano top. They all broke into laughter.

"Since I can't get Shake to go to St. Louis, he's been thinking about teaching. There's a new college opening at home, but he's grappling with the demotion from being 'king of the starving unpublished novelists' to 'poorly paid prince of the classroom.' Hardly a choice to be made. He could probably get some help from Maestro in securing a post, as they say in English movies, but I think I may have jinxed it when I told him that I liked the idea better than my wanting to pack him off to the *Post Dispatch*. The man has difficulty accepting good advice."

"It isn't that," Shake opined. "It's difficult to sort out whether or not it's good advice or a subtle form of capitulation. I've talked to Oliver, my teaching poet friend, and he told me that it's difficult to prepare for classes, grade papers, and still have time to write. Maybe Andora was right; maybe you need to be free of the chores of daily routine to be successful."

"Aw, bullshit," Lonnie said, as she jumped angrily from her chair and stomped into the kitchen.

Rose chuckled. "I think she feels rather strongly about something, don't you?"

"I'll go see," Shake said, heading toward the kitchen. He found her there facing the sink, and when she turned he could see the moisture gathering in her eyes.

"I didn't mean to upset you," he said.

"I'm not upset. I'm angry that you still have feelings for Andora."

"Actually, I don't have strong feelings for her anymore. She was a part of my life, briefly, but I've come to realize I have nothing left for her. It's over and done. It was a summer romance, after all." He reached for her hand and carefully kissed each of her fingers. Then he pulled her slightly toward him and she came without resistance into his arms and they embraced in a deep and loving kiss. When they moved apart, she was smiling.

"Do you think there's a chance that we can be together? I do want to be with you," Leigh said.

"We can work on it, starting now, and test it for endurance. I still have a little work left in graduate school that will keep me in New York, so it won't be easy, but I don't think it's the easy thing we are looking for, do you?" Without waiting for an answer, he kissed her again and his elbow knocked several cartons of Chinese food from the countertop to the floor with a splatter.

"No shagging in the kitchen," Ward yelled. "It's indecent and unsanitary." They laughed and scooped up the food mess and toweled the floor clean and then joined the others in the piano room where Ward had begun a riff on "The Sidewalks of New York."

39

Catching Fish

Several months had passed since the freak microburst of energy cut a path through Trinity Island and Rock Point with surgical precision. The incident had almost been forgotten in the luxury of Indian summer days that followed. Not wanting to close the more positive experience of the summer on a note of destruction and violence, Charles invited Leigh to spend another sunset with him on Cobb Neck.

Driving down from Route 301, they passed fields of corn and soybeans ready to be harvested. As the peninsula narrowed, the air became tinged with the sweet smell of the tidal Potomac creating palpable scents of earth and water unlike any other.

They turned onto a narrow macadam road where pine trees towered over them blocking out the sky, adding their sharp herbal perfume to the bouquet casting a spell over Charles.

The paved road ended within a half-mile and a gravel road took them through tightly packed trees and shrubs until it opened suddenly, as though the curtain in a theater had been swept away revealing the length and breadth of a glittering stage: there before them, awash in sunlight, a panorama of the Potomac River took Charles's breath for a moment. The car swung slightly to the left and stopped by the side of a log cabin sitting amid flowers and trees facing a lawn that sloped gently down to the river a hundred and fifty feet away.

"Ohmygoodness," Leigh said. "Whose place is this?"

"Belongs to a fellow who lives in the city and only comes down every other weekend." Directly before them glimmered a large expanse of river.

"Where are we?" Leigh asked.

"Over there," he said pointing directly across to the Virginia shore, "is 'Marseille.' Don't you recognize it? Down there lies the mysterious Trinity Island," he said, pointing to the left, "and a little ways behind us is a marshy continuation of Neale Sound."

Over his head an osprey screamed a warning as it glided toward its nest sitting atop a pole some fifty feet from the shore. Then Charles saw the head of another osprey rise up from the nest. It nestled down again, almost out of sight, and the mate screamed and flew from the nest and began to fly in a circle directly over Charles. It was measuring the potential threat that Charles posed and screamed again, agitated by human presence. Charles was mesmerized by the huge bird's flight. Taking Leigh's hand, he walked slowly down the lawn toward the river. Charles was quiet, steeping in pleasure, not in the sense of just feeling something of pleasure as one might view a sunset or the cuddle of a smiling child, but he was drowning in it, fully immersed and saturated by it, unable to shut it out or give it up—he had been infected with a disease of delirious joy at the river's expanse and the osprey's cry.

They sat down on the lawn and Charles lay back on the incline, watching the sky. The water lapped the rocks in a soft curl and lisp of sound.

"Why are we doing this?" Leigh asked.

At first she received no answer, until finally he drew in several deep breaths and propped on his elbow, he said, "For the romance of it."

"I haven't noticed any lack of romance, lately," she said.

"I didn't mean the romance we have between us—more of a romance to the rhythm of both our lives."

Before she could respond, they heard the steady hum of an outboard motor drawing closer to them, quickly followed by a boat approximately eighteen feet in length making its way slowly down the river on the outgoing tide. It was running in water fifty feet from shore in what Charles surely thought was water too shallow for fishing. As it drew closer to them, he noticed three rods attached to the stern with lines extended into the water. When it was opposite them, the fisherman at the wheel waved and yelled at them, "You can't catch fish if you don't wet a line," and then he reached into a live well behind him and held up a rockfish, a striped bass that looked to be well over two feet long.

The fisherman smiled and placed the prize back in the box. Charles watched him putter slowly downriver, his back to the glow of the setting sun.

"Trolling in shallow water!" Charles said aloud. "Wow. How about that?" he asked. "Maybe that's one of the reasons we're doing this."

"Could you do that?"

"If I had a boat and a dock and a cabin on the river. I think I could."

His wife smiled at him. "Wouldn't it just be cheaper to buy the fish from that guy?"

"It would, but it wouldn't taste the same," Charles said. "It wouldn't have the stuff you need in it, the good stuff, the things that made you go out there in the first place to catch it. That doesn't come with it when you buy it at the store. You've got to catch it yourself to get that. Otherwise, it's not the same."

She looked at him hard, wondering if he was being serious or making a joke, but the expression on his face told her it didn't matter.

"You brought me here because you want to buy this property, don't you?"

"It's a little more than that."

He couldn't explain it to her in a way that would be fully understandable. He needed the river now, to hold him and give him a sense that the tide of his life might eventually come in again. He wanted a more intimate relationship with surroundings that would replenish rather than deplete him.

"What would we do here?" she asked.

"We'll come here and replant ourselves." he said. He thought for a moment and added, "and grow again."

"And love again?" she asked, trying to see his eyes in the afterglow of the sunset.

"And love some more," he said, "Surely, to love some more, because I have not stopped loving you."

"And will I have more of you this time?" she said.

"More than you can probably stand," he said, looking down at the grass.

How could he tell her that which he barely understood—so ephemeral—so selfish—the pain that he could not describe or share—born of his own ambition. It was the mystery of creation: the more he joyfully gave to his work and the more his reputation grew and his resume expanded, the more of himself he eventually lost. It was not an equation he wanted to continue. Their summer on Trinity Island had been an arrow through the heart of his image of himself.

"How much does the fellow want for it?" she asked.

"I haven't tried to negotiate with him yet, but it's undoubtedly more than we can comfortably afford. I think we could make it work, though, if we wanted it bad enough."

They lay back on the grass in the diminishing afterglow of the sunset. The lights on the Marseille shore began to twinkle, intersected by the silver contrails of aircraft invisible to them.

"Will you give up the presidency?" Leigh finally asked.

"Yes," he said.

40

Maestro Morte

They had pulled his oxygen cord from its source on the wall and taken the plastic tubing with its intrusive fingers from his nose. They waited. His breath came in whispers; small ciphers of life expelled without purpose. His chest rose and fell imperceptibly. He became the osprey rising slowly in a gyre above the nest and then, in a perfect arpeggio of rippling feathers, he carved a long silken arc from the sky and fell with abandon, fell down, down, until, with a great push of wings against the air he rose abruptly in a steep hook, hovered for a second and feathered softly into the darkness. His chest lay still.

Epilogue

I crouched behind the fallen sycamore as low as I could, shivering down, hoping I hadn't been seen, trying to crawl under it, when I felt a hand on my head.

"Come on. Get up from there, Charlie Abell. Come on. We ain't gonna hurt you."

I popped up and searched frantically for my clothes but they weren't on the roots of the old tree where I had hung them. Reuben had taken them with him and dropped them in his escape up the hill. I could see them in the leaves, far out of reach—if only I could reach them—stretch for them—I would be out of the water and safely home. No matter how I tried, they were always out of reach and I was naked. I cried and fell back and tried to crawl under the log when I felt a hand on my back.

"Come on. Get up from there, Charles Abell. Come on." Leigh said, shaking me gently. "You've fallen asleep again and I've made your favorite breakfast of biscuits and molasses, so get up from there before you dream your life away." Then she bent over and kissed my sleepy eyes awake.

Acknowledgements

Many thanks for thoughts and contributions to Danny Mayer, Paul Springer, Les Hubbard, Sam Bowling, Bill Hocker, Chris Hocker, Linda Riggs, the Cobb Island Yacht Club, Dolph Klein, Fred Davis, and Tod Uecker.

CPSIA information can be obtained at www.ICGtesting.com
Printed in the USA
LVOW131143161212

311876LV00001B/125/P